THE REUNION

Helen Cannam titles available from Severn House Large Print

Family Business
An Honourable Man
House of Secrets
Queen of the Road

THE REUNION

Helen Cannam

Severn House Large Print
London & New York

This first large print edition published in Great Britain 2003 by
SEVERN HOUSE LARGE PRINT BOOKS LTD of
9-15, High Street, Sutton, Surrey, SM1 1DF.
First world regular print edition published 2003 by
Severn House Publishers, London and New York.
This first large print edition published in the USA 2003 by
SEVERN HOUSE PUBLISHERS INC., of
595 Madison Avenue, New York, NY 10022

British Library Cataloguing in Publication Data

Cannam, Helen
  The reunion - Large print ed.
  1. Marriage - Fiction
  2. Middle aged women - Fiction
  3. Large type books
  I. Title
  823.9'14 [F]

  ISBN 0-7278-7303-2

Printed and bound in Great Britain by
MPG Books Ltd, Bodmin, Cornwall.

One

Jan wished the clock had a louder tick. It was a pretty green clock, half-moon shaped, which stood on the shelf above the fire that looked like coal but was fuelled by gas. She had never been quite sure what it was that made that faint undertone of a sound, a kind of imitation tick; the clock had no visible working parts, except a battery. A grandfather clock, now, with a proper pendulum and chains and weights to set it whirring and a steady melodious tick – that would have broken the silence in a more comforting manner. The loudest sound in the room would not then have been the clatter of knives and forks on plates and the smack of mastication, as she and Keith chewed their way steadily through a stir-fry of pork and vegetables, served with boiled basmati rice. She longed for the phone to ring. It was nearly twenty-four hours since anyone had rung. The telephone seemed to lurk on the hall table, shiny, black and reproachful, like a temporarily neglected pet. Except that this was not temporary.

It felt, she thought, like a scene from one of those old films, where the estranged couple sit down to dine at a vast banqueting table in a gloomy baronial hall. Yet the dining room at Mill House was not so very large, just a comfortable size, right for a family, or for entertaining guests. It was only today that it felt huge.

Once again, Jan looked across the table at her husband; that familiar figure, whose slight broadening during the past thirty years was only noticeable when old family photos were brought out. Jan recalled her favourite photo, of a slender boyish Keith holding Fiona in his arms on the day they had brought her home from hospital, his face lit by tenderness. The strong brows and dark eyes were as they had always been. But now the lined face was expressionless, concentrated on the food. Of course, one had to concentrate to get through the crunchy vegetables, especially with ageing teeth. And no one, not even the greatest gourmet, would look at a plate of food as he might look at his firstborn child. On the other hand, Keith's expression did not change even when he caught his wife's gaze on him. He looked as if he were lost in some gloomy thoughts of his own.

She wished she could think of something to say, something lively and entertaining, something that would make Keith look at her, not simply glance across the table, but really look, with some sign of interest in what she was saying.

They had eaten alone before, of course, many times, when the children were out or staying with friends. They had taken pleasure in the occasional shared meal at a pub or restaurant, on a birthday or an anniversary. But this was different. This was not a rare treat. From now on this would be the normal state of things. To have anyone else there to share their meal would be the exception. This was the first evening of many, the first day of life without the children. And Jan could think of nothing worth talking about, nothing at all.

Earlier, when they first sat down to eat, she had begun with the usual, 'How was your day?' and received the usual noncommittal reply (Keith hardly ever talked about work). Then she had tried to interest him in the evening ahead of them. 'Why don't you come to the local history group tonight? Philippa Lee's talking – you know she's good. She's been doing research into some early Primitive Methodist preacher in the Dale. I know it's a bit modern for you.' She smiled faintly: Keith used to say that anything later than the mid-eighteenth century felt too much like school history for his liking. 'But it sounds interesting. You used to enjoy the meetings.' In fact, for some years,

7

when the children were small and she had rarely been free to attend the group, he had been its secretary.

'I had more time then,' he said, scarcely glancing at her. 'Besides, I'm going to watch the match tonight.'

She refrained from pointing out the illogicality of claiming too little time, while announcing an intention to spend an evening in front of the television – after all, it *was* unusual for him to be home so early as this, with no meeting to attend later in the evening, no other work to do. She had even found herself wondering if he had come home early so as to prevent her from feeling the full force of Melanie's absence. But if that was the case, then surely he would have made some effort to amuse or entertain her? She searched for some other topic of conversation, but her mind was blank, or rather, not blank, but full of all kinds of thoughts and feelings she felt unable to put into words.

It was Keith who spoke next, his tone without emotion. 'Melanie get off all right?'

'Yes. The train was on time.'

'Good.'

So that was it. End of conversation. End of Melanie, waving from the train with a mixture of nervousness and excitement evident on her face, at least to her mother's eyes; off to begin a new job in a strange town.

Until today Jan had usually shared her evening meal with her younger daughter, since Keith was so rarely back in time. She could talk about anything at all with Melanie, as with any of her children – religion, politics, the environment, gossip, feelings, everything that came up. With Keith, she had only ever discussed what must be discussed – family plans, what their position should be in some crisis with the children, what large item to save up for. Now she found that she seemed to have forgotten how to hold an ordinary conversation with him, after the years when the needs of the children had come first. Or was it rather that they had never really shared things in that way? She could not now remember. There had been so little time when they had been together without the children, just the year and a half between their first meeting and their marriage, and a scant nine months afterwards, before Fiona arrived.

Then she thought of something that was of real interest, though Melanie's departure had put it out of her head until now. 'Oh, I forgot, I had all the stuff about the reunion today. It looks good. There's a dinner and a sixties disco. Wonder if I can remember how to dance?' Keith said nothing, and though his manner – face turned towards her, eyes watching her – told her he had heard, he did not look greatly interested. 'Are you sure you wouldn't like to come? I'm sure they'd fit you in. I could phone tomorrow, first thing.' She was ashamed of the tension coiled inside her, in case he should accept her offer. She did not in the least want him to come with her next weekend. She hoped her feelings were not audible in her voice.

'I'd be like a fish out of water. I bet there won't be any other partners there. No thanks. You enjoy it. It'll do you good to have a break.'

Jan was certainly relieved, yet she felt irritated too. Why could he not be more positive, show more interest or enthusiasm? Conscious that she was trying to provoke some stronger display of emotion, she went on, 'Auntie Hilda didn't seem to take it in, that I wouldn't be here next Sunday.' She wondered if, just this once, he would acknowledge that his aunt's mind was going, that it was more than just minor memory loss.

'Oh, she did, I think. But she was dishing up at the time. It wasn't the best moment to tell her. You should have waited. She can't cope with everything all at once.'

Always, always, that refusal to acknowledge what was obvious to everyone else! She tried to keep her anger under control. 'That's an understatement, if ever there was one,' she said, more mildly than she felt. 'She can't cope, full stop. I wish you'd see it. It's all getting too much for her.' Too much for all of them, she thought, those Sunday dinners – roast meat and all the trimmings, served in Auntie Hilda's little terraced house in Coldwell, an unlovely East Durham town about twenty-five miles away, where the old lady puffed and panted her way through the weekly routine, refusing all offers of help, yet becoming progressively more exhausted and confused. Nowadays, there was inevitably some small disaster before they had done – a plate dropped, food burnt, something forgotten, even courses muddled up, with custard served in place of gravy or salt replacing sugar in the apple pie. Each week, they found the house more untidy, squalid even; last week the dinner had been served on plates that had clearly not been washed since the last meal; Jan had begun to fear for their own health, as well as Hilda's. Even when they had been at home, the children had started to find excuses not to be there. Jan wished she had an excuse, too. Now, she thought, perhaps one of the things she looked forward to most about next weekend was missing the inevitable Sunday visit to Auntie Hilda's house.

The silence closed over them again. She stole a look at Keith as he forked up the last of his stir-fry, trying again to gauge from his expression what he was thinking, what he felt. Was he conscious of awkwardness, uncomfortably aware of the silence; was he bored by every word she struggled to speak, or was he simply tired and hungry and glad to be home from work and able to relax? He did not look glad, or even relaxed, but how could she tell?

He's a stranger, she thought: we've been married for thirty years, and I know what he most likes to eat (steak and chips) and which is his favourite shirt (the blue cotton one with the broad white stripe, at the moment anyway – he's not wearing it today because it's in the wash) and what he likes to watch on television (football most of all, so he should be happy tonight), but nothing at all about his deepest feelings – least of all, what he's feeling now, on this day when the last of our children has left home.

And perhaps, when all was said and done, that was what troubled him; the departure of his children. Who was to say that fathers couldn't feel their loss as much as did their wives? Perhaps in making no allowance for this she was being insensitive; perhaps he was only waiting for her to prompt him to talk about this great change in their lives and what it meant to him. 'Keith,' she said, gently, coaxing him to throw off his masculine reticence. 'What's wrong?'

'Nothing.' He looked surprised at the question, and then irritated. 'Why should there be?'

'You seem a bit – well, quiet, I suppose.' It was the wrong word, but she could not think of the right one. In any case, she was by no means sure that there was anything in his manner that was different from usual. Perhaps it was simply that for the first time in years she had the time and leisure to observe him. But, she thought, surely he had not always been like this? And if not, when was it that he had changed from the man she had married? She could no longer clearly remember that man, but she knew he could not have been like this or she would surely not have married him.

'Since when was being quiet a crime? Stop hassling me, Jan. There's nothing the matter. I just want a bit of peace after a hard day.' He rose from the table and, as usual, helped her clear the dishes into the kitchen, so she could load the dishwasher. He was settled in front of the television with the *Independent* and the impending football before she left the house.

Philippa Lee was a retired headmistress, who had settled in Meadhope ten years before and at once applied herself to researching any unexplored aspect of the area's history that caught her fancy. She was usually a lively and instructive speaker to the local history group, however unpromising the subject might appear beforehand, and this evening was no exception. A small audience in the rather bleak surroundings of the church hall listened enthralled to her description of a wilder past, when eccentric itinerant preachers won over a lawless population. The Dale, so rural now, had then been an industrial powerhouse, centre of lead mining and quarrying. For a little while, her hearers – many of them, like the speaker, drawn to live in the Dale because of its supposedly unspoiled charm – felt that they had been transported back to that very different past, its grimness veiled by time and nostalgia. The applause that followed was enthusiastic. Afterwards, over coffee and biscuits, Bill Mulliner, the secretary, came over to Jan. 'My penultimate meeting as secretary,' he reflected. 'I shall miss all this.'

'I saw the For Sale notice on your house,' Jan said, sipping the watery, synthetic tasting coffee (you could tell Brenda Porter was on refreshment duty tonight). 'But I didn't know you were actually leaving us.'

'We've been wanting to move nearer our son for a long time. Chance to see more of the grandchildren. I'll be sorry to go, in many ways, but we're looking forward to it, too.' He took a sip of his coffee, then said casually, 'Tell me, does Keith think of joining us again?'

Jan could see what was coming. 'You think he might be persuaded to stand as secretary again? I'm sorry, he's so busy these days.' She did not mention the football.

'All the local authority reorganization, I suppose. Pity. He was the best secretary we had – and useful, too. Look at all the work he did to get the Holy Well restored. It helps to have friends in the right places.'

'Ah, but he was working for the county council then.' Some years before, Keith had moved to a better paid post with the planning department of a large urban regional authority in the east of the area.

'True. And now they're changing it all again. It must be unsettling. Sometimes he must wish he'd stuck with the devil he knew, instead of moving.'

'Oh, I don't imagine the work will change much really. Though he'll be responsible for a smaller area. But then so will the county council. At the moment, of course, there's a lot of extra work for everyone.'

'Still, we all need recreation. Try to talk him into coming back to us. Unless, of course,' he added, 'you fancy taking on the job yourself?'

I just might, thought Jan, watching him walk away; it wasn't an afterthought either. Anything might be possible, even larger, more ambitious projects than booking speakers for the local history group, if she were seriously to consider working part time. Not that she had as yet put that

15

possibility to anyone.

At about half past nine, Jan found herself walking home in the company of Sheila Brandon and Anne Heywood, who both lived in the same part of the village as herself. Sheila, about her own age and a grandmother, was one of those vigorous volunteers who keeps local organizations going; Anne, some years younger, was practice nurse with the medical group to which Jan was a senior receptionist. Talking of the evening's lecture, they followed the ancient lane past the honey-coloured stone of the churchyard wall, topped by elder – dark with berries – and the heavy shadowy foliage of a chestnut tree, under which the street lights picked out the gleam of ripe conkers.

'I can't get my head round it,' said Anne. 'They were such a barbaric lot. Then just like that someone comes preaching hellfire and damnation and they've all turned teetotal and God-fearing. Ten years or so, no more, it took. Weird. I believed it while she was talking – like you said, she can make you live it. But it's hard to credit all the same.'

'I don't know, though,' said Jan. 'Look how things have changed in this country since the sixties – or the late seventies, come to that. Not because of religion, of course, at least not in this country, but you get these swings for all kinds of reasons. I suppose there comes a time when change is in the air.'

The lane emerged into one of the main streets of the village beside a low modern block of buildings, discreetly concealed by shrubs, though a grey and white sign declared that it was the medical centre. 'The ad's going in for the practice manager next week,' said Anne. The present manager had recently announced her retirement, and there was to be some considerable reorganization of the large rural practice.

'I know.' Jan grinned. 'And no, I don't think you'll be seeing my application dropping on the mat.' She wondered if Anne knew that Dr Mead, one of the senior partners in the practice, had suggested she apply for the post.

'You should. You'd do it well.'

'You're the only receptionist I know who isn't an unmitigated dragon,' endorsed Sheila.

'Ah, but I'm looking to be a lady of leisure. More leisure, anyway. Now that the kids have all gone.'

'Why, of course, your Melanie's left home now.' Sheila's ready sympathy quivered on the brink of expression. 'How's she getting on?'

'I don't know yet. I only saw her off this morning. But she'll be all right. She's very competent. Much more so than I was at her age.'

'I stayed in one of her hotels once,' said

Anne. 'Dead posh it was too – one night was all we could afford. You must be so proud of her.'

'You'll miss her though,' said Sheila.

'Oh, not Jan,' put in Anne. 'She's making the most of her freedom. It's your reunion this weekend, isn't it?'

'Oh, that means you won't be here for the flowers!'

Jan, who enjoyed being the most valued member of the church flower-arranging team, caught the alarm in Sheila's voice. 'Is it harvest festival this week? I thought that was next week.'

'It is. I'm talking about the wedding. You know, Sharon Bewick's, from the hairdressers. This Saturday.'

'Oh – oh yes, of course. No, I shan't be here. I'm back Sunday night.'

'You looking forward to it?'

'Yes – yes, I am. It was an impulse thing, deciding to go. But the closer it gets the more it seems a good idea. We'll all be fiftysomething, families more or less off our hands and so on. Just the time for taking stock.'

'I wonder,' said Sheila, 'if you'll be able to recognize any of them, or if they'll have changed too much?'

'Who knows? I'm sure I've changed.'

'I suppose the most interesting thing is to see what they've all done,' said Anne. 'You know, will the high-fliers have flown high, or will they all be dull middle-class matrons—'

'Like me,' Jan put in.

'Not dull. Not any of us,' said Anne staunchly.

They had reached Sheila's house, a blue-painted front door opening directly on to the pavement from what appeared to be an ordinary terraced cottage, but was in fact two knocked expertly into one. 'Coming in for a coffee?' Sheila asked. Anne accepted, ('Got to take away the taste of Brenda's brew'), but Jan shook her head.

'I'd better get back. I want to ring Fiona tonight. She doesn't keep very early hours, but there are limits.'

She walked on alone, past the primary school and then a few yards along the path beside the burn towards Mill House. When she and Keith had first seen it, fifteen years before, it had been near-derelict, a grim high building surrounded by a rubble-scattered yard inside a larger, weedy enclosure. Even the things that might have made it attractive – the mill race and the old wheel – had long since gone, carried away by thieves or simply left to decay. She and Keith had seemed to be the only people to see the potential of this near-ruin, to see what might be done inside the still sturdy walls. Keith was good with his hands, and though he had little spare time had found enough to do the simpler work.

Jan had worked on the yard and the garden. For years they had lived in chaos, but there had been excitement in it, and immense satisfaction. Jan well remembered the day Keith had uncovered the seventeenth-century fireplace, hidden behind the ugly mottled fifties tiles, which was now the glory of their sitting room. By the time their children were in their teens, and cared about such things, it had become a house fit for them to bring their most respectable friends home to.

She opened the gate and crossed the garden. It was too shadowed for her to make out more than the outline of the beds and shrubs – her outline, her design – but she caught the scent of late pinks and lavender, and a trace of the Iceberg rose Auntie Hilda had given them for their silver wedding. Iceberg: a lovely rose, but with such a name, to mark a long union – had there been some warning there, if she'd cared to take note of it, of coldness, of hidden dangers beneath a placid surface? No, that was silly. It had never even occurred to her before.

The lavender's taken well, she thought. That had been grown from a cutting Dr Mead had given her.

Once in the house, she hung up her coat in the understairs cupboard. She could hear the sound of the television from the sitting room – Keith was still up then. She picked up the silent phone and pressed the memory button, and then number 1, in close succession. The tones raced through Fiona's number. Five rings, and a male voice answered, deep, wary, with a strong Leeds accent.

'Sam? Is Fiona there?'

'She's moved out.'

There was, Jan thought, a note of desperation beneath the otherwise matter-of-fact words. Even so, they made little sense to her. 'Moved out? But why? Where has she gone?'

'Sorry. Can't talk now. I'll give you her number. I warn you though – you'll only get the answerphone.'

She did too, with Fiona's recorded voice exhorting her coolly to leave a message. She waited for the beep, said, 'Fiona—' and heard her daughter, live, cheerful, break in.

'Hi, Mum.' She did not sound as if anything untoward had happened to her. 'I'm just back from the gym.'

'What's going on? Sam sounded odd, but he wasn't talking.'

'We've split up. We agreed it wasn't going anywhere. I found this place and moved out. I'll tell you all about it on Friday. You are coming still?'

'Yes ... Yes.' Jan felt distracted, unsettled. Her head was full of unanswered questions. But Fiona was about to go out again (at *ten o'clock*, when she'd already spent an hour at the gym!), so they simply settled the

21

arrangements for their meeting. Then Jan went to the sitting room, where Keith was half asleep on the sofa in front of the television (the football had given way to a film full of noisy action). She sat down on one of the easy chairs.

'Fiona's split up with Sam.'

Keith looked, for a moment, genuinely distressed – enough indeed to flick the remote control and plunge the room into quietness. 'What brought that on?'

'She says they just decided it wasn't going anywhere.' By which, Jan had guessed, Fiona meant that she, not Sam, had decided. 'She's moved out of the flat and found somewhere else to live.'

'Already!'

'You know Fiona. Never one to let the grass grow under her feet. But it's a shame. I had hoped they'd stay together. He's such a nice lad.' I sound just like what I said I was, she thought; a dull middle-class matron of conventional views.

'Yes.' Keith appeared to have stopped listening again. Well, it had been nice while it lasted, that show of life.

'I'll go straight from work on Friday,' Jan went on. 'I'll order a taxi, so you don't have to worry about getting back on time.' As if he would, she thought. 'I should make the train that gets into London about six. Fiona says she can meet me.' She paused, watching

Keith. 'You don't mind?'

'Of course not. It'll be nice for you,' said Keith, without any great enthusiasm.

Jan leaned over and gave him a perfunctory kiss on the forehead. 'I'm off to bed then. I expect I'll read a bit.'

'That's all right. I'll not be up just yet. Good night.'

She was not quite asleep when she felt the bed heave under his additional weight. She turned towards him for a final kiss. There would be nothing more tonight, she knew: it was Monday. Except when away on holiday, they only ever made love on a Saturday night, if he felt like it, which was not that often nowadays. On week nights he was always too tired, on Sundays too wearied by the unadmitted stress of the weekly visit to Auntie Hilda. Tonight, striving to find some sort of closeness, she caressed him for a while, just in case, but she knew she was wasting her time. It would not lead anywhere, except perhaps to his falling asleep more quickly.

Which was precisely what happened. Much later, she lay with her eyes shut, half listening to his gentle snores, trying not to worry about Fiona and her broken relationship with Sam, wishing her children were not all so far away; and wondering if this was how it was going to be between her and Keith, today and for ever, as long as they lived.

Two

'There's the white horse,' said the old lady facing her across the table. Jan had been casting furtive glances in her direction for some time. She had white hair and frail refined features, and a rather battered CND badge on the lapel of her heathery tweed jacket (worn for sentimental reasons, presumably – or did the Campaign for Nuclear Disarmament still exist? Jan realized she had no idea). There was a well-worn paperback edition of George Eliot's *Middlemarch* lying on the table in front of her, but she was reading this week's copy of *The Big Issue*.

Jan glanced out of the window of the train, across level farmland to the long ridge of the Hambleton Hills on which the white horse could clearly be seen. 'Oh yes.' She felt relieved to be distracted from her thoughts. The past week had left her feeling bruised and exhausted and utterly depressed; in no mood, really, for a weekend of nostalgia and socializing. She had tried very hard to bring some enjoyment into the time she shared with Keith (could you call it sharing, when

one party was so unresponsive to everything?). She had cooked his favourite dishes,
urged him to come with her to a pub or a
film just once during the week, tried to initi-
ate cheerful conversation. But he had remained resolutely entrenched behind some
invisible barrier – or behind sheaves of paper
he'd brought home from work – and had
merely seemed irritated when she tried her
hardest to draw him out. The most agreeable
evening had been Wednesday, when he'd
been delayed by a meeting after work and
she had been able to eat alone, without his
silent presence across the table, without that
desperate search for something interesting to
say. She had even found herself wondering if
he had another woman somewhere; and if
she would mind all that much if he had. On
the other hand, he had recently been working late rather less often than usual. Perhaps
that meant there *had* been another woman,
but the affair was now over; that might
explain his gloomy mood. But she could not
seriously give countenance to such an idea.
It was just not Keith. In any case, there had
been no sudden transformation from good
humour to bad. She simply could not
remember when he had last been truly good
humoured, or what it had been like when he
was.

Daily, she had found herself missing the
children more and more. It was not precisely

that she felt bereft by their absence – in fact, it was a relief not to have to take constant account of their comings and goings and their dietary requirements (Simon had been a vegetarian since his mid-teens, Mel occasionally ate chicken or fish, but insisted everything was rigorously low fat). It was pleasant to find the fridge still full when she came down to breakfast in the morning, and bread left in the bread crock; there were no mouldering coffee mugs in odd corners of the house, and she could take the car whenever Keith had no need of it. And there would no longer be sudden calls from Simon at most inconvenient times asking them to come and collect him from Durham station eighteen miles away, as he'd decided on impulse to come home to see his twin. It was certainly a relief not to lie awake half the night, listening for the sound of the car, because Mel was out and would be driving home late and might have an accident and never return at all. Much better not to know what she was doing at any given time. It was certainly not that Jan wanted to keep her children with her for ever, or to continue to play an integral part in their lives. But it was only now that they had gone that she realized how much she had depended on each of them for companionship, friendship, support, for a readiness to listen as well as to talk. They were no longer her dependants, nor did she want them to be, for they were equals now, adult friends closer to her than any others. She shared things with them as she had never done with Keith, even, she thought, in the early days. In going, they had left her with a stranger from whom she seemed to have grown apart without even noticing what was happening; and one whose nerves seemed at present to be set on edge by her every word.

But this weekend was hers. She had been looking forward to it for weeks and she was not going to let anything spoil it, she decided. She opened her shoulder bag and took out the envelope with its cache of photos, sorted from their tattered folders in the week before she left home. Faded and yellowing, they showed grey glimpses of new concrete buildings, with small grinning grey and white figures awkwardly posed in front of them. They seemed as old, from as distant a past, as Victorian photographs.

She smiled to herself; looking up, she caught the eye of the woman opposite. 'I'm on my way to a university reunion. I've unearthed these old photos. Funny how you don't really feel any older most of the time, but just look at these! I look so absurdly young. I suppose I was younger then than my children are now. Thirty-five years. It's terrifying.'

'Wait till you've lived as long as I have.' The

old lady was clearly not immune from the common practice of the elderly of boasting about their age; it was a waiting-room topic only too familiar to Jan. 'I'm eighty-seven.'

'Really? You don't look it.' For once, that was true; she was only a year older than Auntie Hilda, but seemed years younger. 'You must have seen some changes in your life.' Jan wondered as she spoke how often her companion had heard that remark, and whether it irritated her to hear it yet again.

If she was irritated she hid it well. 'Not all for the best, of course – but most of them, yes, on the whole.'

'Have you a family?' She could not see a wedding ring.

'Nieces and nephews, great-nieces and nephews, lots of them. But none of my own.' She spoke very clearly, just a little more loudly than Jan found comfortable – she did not really want the entire compartment to overhear their conversation. 'I was a teacher, you see, a biology teacher. I loved my job too much to marry. In those days you had to leave if you married. By the time they changed the rules it was too late.'

Like Auntie Hilda, Jan thought, who had been a junior school teacher, latterly a headmistress, her whole life devoted to her pupils, who had continued to write to her and even visit her for years after her retirement – until lately, when her mind began to go. 'That must have been hard. A painful choice to have to make.'

The old woman shook her head. 'Oh, not really. Friendship is a pretty good substitute for love and passion. I'm not sure it doesn't wear better in the end.'

That, Jan thought wryly, was probably true. After all, it was friendship that seemed to elude her where Keith was concerned.

'To be honest with you,' the old lady went on, 'I'm rather thankful I didn't have the choice to get married *and* go on teaching. It seems to me everyone tries to do too much these days; they all want to have their cake and eat it, and then they find themselves being pulled in all directions. Much better to be able to concentrate on doing one thing at a time and doing it well – being a mother *or* working at a career, whatever your vocation is.' She chuckled. 'Vocation: now there's an old-fashioned word!'

'Perhaps nowadays we're more concerned with seeking happiness,' suggested Jan.

'And that's a project doomed to failure. The surest way not to find happiness is by setting out to find it, don't you think? It can only ever be a by-product. Live your life to the best of your ability, and you'll probably be happy. Of course, there's no point in being unhappy for no good reason. But so many people seem to think they'll find fulfilment just by never allowing themselves

29

to be bored or uncomfortable, even for a moment. In my experience they only end up thoroughly confused and miserable. We all need a purpose, of some kind, something to work for.' She smiled suddenly. 'There, don't I sound like any old woman bemoaning the faults of the young? I would except a good many of the very young, however. They're all right, whatever you read in the media. I'd be out there with the anti-globalization protesters if I were a wee bit younger. It's the middle-aged, the ones who put self before everything, they're the ones who worry me, obsessed as they are with material things. Yourself excepted, I'm sure,' she added, her eyes twinkling, though Jan wondered if she really made that exception or was simply being polite.

'I could imagine you at Greenham Common,' she said suddenly.

The woman chuckled. 'So I was. Wonderful years.' She began on a series of startling reminiscences of that heroic era of anti-nuclear protest, which kept Jan enthralled all the way to London.

In the small, flower-crammed office at Faraday, Willet and Sneyd, the telephone rang suddenly, breaking into Fiona's concentration. She read to the end of the sentence (it was in French, so took a little longer than it might otherwise have done) and then reached over a knot of pink rosebuds and lifted the receiver. 'Call for you, Miss Grey,' said a brisk female voice. 'Mr Preston.'

Fiona sighed with exasperation. 'Tell him I'm in a meeting.'

'Shall I ask him to call back later?'

'No. He knows well enough I don't want to speak to him. Or he should do. If he doesn't get the message this time, fob him off with something else.'

'Right. I understand. Leave it to me.'

At least there had been no more flowers today. Fiona moved a vase of lilies to the floor, giving herself more space, and return-ed her attention to the documents on her desk. She had to assimilate all the essential points before she set out for France, if she was to gain anything from the trip. But Sam's face seemed to hover over the page, obscuring her view of the dry legal words, pale as when she had last seen it, nearly two weeks ago, when he had been so shocked by her decision to end their relationship. She refused to feel guilty about it. For a long time now the relationship had been dead in all but name, stale and going nowhere. The fact that they shared a flat was all that had kept it going for so long; it had simply seemed too complicated to untangle her life from his. But in the end her patience had run out; she had seen that there had been no point at all in trying to prolong the relationship any further. If Sam couldn't see that now, he would, given time.

Yet there was an ache inside her at the thought of him. They had been together for five years, and she supposed she would always be fond of him. She did not like the thought that he might be hurt, however unavoidably. On the other hand, his persistence made her feel rather less uneasy about him, fast replacing her guilt (for she had felt guilty, in spite of her good intentions) with irritation. He had phoned her several times a day since their parting, bombarded her with e-mails, sent flowers both to her flat and the office, so many that she had been forced to buy new vases to accommodate them, since she hadn't quite the heart to throw them out. She had been surprised by his behaviour. He had always seemed the most placid of men. She'd thought he had more self-respect than to indulge in these undignified tactics.

Before Sam's call, in the intervals when her attention had not been wholly given over to the documents, she had been looking forward to the coming weekend, and wondering if anything would develop from her meeting with Éric Fournier, in whose Paris flat she would be staying (why, she wondered, did the French have a taste for the most unfashionable of English Christian names?). He was one of the senior partners in the firm with which her own legal practice dealt in France. They had met twice before, and she was sure he was attracted to her – as she was to him. But when they had last met she had not been free; now she was, though she suspected that he was not. Nothing had been mentioned, but she had sensed the existence, somewhere, of a wife. That only made the prospect of their meeting more exciting. Forbidden fruit, she had thought, full of anticipation. Now thoughts of Eric had been dislodged by those of Sam and she could not get him out of her head.

She glanced at her watch: nearly half past four. She had a little time left before she had to set out for King's Cross to meet her mother. She tried to force her attention back to the documents.

When she left the office, Sam was waiting outside, and pounced on her as she came through the door. 'Piss off, Sam!' she said, but he simply held her arm, lightly enough, but preventing her from easily walking away.

'Please, Fee! I just want to talk to you.'

'There's nothing to talk about, Sam. Leave me alone.' She looked into his wounded eyes. They were limpidly blue, but still made her think of a dog's. 'Look, you admitted we weren't going anywhere. We talked about it long enough. It was you who said it had gone stale.'

'That was an argument for trying to liven

things up, not end them.'

'Flogging a dead horse.'

'Fee, what we have has never been that! We used to have such good times.'

Fiona knew he was trying to encourage her to look back, to remember, thinking he could soften her with sentiment. But she had never been one for nostalgia. It was pointless – after all, you could not live in the past. 'We did,' was all she would say. 'And I'm grateful. I'll always be fond of you. But that's why we must end it now. So we can both get on with our lives.'

'I don't want to get on with it without you.'

'You haven't tried, have you? Just back off, leave me alone. You're a nice guy, and I want to be able to think of you kindly. But if you go on like this I shall start to hate you. Now, I've a train to meet, if you don't mind.' She shook off his hand and began to walk away.

He hurried to keep up with her. 'Then there *is* someone else. You said there wasn't.'

'And there isn't.' *Yet*, she thought. 'My mother's coming to stay.'

She saw regret pass over his face, a suggestion of happy times recollected. Sam had always got on well with her parents. She knew they had seen in him the ideal son-in-law, friendly, helpful without being obsequious, at ease in their company. She knew he had begun to feel that in them he had found substitutes for his own parents, who lived in the Far East. 'A lovely woman, your mother.'

'All the more reason not to keep her waiting.'

'Give her my love.'

He let her go then, but she knew he was watching her all the way down the street until she turned the corner into Gray's Inn Road and was lost to sight. She had no intention of passing on his message to her mother. She knew quite well that Jan would want to talk about Sam, but she hoped to limit the subject as much as possible. She decided she would not mention Sam's present persistence. In any case, she hoped fervently that he might at last be about to accept that things were over and leave her alone, though she feared it would not be as easy as that. In an odd way she felt almost flattered by his attentions, even while they exasperated her. Yet at the same time she despised him for them.

She walked briskly in the direction of King's Cross, trying by the exercise to shake off her agitation and brace herself to face her mother's questions. She had been looking forward to Jan's visit, happy to show her a glimpse of her life here in London. Now Sam had spoiled it for her. She hated the feeling that things – however temporarily – had slipped out of her control.

The moment she stepped off the train, Jan

glanced along the platform to the small knot of people by the barrier; she could not make out anyone she knew. She had to break off then to help her companion with her luggage, but as soon as she could she looked again. 'There's Fiona!'

The old lady followed her gaze to the poised figure in pale linen. 'What an elegant young woman.' They began to walk towards the barrier.

'Yes,' said Jan with pride. 'She is, isn't she?' As so often, she wondered how she and Keith had managed to produce this beautiful, assured creature. She was, on the face of it, not much like either of them. But then in spite of all their worries over the years, all their children had somehow turned into likeable and attractive adults.

'And there's my friend.' Another lively old lady – rather younger, Jan thought – came to greet her companion. 'Do enjoy your reunion. Nice to have met you.'

Jan watched them walk away. 'I hope I'm as sprightly at her age,' she said aloud, then she kissed her daughter. 'You do look well. Blooming, in fact. You're obviously not pining for Sam.'

'No, he's doing the pining.'

'Poor Sam.' She felt a genuine sadness.

'He'll get over it. Now, we'd better get a taxi. I know you like walking, but this bag would feel very heavy by the time we got there.' In the taxi, she said, 'I've booked a table for us in a little Italian place round the corner from the flat. You see, I'm off to Paris first thing tomorrow—'

'You didn't tell me that! Oh, Fiona, I must be the last thing you want under your feet tonight!'

'Don't be silly. I love having you. I'm only going till Tuesday, and everything's ready.'

'It's work then?'

'Yes. One of our clients inherited a property in France, so I have to disentangle it from the French legal system. It seemed sensible to do it in person. Just routine and very boring.'

Jan looked at her daughter's face, and was not deceived. 'You'll love it.' How good it must be to enjoy your job so much, she thought.

Fiona laughed. 'Yes, I probably will.' She peered out of the taxi window. 'Here we are.'

Her new flat, in a quiet road on the fringes of Islington, was roomy and comfortable. If she can afford this, Jan thought, looking round with eager curiosity, then she's clearly doing very well for herself, better than I realized. The flat was already marked discreetly with her personality, and filled with flowers. There were flowers too in the spare bedroom, freesias and carnations and irises and lilies, cramming the small quietly furnished room with colour and fragrance.

Jan gave a cry of delight. 'Oh, how lovely! You've gone to a lot of trouble.'

Fiona laughed. ' 'Fraid not. That's Sam for you. He's driving me up the wall. But at least it's saved me buying flowers for you. You'd have had to make do with just a bunch of freesias.'

'Oh, poor Sam!' Jan said again, with more feeling this time. 'Has he found someone else to share the old flat?'

'I don't think he's tried yet. But never mind Sam. Let's have a drink. I'm gasping for one. What will you have? Tea? Coffee? Wine? Whisky?'

Jan accepted a glass of Australian Merlot, and sipped it while her daughter changed, put away her briefcase (Jan glimpsed the open suitcase on her bed, already half-packed), sat down herself with a glass of wine. Jan told Fiona about her companion on the train, and how sad she felt that Auntie Hilda was not so mentally alert in her old age, and how she felt sure that Keith was worried about his aunt, though would not admit to the fact.

'It must be hard to think it's happening to someone you love very much. After all, she brought him up. Just imagine if it was Granny.'

Jan had already done so, many times, though her own mother, still living in their Surrey home, was younger than Hilda Grey, and very fit. They had been close during her childhood, while her mother, a war widow since Jan was a few months old, had struggled to bring her up single-handedly. The closeness had diminished later, when, just after Jan left for university, Audrey St John had suddenly married again. Jan was glad for her mother's sake and liked her stepfather, but had never known him well and inevitably she and her mother had grown apart as a result; yet the love between them would always be there, and a deep gratitude for what her mother had given her. She wondered if, at this moment, Fiona in her turn was trying to imagine how she herself would feel if Jan were to grow senile. Jan had a sudden sense of overlapping generations, of her own understanding of her mother enlarged by her experience of motherhood, of her understanding of her daughter enlarged by her knowledge of what it was to be a daughter, of that same pattern repeating itself with Fiona; and with Fiona's children, were she ever to have any. Which, inevitably, brought her thoughts back to Fiona's recently ended relationship. 'I'm sorry about Sam,' she said, though she feared her daughter was not very willing to discuss the subject.

'Don't be. It's for the best, believe me.'

'I shall miss him though. He'd got to be part of the family. A nice lad.'

'I know. But that's not enough is it? Nice

can be very boring, you know.'

'Oh, I know that. But you must feel it a bit after so long.'

'Not in the least. I wish he could be happier about it – I don't like to think of him being miserable. But he'll be all right. As for me, I'm just relieved. It's great to be free. I like having my own place again too, all to myself.'

Jan looked about her, remembering the large living room of the old flat, full of Sam's clutter – sports gear, computer (there had been one in every room – Sam was a software engineer, working for a small firm that designed games), shoes, CDs, electronic equipment of all kinds, so that one scarcely noticed Fiona's books and ornaments and pictures. Yet, here, they were what brought the flat to life. How odd to be able, so suddenly and completely, to eliminate all traces of another person from your life!

'I was thinking the other day,' Jan mused. 'I'd been married to your father for four years and had three children by the time we'd known each other as long as you and Sam have. But it was different then of course.'

'And that was you and Dad anyway. You always were different.'

It was something Jan had always accepted as appropriate, her children's assumption that their parents' marriage was a model of what marriage should be. Now she found herself wondering what they could possibly have based it upon. Or did all children think like this of their parents' relationship, unless events proved them wrong? She, of course, was in no position to judge, or not from her own experience anyway. After all, she had grown up without a father. Not that it had seemed odd to her in any way, for her mother had somehow never allowed her to feel that anything was missing from her life. It was only when she became a mother herself that she realized how hard that must have been.

'But there must be a lot of people who married like you did,' Fiona was saying, 'because it was expected of them, and then woke up a year or two afterwards wondering what on earth they'd done.'

Had they? Jan wondered. True, many more marriages now broke up, even ones as long-standing as her own, yet many still survived, and not always unhappily. 'Are you saying you don't see any point in marriage?'

'Oh yes, when there are children, I think so. Children are better for security. But when there aren't any children, or once they've grown up and left home – well, that's different. After all, a woman wants different things from the father of her children than she does later on. Why tie herself for ever to the ideal father, when there might be the perfect lover just round the corner? Or, better still, free-dom, with the occasional perfect lover when you feel like it?'

'You don't think it's possible to find both in one man then?' She wondered what Fiona would say if she were to realize that Jan did not after all know the answer to this question. Even her own mother's experience did not help here, since her late second marriage had produced no children and seemed happy enough without them. She wondered if her mother had looked for something different in this second marriage than she had in her first. Perhaps she would ask her one day.

'Maybe,' Fiona said. 'You and Dad for instance. That's obvious. But you're the lucky ones. It's not true for most people. And certainly not for me and Sam.' She stood up, dismissing the subject, to Jan's relief – her head was spinning with all the unanswered questions thrust upon her. 'Let's go and eat. I booked an early table.'

'Good,' said Jan. 'I'm starving. I was afraid we'd be waiting till nine.'

Early though it was, the restaurant, an un-pretentious family-run business, was already full of noisy families. Marco, the proprietor, a round cheerful man who clearly knew Fiona well, showed them to one of the quieter tables by the window, and handed them their menus. 'Nothing pretentious,'

Fiona explained. 'Just good simple Italian family food. Their pizzas are great. But then so is everything.'

'Then I shall have a risotto. I've never yet made one that was really satisfactory. Maybe it'll inspire me.'

Fiona advised the mushroom risotto, and then ordered a creamy spinach pasta for herself – Grey family tradition insisted that, when eating out, everyone should choose a different dish so they could all taste as many as possible. To go with their meal, Marco recommended the house red, a good country wine.

'Are you going to apply for that job?' Fiona asked, as she filled Jan's glass.

'What, as practice manager?' Jan shook her head. 'No. I don't think it's me really. A few years ago perhaps, but I'm looking to slow down a bit now, not take on extra work.' She was surprised by what she saw in Fiona's expression. 'You're disappointed.'

'I think you'd make a splendid practice manager. After all, Dr Mead must think so, or he'd not have said anything to you. Hell, Mum, you're only just over fifty! You don't want to think of slowing down yet. Besides, you've not got any of us under your feet any more.' She grinned. 'You've got to fill all those empty hours.'

Jan knew it was a joke; as was obvious, for she had plenty to do. Yet she did not want to admit that there was an emptiness. She tried to keep her smile carefree. 'True.'

'What does Dad think?'

'Oh, that I should do what I think best. If he has any other opinion he hasn't said. You know your father.'

'Well, I don't mind telling you what I think: I think you should go for it. You've been an old-fashioned traditional wife and mother all your life. You've never really done anything that uses all your gifts. Now's your chance!'

'That's all very well, but being a receptionist was meant to be a stop-gap – a useful little fill-in while you were all small. I never meant to make a career of it. Archaeology was my subject, remember.'

'That doesn't mean you can't make a good career out of something else. You're very good at organizing things, aren't you? But it's up to you, of course.' Fiona raised a forkful of shell pasta to her mouth. 'Have you heard how Mel's getting on?'

'Fine, I think. I was a bit wary of phoning. I'm not sure whether or not she still works shifts, and I didn't want to pick the wrong time – it wouldn't look good for the new manager of a grand hotel to be phoned up by her mother in office hours. I finally got hold of her at her flat on Wednesday night. She's very busy but enjoying life, I think. She says the flat's nice. I expect it'll all be a bit strange at first.' She was on the verge of telling Fiona of her unease, her sense that Melanie was, very skilfully, putting a brave face on things. But she had already told herself she was being over-anxious, so she said nothing. After all, it was inevitable that Mel should feel unsure of herself on first leaving home, at least until she had made new friends.

'You and Dad'll have to go and stay at the hotel.'

'When she's well settled in, that would be nice. Expensive though, I think. We'll have to save up.' The thought of staying anywhere – even in luxury – with Keith as her companion was cheerless in the extreme, as things were at present. Her thoughts veered sharply away from the subject. She *was* going to enjoy herself this weekend. 'You were right. This risotto is wonderful.'

They had coffee at the flat, to a background of some soft music unfamiliar to Jan – she liked it when the children introduced her to some favourite piece. 'You'll like this, Mum,' they'd say, as Fiona had just now. Then she'd added, 'I got it in France. It was recorded at a big Aids concert they had a few years ago.' And Jan did like the gentle, husky-voiced singing. As she listened, she reflected on the continuity of French pop music, for something about the song made her think of Franoise Hardy, whose records used to haunt her student days.

It was an agreeably companionable evening, which at last drove away all the tensions of the past week. Fiona talked about her work in a great deal of detail. Jan loved these glimpses into her daughter's world, which seemed amazingly exotic to her. She herself might be in touch with birth and life and death, but it was all very domestic and familiar and circumscribed. Fiona often travelled, and was familiar with the intricacies of foreign law.

'I've often wondered why you opted for Roman law,' Jan said, when there was a pause in the talk. 'Did you see the possibilities, or was it from choice?'

'Hm. I don't know. I suppose it seemed like a good career move, what with being good at languages as well. But sometimes I think it goes back a lot further than that. You know how Dad used to take me to Roman sites when I was little – after the twins were born, and he used to get me out from under your feet at weekends. We went to Hadrian's Wall, all over, a different place every week.' Jan had forgotten that phase. It had not, she thought, lasted very long, but to a small child like Fiona it must have seemed like years. 'I got hung up on the Romans then. I think that was in my mind when I went for Roman law. So you see, it wasn't a rational choice at all. I've Dad to thank for it.'

Jan was surprised to think of Keith having

so profound an affect on his daughter's life. She could recall no other occasion when he had so directly influenced any of them. 'He'll be glad to hear it.' Or would he? Would he just make some non-committal remark when she told him, and then return to eating or reading his paper or whatever he had been doing? To push thoughts of Keith away, she began to talk of Simon, and what she knew of his present job as part of the management team of a nature reserve in the Yorkshire wolds. 'They'd been having trouble with poachers, last we heard – they'd had to call in the police. But you know how bad he is at keeping in touch. I have a feeling we'll never hear from him now Mel's left. She was all that kept him coming back. And of course, he's never in if you phone. But then I always wanted an excuse to go and visit him...'

On Saturday morning, Jan caught an earlier train than she had intended, anxious to be out of Fiona's way as soon as possible; her daughter had to be at Waterloo by mid-morning, to catch the Eurostar to Paris, though quite why she had to be there so early in the weekend Jan was not sure; Fiona had somehow managed to avoid answering that question. Jan wondered if there was a man in the picture somewhere.

Fiona saw her off, waving as the train left the station. Then she walked briskly back towards the Tube, glad that was over. She loved her mother dearly, and she had enjoyed the visit. It was good to know that her parents were always there, a secure base, to be depended upon for love and support, in everything. But to be in their company was to take a pause from life, to sit back for a moment from its demands, as if one had briefly moored one's boat in a familiar and tranquil backwater – and even so well-loved a place could get on one's nerves after a while. Now, with Jan gone, Fiona moved back into the mainstream of her own life, looking forward with eager anticipation to the weekend ahead, a weekend uncluttered by old ties.

Three

Jan was the only person to get out at the small station that still served the university. It was probably much too early for anyone else to be arriving. She stood on the platform in the crispness of the autumn morning, and remembered how she had first stood here, a seventeen-year-old in an appalling powder-blue interview suit, on the day that had decided her future; or the next three years of it, at least. The station seemed to have changed very little, but then it had always been the most basic of affairs, two unadorned platforms linked by a narrow footbridge. She supposed there must have been some sort of ticket office in those days, but there was no trace of it now and she could not recall where it had been. She made her way down the path that led to the grand pillared entrance to the university. That was new. In her day the authorities of a visionary new venture would have despised such backward-looking pomposity. Besides, when she first came, most of the campus had still been a building site.

Now it was hard to find traces of the campus she remembered, all wide spaces and concrete. The acres of mud had given way to swathes of well-tended lawn, tastefully softened by reed-edged pools and stands of mature trees. In her day, there had been only a few very new saplings – the infants of these same trees, she supposed, which only underlined how very long ago it had all been. There were buildings all around, where there had been none before, not constructed in the fashionable sixties concrete, but in the brick that marked them of the eighties. She recognized the nearer building, its concrete now aged by lichen and water stains, but it no longer had the look of assertive prominence that had once marked it as the focal point of the campus, the students' union building where all social activity was centred. She hesitated, looking around her, wondering where she should go. She felt as strange and awkward as any new undergraduate.

The next moment a blonde young girl, smartly casual in appearance, approached her: Emma Percival, declared the badge on her lapel. 'Can I help? Have you come for the reunion?'

She led Jan along paved paths through the small town that the campus had become, pointing out this landmark and that – 'You'll remember the library, I expect, though it's been extended a few times, and the chapel. That's the medical centre over there. There's a nursery attached. The shops are nearby – the supermarket's not bad.' Jan gathered she was a second year English undergraduate, though she looked absurdly young, younger even than Jan's own children. As Jan had been, when she first came here...

Somewhere near the physics laboratories, Emma left her, directing her to an octagonal block far beyond the early sixties limits of the campus, where another girl, equally youthful, equally self-assured, assigned her to a study bedroom overlooking a courtyard. It was rather smaller than the accommodation she recalled as a student, though it had the familiar pin board and bookshelves and table. But the wardrobe was larger and there were private washing facilities. In another ten years, she guessed, every room would be expected to have its own shower.

Yet there was enough that had not changed for her to stand at the window, her eyes on the courtyard, hearing the voices beyond the door and wondering who they might belong to, whether to those who might (potentially) be her friends; enough for her to recall suddenly, in a great burst of feeling, what it had been like to be a new student here, all those years ago. Nervous, excited, full of hope and fear in equal measure, and in some ways (oddly) more self-confident than she was now, at least on the surface: Janet St John, first year archaeology undergraduate, fresh from her Surrey home, ready to take on the world. Now, she wore well-fitting jeans and a cream silk shirt and a navy jacket. Then (if not on the first day, then some time soon afterwards, according to the photographic record) she had worn a short skirt in some kind of tweed, and a loose grey jumper. She would not have remembered that detail, had she not looked out the photograph. Of course, the jumper might not have been grey; that might just be the photograph. It was hard now to recall the past in any kind of colour.

The courtyard was filled with a decorative mass of shrubs, carefully judged to give year-round foliage without providing cover for intruders. Otherwise, it was devoid of interest. She could not even see into any of the other windows that looked on to it – the building was arranged in such a way as to prevent any invasion of privacy. How unlike the uncompromising rectangles of her own hall of residence, which she had passed on the way here but scarcely recognized, so well-screened was it by more acceptable modern buildings.

She turned back to her own room and discovered a large envelope on the bedside cabinet, containing a sheaf of helpful documents – a list of those present (or expected to be), a map of the campus (only too necessary, Jan thought ruefully), a detailed timetable of events, and a printed plastic name tag, complete with pin. Janet Grey, née St John, hers said, and, underneath, Arch, for archaeology, her degree subject. She pinned it on the lapel of her jacket.

Then she unpacked, hanging her few clothes in the wardrobe, placing her washing bag beside the basin in the cubicle, slipping her folded nightshirt under the pillow, arranging other items on the shelves or the bedside table. She revelled in the sensation of having a room to herself, entirely for her, with nothing in it that was anyone else's. Not that it had much that was hers either, beyond her bag, her folding alarm clock, the bedside photo of her children. But for these two days it was her own place, hers alone.

She had a sudden tempting vision of this as a permanent state – not herself in this student room, but herself alone, as Fiona was, independent, able to arrange her life and her surroundings entirely as she pleased, without reference to anyone else at all. It seemed an alluring prospect. Was Fiona right, she wondered? Was this the more natural state, to want something very different from life as one grew older, as one's children left one's care? And if so, did that necessarily exclude Keith? Of course, in the old days, many women would not have survived into old age. Now she, like many others, could look forward to years beyond child-bearing. No longer in need of support and protection, was it instead a biological imperative for a woman, unexpectedly given this extra lease of life, to have her freedom, to have the opportunity to try all the things which her maternity had denied her for so long? Jan had always assumed that in old age companionship between life partners would be the natural goal. But if there could be no real companionship from that partner, if the stresses of the intervening years had driven them apart, made them strangers, then what point was there in prolonging the relationship?

She realized that her thoughts were

carrying her to a frightening position, and abruptly dragged them back to the practicalities of her present situation. There was still an hour to go before morning coffee; she thought she might explore the grounds a little. But on her way outside she passed a small communal kitchen. A woman was plugging in a kettle, a tall, very thin woman with well-cut dark hair, and something vaguely familiar about the way she moved. She looked round as Jan passed, and there was a moment's hesitation while they considered one another – they were not quite close enough to read the name tags they both wore. Jan knew they were each thinking: I know her; now who *is* she? Probably, too, they were trying to recall whether or not the original acquaintance had been one they would ever wish to renew; if not, they would simply look away again and continue with what they had been doing. It was the other woman who apparently answered the question first. 'Jan St John! It is, isn't it? My goodness, you haven't changed a bit.'

Jan took a step nearer, put on her reading glasses and peered at the other woman's tag, which confirmed what at that moment she remembered: Rosemary Chawton. Eng. A brief confused succession of scenes passed through her mind: a tall figure holding forth during students' union elections; a performance of *Tis Pity She's a Whore*, in which

Rosemary, in full Jacobean black and gold, had the leading role of the incestuous sister, and milked it for every ounce of passion (not difficult perhaps, when her male protagonist had been the dazzling Roger Helme) – Jan, playing a minor walk-on role, had been awed by her; a tutorial partner (what on earth had they been doing in the same tutorial?) explaining with plausible fluency how she had been utterly prevented by circumstances beyond her control from writing the requir-ed essay. She also remembered a great deal of wild laughter. Rosemary had been fun.

'You look stunning,' Jan said. She felt a surge of envy. 'What are you doing now?'

'Oh, this and that. Mostly running a bou-tique.'

Successfully, Jan supposed, noting the many rings on her fingers, the gold chains about her neck, the well-cut clothes. She still looked good in the black that could be so ageing to women over fifty.

'I'm gasping for a cup of tea,' Rosemary went on, surprisingly; Jan would have thought whisky was more in her line. 'You, too?'

'Why not? We've got a while before we start.' She glanced again at Rosemary's name tag. 'You didn't marry then?'

'Oh yes, I did, I'm afraid. Worst thing I ever did, though at least it didn't last long. I went back to my maiden name after the divorce.

55

Thought it might help me forget he'd ever had any part in my life. He was a shit, frankly. But you're still married to the same person?'

'Yes.' Jan wished she hadn't mentioned marriage. She wanted to forget Keith, and home, for these few hours at least.

'Quite something these days.' The kettle boiled and Rosemary poured water on tea-bags in two mugs – Jan wondered where she had found them; or had she brought her own? 'Milk? Then you probably don't take sugar either. Just as well – I haven't any. I go for less banal vices.' She leaned back against the worktop, sipping her tea. 'I was looking through some old letters the other day. Can you believe it, I kept them all? Or I did then. Not any more. I found one from you.'

'Never!' Jan had thought they had lost touch as soon as they left university. Rose-mary had never been much of a letter writer, and she herself had soon been distracted by domesticity. She had meant to search the boxes in the loft for old letters before coming here, but had not had time.

'Very important one too, though I bet I never got round to answering it. You were telling me you'd met this wonderful man and were going to get married. "Keith makes me laugh", you said. "We laugh all the time." Sounded good to me.'

Jan looked startled. Had she really written

that? Had it even been true? She could not now remember when Keith had last laughed, not really laughed.

'I should have taken note of that,' Rosemary was saying now. 'No marriage is going to work without a sense of humour, on both sides. Lance had all the romantic charm – looked wonderful, brought flowers and gifts, flattered me. But no sense of humour, not a glimmer. Took himself completely seriously and didn't care twopence for anyone else. Boring too, once the first excitement had worn off. I should have seen the signs. But I suppose no one thinks of these things when they're in love. You were lucky to stumble across a good man.'

'Yes,' said Jan. She hoped there was no indication of doubt in her voice. She did not want to have to explain that everything was not quite as wonderful as Rosemary might think. After all, it was something she had scarcely begun to face herself. She glanced at her watch and was relieved to see what the time was. 'Shall we go over to the common room now?'

'Not *the* common room – the junior common room in Egremont House. They've got about six common rooms now, as far as I can see. Oh, how things have changed! It was all so much simpler in our day. Have you noticed all the car parks? Car parks! I can't remember anyone having a car, can you? But then it was the thing to be working class and poor.'

'And what a lot of trouble we middle-class students went to, putting on accents and dressing down. Of course, you wanted to be northern too, preferably from Liverpool.'

Rosemary chuckled. 'Do you remember Carol Wright? She really was from Liverpool. We all cultivated her.'

'Ah, but what no one knew was that her family owned a whole chain of department stores and she'd been to some posh public school. I had a room next to hers in the first year and she had no accent at all then, at least not until she'd been here a week or two.'

'I wonder what became of her?'

'She died of cancer, not long after graduating.'

'Oh God, I didn't know.'

They found their way to the oldest of the buildings on the campus – the one they had known as the Students' Union – and through vast open halls and stairways and passages to a common room that was in some ways still as they remembered, though the orange and brown furnishings of their day had given way to cooler, more neutral tones. It was all odd, half-remembered, like some once well-loved face now recalled only partially, the shape of a nose here, the expression of an eye there, never quite able to be grasped as a whole.

The room was already filling with people like themselves, all with that look of half-familiarity, all peering at name-tags, some with continuing blankness, some with a cry of recognition: 'I *thought* that's who it was!' Jan smiled to herself. Her first impression had been how reassuringly little everyone had changed, once you remembered who they were. Her second, that in one respect their age was immediately apparent. Nearly all of them, male or female, had those telltale reading glasses on a string or chain about their necks, or tucked into a breast pocket.

Along one wall there were screens covered with old photographs, programmes, student magazines. Jan and Rosemary went to examine them, reading, musing, laughing, commenting. 'It's funny,' Jan said to Rose-mary, 'you think students have always worn jeans, as a matter of course. I'd quite for-gotten that we didn't. Don't we look staid in all those skirts? So much for the swinging sixties.'

'At least they were miniskirts. I suppose that was the rebellious bit. Do you remem-ber how awkward it was with stocking tops, until tights came in? You always thought your suspenders were showing.'

Jan was surprised to think Rosemary might ever have worried about such things. She had always seemed supremely indifferent to the banal anxieties that afflicted the less confident. 'They were too, most of the time.'

'Thank God for tights,' said a woman out of Jan's sight beyond Rosemary. 'The best thing that happened to fashion.'

'Sandy Portman!' cried Rosemary, turning to embrace the woman. Jan, who had not known her particularly, smiled a vague greeting and moved off in another direction, pleased to be alone again. It had been good to meet Rosemary, but she wanted to meet others too, perhaps those who had meant more to her.

Coffee was being served in the refectory beyond the common room. Jan wandered through and took a cup and talked to one or two people she remembered – most of her contemporaries seemed, dispiritingly, to have become teachers or social workers. It made her feel slightly happier about her own career path, such as it was. Not having found any really close acquaintance from the past, she looked around the room, trying to decide where to sit, then glanced towards the windows that lined one wall.

Wasn't that Roger Helme, talking animatedly to two women on a group of chairs by the window? She could hear their laughter. His hair was still dark blonde, though thinning a little on top, and she well remembered the arrogant poise of his head, the nonchalance with which he flung his arms along the backs of adjacent chairs. She had never known him well, but had nursed a hopeless crush on him during her entire three undergraduate years, in spite of various not very satisfactory boyfriends. She moved towards him, but could not quite find the courage to join the group – they were so obviously absorbed in one another, and would probably resent an intruder. Instead, she sat down on a nearby chair, facing another man, who was sitting alone with his back to the group, gazing out on the view of a lake enlivened by ducks and a pair of swans. He looked round at her. He was sturdy, with tousled greying hair, a tanned weatherbeaten complexion, a look of rough-hewn eccentricity. She smiled, put on her glasses to read his tag: Don Hadley. She thought she had heard the name somewhere, but that was as much as she could say about it. Arch, it said underneath the name – so he had been in her department. She had no real recollection of him. But then the male archaeology students in her year had been an unprepossessing lot on the whole. It was hard to believe that this man could ever have been one of them. 'We must have met, I suppose. But I'm ashamed to say I don't remember.'

'We had the odd seminar in common. I do remember you.'

She had seen him narrowing his eyes to

read her name – no reading glasses in evidence, for once; she wondered if it was vanity or exceptional sight. 'What are you doing now?'

'Professor of Archaeology at Oxford, St Mark's College.'

She was impressed. 'You must be one of the few who's ended up doing – well, I was going to say the obvious, but that sounds a bit dismissive.'

'Following the mapped-out path. Yes. Sadly predictable.'

'Not at all, I imagine. It's what I dreamed of doing once. And what am I now? A doctor's receptionist.'

'What happened to the dreams? Marriage, children?'

'Something like that.' Janet St John had imagined herself marrying an archaeology professor (Roger Helme had always seemed beyond her reach, and was in any case too unconventional for marriage), someone exciting and charismatic like their own Professor Mike Hardwick, who (disappointingly) was at the time happily married with a large young family – he was now too infirm to attend the reunion, so she had been told. She had dreamed of a life of shared endeavour, shared achievement, of which hers might be the less, but only because of the inevitable interruption of children – she had always wanted children, children and marriage. 'Are you married?'

'Was. My wife was killed in a car crash four years ago.'

'I'm sorry.' She wished she had not asked, though he seemed unperturbed.

'We were about to divorce. I don't know if that made it worse or better.'

'I suppose you'd feel guilty.'

'Oh, I'm not much given to introspection. My work's always come first anyway. Which I suppose was the trouble.'

'But you've taken time off for this weekend.'

He looked as if he had not considered that point until now. 'So I have. I wonder why? Curiosity, I suppose. Or a vain attempt to recall one's youth. Isn't that what it's all about?'

'I don't know,' she said. 'Isn't it rather that we're all beginning to feel we've come to – well, I suppose, some sort of watershed in our lives? We want to look back at what we were, and what we've become, and then maybe look at where we're going next. It's the right moment – for many of us, the first time we've been able to pause for breath and take stock; to be something other than a wife and mother, or whatever. Though perhaps men don't feel that need. They're rarely in the nest long enough to notice when it's empty.'

'Ah, so that's it, is it? Your family's just

flown?'

'The last one, yes, on Monday. Melanie's twenty-five, but she chose to do her degree at our nearest university, then she worked for a local hotel chain, so she's always lived at home, up to now.' This is boring, she found herself thinking; why am I droning on like this? But her companion did not look bored, which was perhaps why she continued to ramble on, pouring out the small details of the recent past. 'She and Simon are twins, so though he works away, he was always coming back to see her. Now she's been promoted to manage a hotel in the Midlands, so it's as if they've both gone at once. I'm not sad exactly, but it's taking some adjusting.' She decided not to mention that it was not adjusting to the empty nest that was the main problem, but to the stranger who had helped her to build it.

'So, is this weekend going to be a success? *Are* you rediscovering yourself?'

'Too soon to say, I think. It's odd though: so much seems the same, and then you get a jolt because something else isn't.'

'I know what you mean—' He glanced round as someone came up to them.

'Jan! Sorry to interrupt, but I had to come over.'

Jan stood up. This time the face was wholly familiar. They had shared a room for a year, a flat for another, and had kept in touch ever since; someone very like herself, in standard high-street trousers, shirt and jacket, with tidy hair and clean shoes and a general look of ordinariness. 'Sue!'

They kissed, and Sue Haswell said, 'I've just found Patty Freeman. I promised I'd bring you over. She's over there.' She gestured towards a large woman in a wheelchair, talking to two others near the coffee hatch.

Jan glanced round at Don Hadley. 'Excuse us – we've a lot of catching up to do. See you around.'

'Sorry to drag you away,' Sue said as they went. 'I don't remember him, but he has a certain rumpled charm.'

'Yes,' said Jan, surprised to realise the truth of the remark. 'I suppose he has.' She glanced behind her, and saw he was already in conversation with someone else. 'To tell you the truth,' she confessed in a conspiratorial undertone, 'I was rather hoping to get talking to Roger Helme.'

'Not him still! I thought you'd have learnt by now – he always was a lost cause. You were wasting your time.'

'Oh, I know I was never really exciting enough—'

'Jan, he's gay!' She studied Jan's astonished face. 'You must have known!'

Jan felt unutterably foolish. Looking back now it seemed obvious. True, he had often been seen in the company of the most glamorous female students, but then in those days active homosexuality was still illegal and most men of his kind tried to create some kind of impression of hetero-sexuality, as a protection. But she could not recall that any girl's name had ever been closely linked to his for long. On the other hand, there *had* been inseparable male friends, one at least of whom she had known, even then, to be homosexual. 'Funny, I saw myself as Mrs Worldly-Wise in those days,' she admitted ruefully. To cover her discom-fiture, she changed the subject. 'You were still teaching, last I heard.'

'For my sins, yes. But I plan to be out by the end of this year. Retired, a lady of leisure. I've had enough.'

Jan wondered how many times she'd heard that lately, from those of her friends who were teachers, worn down by regulation and prescription and constant changes in gov-ernment policy.

They reached Patty in her wheelchair. Disabled by polio from childhood, her cheerful presence as a student among them had been something worthy of note, a sign of the progressiveness of the university. Now, commenting favourably on the improved disabled access of the campus since their student days, she added, to Jan's surprise, 'I always felt I was here on sufferance, no matter how kind everyone was.' She had for many years been an active campaigner for the rights of the disabled. Jan had occasionally heard her interviewed on the radio, when an expert opinion was sought.

There were so many people to meet, so much talking to do, so much catching up, that the official welcome in the main hall seemed like an intrusion, as did the guided tour of the campus that followed. The guide, an eager, confident student, gave up trying to speak through the chatter of his unruly group, and let them simply walk and talk. Jan reflected that he must be unused to seeing his elders behave in so undisciplined a manner.

Lunch was a buffet meal in the refectory, and then came meetings of the different subject groups, with those of their old lecturers who were in sufficiently good health to attend. Jan talked until her throat hurt, and laughed and shared confidences, and was surprised, touched, bored, delighted by turns. All the time memories came tripping over one another to the front of her mind, incidents from her student days, things she had felt and thought all those years ago. It was almost as if she were Janet St John again, as if the years in between had been effectively swept away; almost, but not quite, not completely. She could see now, as she had somehow failed to do then, that it had been a period of infinite possibilities, of unparalleled opportunities; of possibilities not taken up, of opportunities missed.

There was a grand formal dinner that evening, and then a disco. Jan wondered if many others, like herself, were unused to staying up so late, and to cramming so much into so short a time. But excitement gave her energy and stamina.

She had thought to sit in a group with Sue and Patty, but Sue developed a crippling headache and went to bed, and Patty had arranged to go home overnight and left after dinner. Jan found a seat with other rather slighter acquaintances, and danced with a junior civil servant called Alan Pike, whom she had once, briefly, been out with all those years ago, though it had never developed into anything much. How innocent they had all been, she thought now; how wary of taking risks, in those days before the pill became widely available and the old double standard still ruled the lives of most women. Alan was not much of a dancer anyway, still less of a conversationalist, and she soon found an excuse to move to the far side of the room where she could sit down and watch the dancers in peace.

The room was a vast dim cavern, low-ceilinged, stretching away into shadowed corners and alcoves which the flickering disco lights could not quite reach. Faces glimmered, moved into focus, faded; sounds came and went in bursts. Some way off she glimpsed the one obvious success story of their year, a writer of raunchy best-sellers, who sat alone, like Jan herself, sombrely watching the dancers. Perhaps, Jan thought, she was simply observing, gathering material for her next novel. Perhaps she was just not very good company. After all, there was no law that said people who wrote entertainingly must necessarily be entertaining themselves; perhaps the writing of fiction was a substitute for life. Not far from her, loud shrieks of laughter came from a wildly gyrating group at the centre of which was a woman whom Jan knew to be a worker with disturbed children. At least she seemed happy, her high spirits infecting everyone around her.

Jan suddenly felt alone and tired and even a little despondent, and considered making her way back to her room to go to bed – it was nearly midnight, after all. But she was reluctant to let the day simply peter out like this, leaving so many tacit expectations unfulfilled. To her astonishment she even found herself wishing for Keith. He danced well – or he used to – and with him as her partner she used to love dancing. In that, at least, they had always found a natural harmony, an instinctive compatibility. Together, they would do a superb jive, which on occasions had even impressed their children, otherwise embarrassed to see their parents displaying themselves in any way.

Someone slipped into the seat beside her, breaking into her thoughts. She looked round to see Don Hadley. 'Never was much of a one for dancing,' he said. 'You don't mind if I join you?'

'Not at all.' Another lonely individual, she thought.

'Can I get you a drink?'

She indicated the inch or so of white wine and soda still in her glass. 'I'm fine thanks.'

'Such energy!' He nodded towards the worker with disturbed children. 'Have you noticed, it's the people with the most worthy jobs who really seem to know how to let their hair down.'

So he's realized that too, thought Jan. Aloud, she said, 'Before I came, I was wondering who the high-fliers would be. The odd thing is that in present day terms there don't seem to be any. Nearly everyone's doing worthwhile, socially useful things, like teaching. No financial whizzkids, no entrepreneurs.'

'We have the odd politician to our name, and an actor or two – not that they're here this weekend. But you're right. But then that's our generation for you. The early sixties: not sex and drugs and rock and roll, but an irritatingly strong social conscience. Not that much of that ethos rubbed off on me.'

'But what you do, you do for love of the work, not for money or recognition.'

'True. If I'd wanted fame and fortune I'd darn sure not be in archaeology. Or I'd become a media figure, a Julian Richards or whoever.'

'That doesn't tempt you? I could imagine you doing it well.'

'But then you have less time for getting your hands dirty on the ground. That's what I really enjoy. Not the papers or the conferences or the teaching, but the moment when you scrape away centuries of dirt and suddenly find a living artefact staring back at you, just as it lay hundreds of years ago. Or that subtle variation in soil colour or texture, when you know you've got a post hole, and there really was once a building on that site. Wonderful. There's nothing like it.'

Jan suddenly recalled that feeling too, as she had experienced it herself during her undergraduate and early postgraduate years. 'What period do you specialize in?'

'Saxon. Early Saxon, for the most part. We're about to start a new dig in the Thames valley. One of these six-weeks-working-flat-out jobs, since they want to develop the site.' He told her of the accident of the site's discovery, and what he hoped for from the dig. His excitement easily communicated itself to her, and she listened enthralled. It was not simply what he said that fired her, awakening all her own dormant enthusiasm for the subject, but she found herself fascinated too by the expressiveness of his face and the lively tones of his voice – deep and husky, verging on the craggy, like the rest of him. Sue was right, she thought; he did have a certain rumpled charm. She found herself wondering if his students found him as charismatic as she had found Professor Hardwick, all that time ago. It was an odd thought – had she missed a chance here, too busy looking for instant glamour to notice the potential of someone superficially less appealing, or who was, perhaps, simply a late developer? Or had she been the one who had been late in developing?

'You know your stuff still,' he said, at the end of some long explanation in response to her probing questions. 'Did you never think of getting back into archaeology?'

'Not really. When the children were small I simply wanted something that fitted in with their lives – receptionist to our local doctor seemed just right. Later, I took it on full-time. It's convenient, and I know I do it well.'

'It's not too late to change tack,' he suggested.

'Oh, I can't see anyone offering me a university job now, can you?'

'That depends. Tell you what, come and visit my dig. We start in three weeks. Come for a weekend. Get your hand in again; see how it goes.'

She looked at him in astonishment, realizing he was in earnest. Then, before she could say anything, the DJ announced the last dance. 'Yesterday', sad, nostalgic, slow, began to play. 'I suppose we'd better show willing,' said Don, standing up.

Feeling disproportionately excited, Jan let him take her hand and lead her to the centre of the crowded floor. She felt his arms slide round her, pulling her close, very close, as he began to edge her round the room. Not since her marriage had she been so near to another man. She could feel the angularity of his hips against her belly, his shoulder beneath her cheek. He smelled quite different from Keith, though she could not have said precisely how. Keith was so familiar in every way, at least in all that was external to him, so that, physically, he now seemed almost an extension of herself. This was new and different and somehow very exciting. She was guiltily aware of her own arousal. She wondered what it would feel like were he to kiss her. She wished he would, but hoped he wouldn't. She felt his hands move on her back, the beginnings of a caress. She was sure that at any moment he would bend his head towards hers.

But it was too late; the music came suddenly to an end, and they drew apart and stood politely clapping. Inside, she was in turmoil.

'Another drink?'

She shook her head. 'Too late for me. It's past my bedtime.' She instantly regretted the remark, which suddenly seemed flagrantly suggestive.

'I'll walk you back to your room.'

'Oh, there's no need,' she said, her voice breathless, and then heard herself add, 'only if it's on your way.'

Which, of course, gave him all the excuse he needed.

At first they walked decorously, side by side, in the patchy shadow beneath the trees. Once or twice his hand brushed hers. She had forgotten that sensation, the tingle that seemed to run up her arm, earthing itself right inside her. Once, she had felt like that with Keith, but not for years.

They reached the corner of the largest of the new buildings – the library, she thought. There, in a space that was briefly untouched by the light from any of the lamps, he halted, and she felt his hand close about hers. 'Jan, I fancied you the first time I saw you. I've never forgotten. I was much too shy to say anything then – and too wrapped up in my work. I don't want you to say anything now. But you're as attractive as ever you were.'

She heard herself say, 'Oh,' though the word emerged more as a sigh than a comment. Her legs felt absurdly weak, her breathing was almost beyond control. She had never imagined that one could feel like this at over fifty years old, like a girl being walked home from a dance by an attractive youth.

She felt him clasp her shoulders. His touch was cautious, hesitant, and she knew he was watching her face, trying to gauge her reaction, though she doubted if he could see anything. She forced herself to stand quite still, though every instinct urged her to move nearer to him.

There were voices behind them, fast approaching; and laughter. His arms fell to his side and they walked on, quickly now, as if escaping from something.

In the residential block the lights blazed, dampening excitement, discouraging possibilities. She felt absurdly regretful. He halted just inside the main door, looking at her. 'Good night, then. I've enjoyed this evening.'

'Me too. Thank you. See you tomorrow.'

Then he turned and walked away, and she let herself into her room.

She switched on all the lights and went to the mirror and stood gazing at herself. She looked flushed, bright-eyed, younger than her fifty-four years. *He finds me attractive. He nearly made a pass at me.* The realization was exhilarating, and suddenly made her feel beautiful, assured, exciting.

Four

Jan woke to a sense of anticipation mingled with anxiety. Dressing in a fluster, with fumbling hands, not knowing what to put on and in what order, she was swept suddenly back to the awkward student who had more than once woken like this all those years ago. The first time, it had been a crisp autumn morning, much like this one, some time during freshers' week she thought (had they called it that then, or had there been some more English, more traditional name – introductory week or something? She could not now remember).

Her first few days as a student had been terrifying – the talks were all right, as older students laid out the inducements offered by the various societies, in such glowing terms that she was almost tempted to join them all, there and then. But it was the evenings that were difficult, painful even. Then there would be some sort of hop (not a disco, not then), records from the hit parade blasted out to the madly-jigging students, the bar offering the inevitable anaesthetic for the shy (not many drugs around at that date), the lights too unwaveringly bright to induce the sense of anonymity that would have made it easier to reach out to others, to forget her awkward self. She recalled painful faltering attempts at conversation, silly questions that bored the listener, pretentious remarks that were meant to impress but patently failed to do so.

Then, after three days, she had enjoyed her first success; a youth had stayed to dance with her after the first approach, talked to her for some time, clearly liked her. She thought there might have been a kiss – how could one forget something that must, at the time, have seemed of crucial importance? She could not now remember who he was, what he looked like; the whole incident had apparently been quickly forgotten. But now, this morning, that small fragment of her past returned to her, stirred to life by the same feeling, the same sense of wakening to possibilities. She had no idea if she'd seen the youth again then, after that first en-counter. If she had done so, then presumably not much had come of it, since she could now recall nothing else about him, so little indeed that she had no means of knowing if he had come to the reunion.

But it had felt just like this all the same, the waking to exitement, to the knowledge that something had happened last night, to wonder at the possibilities the day might bring; even the air seemed to smell the same. Then, as she dressed, there was the same impatience to be across in the cafeteria, having breakfast, looking out for him, wondering what was going to happen next – if anything was – and the simultaneous fear that nothing might happen or that it might; the wondering what the latter alternative might bring. She had still been a virgin then, all those years ago, and more than a little afraid of losing her virginity. That, of course, was different, except that there was still the feeling that she might be faced with a moral choice, a temptation to something her conscience would not allow.

She looked in the mirror, and was almost shocked to see looking back at her, not Jan St John the student, but a middle-aged woman, who was, for a fraction of a second, almost a stranger. The oval of her face was unchanged, if less well-defined in outline, and the blue eyes were still there, but there were lines at their corners, and grey hairs among the chestnut ones, and just a hint of a double chin. All that eager frightened youth had gone, without trace. She grim-aced. 'You're an old married woman,' she told herself. 'You're not meant to feel like this. That's for silly teenagers.'

She put on her well-fitting cream trousers and a navy shirt, both of which she knew gave the most flattering emphasis to a figure that was still reasonably trim, and made her way towards the refectory building in a state of ridiculously nervous excitement. Rosemary joined her as they went. 'Good night last night,' she said. 'You seemed to be enjoying yourself.' She cast a sly smile in Jan's direction. 'Who was the nicely craggy man?'

Jan told her, though it was clear that Rosemary did not remember him any more clearly than she herself had done. 'We have an interest in archaeology in common,' she added primly, at which Rosemary laughed with a hint of derision.

'I'm going to have the works this morning,' Jan said as they reached the cafeteria; her stomach was churning, but she still felt hungry. While Rosemary helped herself to toast and tea, Jan filled her plate with bacon, eggs, tomato, sausage, mushrooms, fried bread, beans, potatoes, added to her tray a small plate of toast with marmalade and coffee and carried the tray to an empty table, glad that by then Rosemary had found another friend and gone to the opposite end of the room.

'That's what I like – a woman who doesn't spend all her time thinking about her figure.'

Jan looked round; and found herself blushing fierily, embarrassingly, just as she would have done all those years ago, in similar circumstances. 'Good morning, Mr

Hadley.' She glanced at his full plate. 'I can see you enjoy your food, too.'

'We archaeologists take what we can when we can. You never know when your next meal's coming, if at all. At the mercy of whoever's kind enough to cook for us. We get some strange meals, I can tell you. Tinned stuff or brown rice – no half measures. Why is it, I wonder, that those who undertake to cook always seem to be vegetarians at the very least, if not vegans?' He sat down at the other side of the table, and paused, studying her face, 'I didn't mean to imply that you needed to watch your figure. No one less in need of it.' His eye ran down her body, clearly approving the trim waist. Pleased, but embarrassed, she sat down too, so he could no longer see it. 'Am I being sexist?'

'If you are, I'll forgive you. At my age one needs all the compliments one can get, of any kind.'

'Stop fishing!' They ate in silence for few moments, then he said, 'What have they laid on this morning? I've left my programme in my room. All I can remember is coffee and a buffet lunch. But I know that's the final bit, before we go home.'

'I can see you go for the essentials,' she laughed. 'I think there's some sort of slide show or video or something before that: called "Early Days". But they've left us a good bit of time for socializing.'

He swallowed a forkful of scrambled egg. 'You know what I have in mind? Did you ever walk up Mount Tichford?'

'It was one of those things I always thought I'd do one day, but never did. Isn't there an iron age fort up there?'

'Yes. I did get up there, in my first year. But I heard they'd done a dig on it about five years ago. Thought I might go and take a look. Who wants to sit around socializing on a morning like this. Like to come with me?'

There was a pause. She knew she almost said 'yes' at once, without hesitation. She wanted to, but some scruple held her back. Just a walk, she told herself; that was all it would be, a walk on a fine morning with a congenial companion, sharing an interest in the subject they had once studied, though in her case it had been long neglected. But of course that was not all it would be. She had already acknowledged her morning sense of excitement. She recognized too what lay behind the impulse to say yes, and knew it was not simply a shared enthusiasm for an academic subject. If, say, Rosemary had asked, she could have said 'yes' or 'no' without a qualm, simply following the impulse of the moment; she would not have needed then to consider her answer. But it was not Rosemary who was asking her; it was Don.

On the other hand, they were both adults, sensible adults. It would be simply a walk, unless they chose to make it otherwise. But would she want to tell Keith about it afterwards? Should she perhaps suggest someone else might come? Or was she being foolish, reading into it what was not there at all, and never had been?

'What's the problem?' he prompted her at last, clearly sensing her doubts. Did he recognize them for what they were?

She realized then that there was only one answer she could possibly give, and smiled, from relief that was stronger than regret; though the regret was there. 'A very silly one,' she said. 'I haven't any suitable shoes.'

He peered under the table at her feet, in their neat black slip-ons. 'What's wrong with those?'

'Nothing, on pavements or roads. But they're all I've brought, and they couldn't cope with mud.' It had rained heavily during the past week.

'Oh – Oh, I see.' His disappointment was patent, and made her at once deeply regretful and yet relieved that she had found a way out.

After that, the morning's activities seemed tedious. She found herself scanning the gathering for Don, in case he might have decided that without her there was no point in going for a walk, but there was no sign of him and she felt obscurely resentful. Clearly he had not after all had any ulterior motive in asking her to join him; she could have gone with him without the slightest twinge of conscience. Though would she have wanted to, if it had all been entirely innocent?

What is the matter with me? she found herself thinking. I'm a married woman – happily married; yes, of course, in spite of everything, in spite of a temporary difficult patch such as all marriages go through, I wouldn't want anyone but Keith. Why should I even wish, for a moment, to play with fire, as I've been doing today?

Was it because in coming here she felt as if she had entered an existence taken out of time, one that was free of all the normal constraints of life; an existence in which, for two brief days, she could simply act on impulse, please herself? Or was it rather that in coming here she had regressed to a period when she was once again a student, with all a student's freedom from ties, all the eagerness to explore life and to break boundaries that young Janet St John had never quite dared to indulge? The trouble was, as she recognized with an angry sense of frustration, Janet Grey was as much held back by inhibition and scruple from following her instincts to their conclusion as Janet St John had been.

She found herself counting the hours and then the minutes to lunchtime, when she would be sure to meet Don again over the final buffet. But he must not yet have been back from his walk, for there was no sign of him that she could see, and, depressingly, she had to make do with Rosemary's company; her old friend joined her as she took a plate and joined the queue for food. 'You came by train, didn't you? Can I drop you off at the station? It's on my way, more or less.'

Jan accepted with a proper show of gratitude, because it would have been silly to turn the offer down; but her sense of depression only increased at this reminder that her time here was nearly over, taking with it the final opportunities – for what?

They had just sat down at one of the long tables, with their plates of chicken drumsticks, pork pies, sandwiches (what conventional food! Jan thought), when Don was there at her elbow, asking if he might join them. Jan found herself blushing furiously. She bent down suddenly, as if to retrieve her paper napkin (hastily, deliberately, dropped) from the floor, and hoped when she came up again that her heightened colour would simply be attributed to her recent position. Then she sat silent and uncomfortable, her appetite gone, while Rosemary chatted away, clearly charming their companion. For that time Jan hated Rosemary with all the venom of a jealous adolescent.

When lunch was over, the three of them walked together towards the residential blocks. Jan passionately wished Rosemary away, but she seemed quite oblivious to any sense of being superfluous – which was hardly surprising, when she assumed Jan was blissfully happy in her marriage and that Don was simply a casual acquaintance, less welcome as a companion than she was herself. Before long they separated, Don making his way towards the block where he was staying, leaving the two women to walk on together. 'Nice guy,' said Rosemary comfortably, and began to talk of something else. Jan was glad to reach her room and find herself alone.

She had packed most of her belongings before breakfast (to give herself time for more interesting actitivites later, she recognized now, with a renewed sense of opportunities lost) and now finished quickly and carried her bag down to the lobby. There, to her amazement, she found Don hovering by the door. 'Alone at last!' he whispered, with a quick glance up the stairs behind her, in case anyone else was coming. 'Tiresome woman!' Jan realized he was referring to Rosemary. 'Can't she see when she's not wanted?'

"She couldn't see any reason why she shouldn't be wanted,' Jan told him, her tone as neutral as she could make it, though she felt a small spark of girlish triumph at this evidence that she was indeed preferred.

'No.' He stood looking down at her. 'Jan, that offer for you to join the dig – I meant it. No strings. You'd enjoy it. Do come.' He reached into his pocket and pulled out a card, which he handed to her. 'My address and phone number.'

'How businesslike!' Why did one say such stupid things at times like this?

'Got it done in one of those machines at a station somewhere – had an hour to fill in between trains and couldn't face another BR coffee.'

They heard steps descending the stairs. 'Right, I'm off,' said Don hastily. 'See you!' And he slipped away just before Rosemary reached the lobby.

'Ready?' said Rosemary. 'You look a bit flustered.'

'All that rushing about packing.'

Rosemary talked as she drove, while Jan listened, glad that her companion was too much of a talker to notice another's silence. At the station, Rosemary readily accepted her plea not to come and wave her off. 'I'll write,' Rosemary promised.

No you won't, thought Jan. But she waved and called, 'Me, too!'

Jan wished that she could have called on Fiona again on her way through London, but she knew her daughter would still be

86

away. There was too much time for reflection, though she did not feel inclined for the casual, no-strings-attached chat that one has with one's fellow passengers. She could not shake off that other persona she had found at the reunion, young Jan St John, with all her life before her. There had been many train journeys like this in those days – parents were not then expected to transport oneself and all one's belongings at the beginning and end of term in the family car, even if there was a family car.

All her life before her, and no Keith at all, for they had not met then ... Life before Keith; without Keith – it was something she had never thought about before, would have found impossible to imagine. Now, at this time of regression, it *did* seem possible. It had, after all, been pure chance that had brought them together, if there was such a thing. They had been married young, as people were in those days, but even so there had been twenty-two years of her life before he came into it, and those the significant formative years. She had come to university from her comfortable Surrey home, leaving behind a mother she loved, a childhood that had been happy in spite of occasional minor hardships. As a student, she had affected to despise those things as bourgeois, respectable, but as much as the influences of her student years, they had made her what she was, then – and now? Was she still in any way the same person as that girl of long ago, or had she changed so much that nothing was left? How did you tell?

At Durham, this person she no longer knew got out of the train, apprehensive, yet full of hope; surely Keith would have missed her, would now be glad to see her, come lovingly to greet her? She scanned the crowd for him as she walked up the platform, skirting children hugging parents, couples embracing. Then she saw him waiting dutifully at the barrier, his expression patient. He waved when she caught his eye and came to take her bag, but did not smile. 'Good time?'

She had thought she would kiss him, she wanted to, but somehow the moment had passed and it would have seemed awkward, even odd to do so now. 'Yes, thank you.' She studied him as they walked together in silence to the car. He looked no older than Don, but had none of the archaeologist's air of relaxed ease with himself. Keith looked so careworn, so sombre; even his clothes – neat pullover, casual brown trousers – seemed worn for convention rather than comfort or ease. She could not now bring to mind what he had been like when they first met, but caught herself wondering what she could ever have found attractive in this man who was so intrinsically middle-aged. Had she really written to Rosemary 'Keith makes me laugh'? It seemed impossible to imagine it might ever have been true. 'Everything all right with you?' she asked, more from a sense of duty than from any expectation that she would learn anything from the answer.

'Yes, thank you.' He opened the car door for her. Shortly afterwards, with no more said, they were making their way home.

Always before when she had come home after an absence, she had come back to the familiar. It had folded her round, reassuring, safe, unchanged, its details unnoticed because they were a part of her.

This time it was different. The woman who returned had been recalled to an earlier time, to a person long gone and forgotten, setting out on a journey into the unknown. She did not feel this time as if she were simply returning, but almost as though she were coming to Meadhope and Mill House for the first time. She saw them with the eyes of the naive and hopeful girl she had been thirty-five years ago, a girl who was scarcely aware that County Durham existed, still less this Dale full of old industry and struggling hill farms. She saw the grey streets in the rain with the eyes of a stranger, the ugliness of the red brick council estate that edged the village, the way the weather dulled the honey-grey stone around the market place, blotted out the high green hills beyond its borders. Love and familiarity no longer soft-ened her view.

The house seemed cold, cheerless, suffused with a dreary light. 'I'll turn the heating up,' Keith said, going to the understairs cupboard where the controls were. Jan took her bag up to the bedroom – the room looked exactly the same as it always had, with the soft warm colours she and Keith had chosen together, yet somehow it no longer seemed quite to belong to her. She changed into jeans and sweatshirt and slippers, but still did not feel as if she had put on the old married Jan with the old clothes. She went downstairs, and found Keith in the kitchen. 'There's a pizza in the freezer,' he said. 'Will that do?'

They prepared the meal in silence, with the coordination of an old married couple, used to sharing tasks, though as usual it was Jan who did most of what might pass as cooking. She forced herself to be the wife again, to care about what most affected her husband. 'How was Auntie Hilda today?' She knew Keith had been going to visit his aunt without her.

'Fine.' Jan doubted it, but did not pursue the matter. In a way, this strangeness was pleasurable, exciting, and she wanted as long as possible to put off the resumption of her old self, her old life.

Over the meal, Keith asked her again about

the reunion, wondering if she had met many old friends, whether they had changed. His tone did not suggest any real interest in what she had to say – she thought he had spoken simply to fill the silence, but at least he'd noticed that there was a silence, which was more than he usually did, and for that she was grateful. Besides, it gave her an opportunity to try and draw him back into her life; into what she was beginning to see might be a new stage in her life.

'It's amazing how little everyone had changed. There was hardly anyone I wouldn't have recognized, even if I couldn't have put names to them without name tags. They said the same about me too, but maybe they were just being polite.' Keith, she noted, did not try to contradict her. She tried resolutely to describe the weekend in her liveliest manner, who she had met, what they were doing now, the more amusing things that had happened, but not once did he smile or appear to be truly interested. But then of course he had never known any of them, except Sue Haswell, who had come to their wedding, though they had not met since. Jan took a deep breath and ploughed on. 'There was one person who'd changed – for the better, I may say. He used to be one of the dullest archaeology students, very boring, I suppose because he lived for his work, which is what makes him interesting

91

now, to me anyway. He's an Oxford professor, and clearly loves what he does. We got
talking about archaeology – I'd forgotten
how much I used to love it. He's about to
start work on a Saxon site near Oxford – he
invited me to go for a weekend, once it's up
and running.' There, she had said it –
mentioned Don, and the invitation. It was all
quite innocent, of course; there would have
been no reason at all to keep it from Keith.

'You should go,' said Keith. 'You'd enjoy
it.'

Jan lowered her knife and fork and stared
at him. 'Do you mean that?'

'Of course. I wouldn't have said it otherwise.'

'I can't though, not really – there's too
much else to do.'

'That's up to you. I can't see a weekend
would matter.'

No, and she would escape Auntie Hilda
once again. But what would she be walking
into? With her eyes open too, as Keith's were
not. 'I'll see. I'll think about it.'

She had thought that Keith might be so
glad to have her back, might have missed her
so much, that he might even want to make
love to her for once. But the day ended like
any other Sunday evening, with an hour of
television, a mug of cocoa and then bed and
sleep – except that she did not sleep for a
long time, simply lay going over the weekend

92

in her mind and finding that Don's face and not Keith's was persistently at the centre of her thoughts.

Fiona always felt intoxicated by Paris, by its buildings, the sky, the river, the noise and bustle, the secret sunlit squares, the shops, its very air. It would have been enough to be there alone, with nothing to do and no one to keep her company. But to be there, as she was now, with the prospect of nearly four days in her favourite city as a guest of one of the most fascinating men she knew – that was sublime, perfection.

Éric Fournier was tall and well made, with silky fair hair and that air of casual elegance which only a Parisian seemed quite able to achieve. Unlike many of his contemporaries, he had learned his English during successive visits across the Channel, so he spoke with no trace of an American accent, fluently yet with a throaty lilt that Fiona found irresistibly erotic. His flat, in a quiet street not far from the Champs Élysées, was decorated in a style that Fiona could only describe as one of restrained opulence, the furniture in its grand rooms large and traditional, but the walls pale, the shining boards of the floors uncluttered except by a few judicially chosen and very expensive oriental rugs. There were a number of fine modern paintings, one or two tasteful ornaments and that was it – no

heavy drapes, no gilding or crystal chande-
liers (the lighting was modern, functional
and very well placed); above all, no massed
family photographs. There was no indication
at all that he was married, but she was still
fairly sure of it. He showed her to his spare
bedroom, as elegant as the rest of his flat,
with its own shower room, and when she had
washed and changed took her out for a light
lunch at a very expensive bistro just round
the corner. He was excellent company,
attentive, full of unobtrusive little compliments, amusing. After lunch, they simply
walked through the streets, while he showed
her corners of the city she had never
explored before, showed her treasures she
had never seen.

That evening, after a long and leisurely
dinner in one of the city's best restaurants,
they went to bed, not separately in the flat's
two bedrooms, but together, in his bed; and
he was every bit as wonderful a lover as she
had hoped, even expected.

It was all so easy and uncomplicated, so
unlike anything she had known before. But
in the small hours of the night, when she
woke briefly and for a moment could not
remember where she was or how she had
come to be there, she found herself wondering if she had allowed herself to be taken for
granted, if she had made it too obvious that
she was attracted to Éric, so that he had

been able, rightly, to assume that she was his for the taking. She even asked herself, uneasily, if she had cheapened herself by allowing all this to happen as it had. Then she told herself she was being foolish. What did it matter, so long as they both enjoyed themselves, so long as no one was hurt by it? It was a relief to know there were no demands to be made, no strings attached; just what was needed as a change from Sam.

During the whole weekend they avoided talking of anything personal, or of work either, come to that. On the Sunday, he took her to a lake some way out of Paris, for a picnic in the late September sunlight, eaten under trees already turning orange and red. In the evening, there was, once again, a wonderful dinner and the promise of bed to follow. It was as they walked the short distance back to the flat from the restaurant that Fiona suddenly asked, 'You're married, aren't you?'

He glanced round at her, his expression guarded. 'I think you knew that.'

She had, of course she had, yet she felt unexpectedly chilled; and, yes, guilty. How stupid, when she had known exactly what she was letting herself in for! She wished she had not asked, did not want to know any more, yet found herself pursuing the matter. 'Where is your wife?'

'Now? At home, near Amiens, with our

children. They are at school there, good schools. Normally, I go there for the week-ends.'

'But not always.'

'Not always. She is accustomed to this, you know.'

Because she was French, and the traditional French wife expected her husband to have a mistress, to be unfaithful – all of which Fiona knew, yet somehow putting it into words made it seem uncomfortably real. She wondered how many children he had, whether they were boys or girls, how old they were, what his wife was like; but did not ask. She already knew too much.

They reached the flat, and he became passionate, seductive, and within moments she had put her scruples aside and was in bed with him again. If it had not been her, then it would have been someone else. Or so she told herself.

On Monday, they went together to his office and he was businesslike, efficient, helpful, so that the work she had come to do was completed with the minimum of difficulties, with only a few minor points to be finalised on the Tuesday morning, before she returned to London. 'I shall come with you to the Gare du Nord,' he told her that morning, 'but first, we shall have lunch.'

The meal was as enjoyable as all the others, his company as agreeable. The niggle of guilt slipped away until it was just that, a niggle like a troublesome tooth that was not yet in urgent need of attention but might be one day. It did not really detract from her enjoyment, nor her gratitude to Éric for the way he had welcomed her. At the station, he kissed her goodbye – she had known no one who could kiss so well, with such infectious passion in the lightest touch of his mouth. 'Thank you for everything,' she said.

'No, it is I must thank you. I hope you will have reason to come again soon.'

At the barrier, he kissed her once more, and then waved as she walked away from him. A good weekend, she told herself; a lovely time. Everything had gone exactly as she had hoped it would.

Back at her flat there was no post, and no message on her answerphone. She felt obscurely disappointed, though she was relieved, too. Clearly Sam had at last realized that she meant what she said, that there was no future for them together. She could put that part of her life behind her, as over and done with.

Five

Jan quickly realized during the following week that though she might have changed during the weekend of the reunion, Keith had not, in any way at all.

He came home late from work on three days during that week, but even when he was at home, sharing her meals, sitting in one of the easy chairs near her while she watched television or read, lying beside her in bed at night, he might as well not have been there for all the companionship he offered. Questions on her part were answered with a monosyllable, observations ignored, and he initiated no conversation himself. She soon saw that he had been at his most lively, his most approachable, in the moments following her return home last Sunday night. After that, he had quickly reverted to the silent and morose man who occupied the house with her, but could not be said to live there in any meaningful way. She was, by turns, anxious and angry at his mood, the more so as he answered any probing questions, as usual, with irritated denials that there was anything wrong.

At least, Jan thought, she had her work to go to, which offered her companionship, friends who were interested in what she was doing and who shared their enthusiasms and concerns with her, problems she could solve since she knew exactly what they were. She would set out for work in the morning with spirits lightening every step of the way; and feel the knot of tension tighten within her as she made her way home in the evening. Work was a haven. She even found herself thinking that perhaps she should apply for the practice manager's job after all. But then she thought of the other things she now saw she could do with her life, and resisted the impulse. It was no longer simply the prospect of having time for various pleasant voluntary activities that tempted her. After last weekend, she suddenly saw that a whole new way of life was possible. Don was right; it was not too late to take up the threads of her interest in archaeology again, perhaps even take them up seriously and professionally, after some kind of refresher course – beginning, maybe, with a visit to the newly discovered Saxon site, after excavations started there in two weeks time. That did not solve the problem of what to do about her marriage, about Keith, but it gave her a purpose, something to look forward to.

She wished she had someone she could

confide in about her difficulties with her marriage; but it was too personal a thing to be discussed with work colleagues, and the children, who were her natural confidants in most things, would be too emotionally involved themselves. The only other possible confidante was her mother, to whom she talked on the phone once or twice a week. But she felt that in some way her mother – who had never ceased to mourn her father after his death at the hands of the Japanese, late in the war, and who was now enjoying a happy second marriage – would have found it difficult to understand how Jan could have anything to complain of in her own long and durable marriage. In any case, to complain about Keith's behaviour to anyone still seemed to her something of a betrayal. But she knew that if it went on like this, she would have to take some action, speak to someone, even ask for help. For the moment, however, she could simply get on with her life in her own way, since to do so seemed to affect Keith very little.

The Sunday after the reunion was Harvest Festival at the parish church. 'This is going to be our best ever display,' Anne had declared, as the members of the flower-arranging team met in church on the Monday night to discuss their plans. Most of Jan's spare time in the following days was spent planning, discussing, buying flowers and vegetables or begging them from gardens; and then, for the whole of Saturday, putting them into effect in the ancient church.

In previous years, Keith had always come to church with Jan for Harvest Festival. He had no particular religious affiliation, but enjoyed marking the major festivals in some way or another – or so Jan supposed. He had never in fact talked to her of what he felt or thought on any religious matter, or not that she could now remember. She realized that she had no idea whether in fact he believed in God at all, though she supposed he must, in some way. On the other hand, she was not always sure that she herself believed in God. She went to church as much because she enjoyed the services and liked many of the other members of the congregation as for any deeper reason; it was a social thing.

'It's Harvest Festival tomorrow,' she had said to Keith that Saturday night, though he could hardly have failed to know that, since she had been at the church all that day. But he had done no more than grunt some non-committal reply, and this morning he simply settled down with the *Sunday Times*, effectively shutting her out. 'I'm just off to get ready for church,' she said after breakfast. He did not move, merely grunted again. When she was ready – in very good time – she tried again: 'I'll be off soon.' Then: 'Do I gather you're not coming?'

'If you do, then you'd be right,' he said, without looking round or lowering the paper. She felt painfully disappointed, but said nothing, simply dropped a kiss on the top of his head and left the house; the kiss might have gone unnoticed, but for her it was a demonstration – to herself as well as to him – that she was still trying to reach Keith, that she still cared about their marriage.

The church looked and smelled wonderful. Jan was proudly conscious of the arrangement of corn and flowers beside the font which she herself had done, pleased with the way it looked, though as she passed she tweaked one of the lusciously blowsy dahlias back into place; someone must have knocked it. She wished she could have shown it all to Keith, though in his present frame of mind she supposed that would have been a waste of time; he would not have been interested. She concentrated on enjoying the service; the sermon was mercifully short, the singing jubilant and full-throated, though these days the church, much more crowded than usual, was never packed to the doors as once it would have been at such a time.

'Keith all right?' the vicar asked as she paused at the door on the way out to shake his hand.

'Fine,' she lied, wondering how he would have reacted if she had given any hint of the truth. The Revd Stephen Winston was a pleasant enough man, but not one she felt readily able to confide in.

As she walked home she braced herself for what was to come. Keith already had the car out, and had put on the dark suit he always wore when visiting his aunt – she always used to like to see him looking smart, though Jan doubted that she noticed any more.

It was a fine day, but even in sunshine Coldwell looked bleak and uninviting. It did not help that all Jan's efforts to converse had met with (at best) taciturnity from Keith, at worst a snappish irritability. It had been a largely silent journey and seemed very long.

There was no smell of cooking when they reached the house. Opening the back door, they saw only a deserted, chaotic kitchen. The sink was full of dirty dishes, the draining board covered with an assortment of clean and dirty plates, all higgledy-piggledy, among which stood a half-opened tin of steak, its contents already beginning to stink, and a pan containing water in which lay a few discoloured (and clearly uncooked) potatoes. Jan exclaimed, put a hand to her nose, choked with nausea, and followed close behind as Keith went quickly to look for his aunt.

They found her upstairs, cleaning the bathroom basin, dressed only in a soiled nightdress. She looked round with a vague smile. 'I want to have it nice for my visitors.' She gave a final rub. 'There. That's it.'

Keith took her arm and steered her gently towards her bedroom, which smelt of stale urine. Jan changed the sheets and then, together, they helped Auntie Hilda to wash and dress and then went downstairs. 'Now, let's see about dinner,' said Keith briskly. He opened the fridge door, then shut it again hastily, but not before Jan had caught a nauseating waft of the stench from inside.

'It's been switched off at the wall,' Jan pointed out.

'Then we'll go to the Blue Bell,' Keith decided. 'We can tidy up when we've eaten.'

Jan thought it unlikely that she would be able to eat very much with that prospect before her, but could not see what alternative there was. It was nearly one o'clock, and she was very hungry – or had been at least. The old lady must be even hungrier, since it looked very much as though she had been skipping meals.

The dinner in the pub was as uncomfortable as it could be. They both tried brightly to engage the old lady in conversation, but were soon embroiled in the confusions of her mind, answering endlessly repeated questions, enduring loud, embarrassing comments about what Hilda thought she saw. There was no opportunity to talk to one another.

Afterwards, they settled Hilda in front of the newly lit fire, where she quickly fell asleep, her gentle snores providing an accompaniment to their work in the kitchen. It took two hours before some kind of order was restored, by which time Jan at least felt exhausted. Before they left, she found a corner shop a few blocks away which was open and had bread and milk and other basic foods, so they were able to restock the fridge – now fully working again – before they left. Jan wondered how long it would be before everything was once more in disarray. As Keith drove home, she said, 'We have to contact social services. She can't go on like this.'

'What do you mean, "go on"? This is something different, a one-off, I would guess. Things have never been like this before, you know that. It's my guess she was rather under the weather last week and things got a bit on top of her.'

'A bit! Oh Keith, you must see it's more than that!'

'She was fine last week.'

'You mean she was perfectly normal and everything was in order? I find that very hard to believe, especially as that wasn't even true two weeks ago. In fact, it's been clear for a long time that she's not coping. At the very least, she can't be eating properly.'

'What are you suggesting? That we dump

her in a home? She's an old lady, so she gets muddled sometimes. That's all.'

'Then we should get social services to do an assessment, at the very least. Just to be sure. If nothing else, they can give her some help.' Why did they have to pretend like this? Surely even Keith must see that things were in a bad way?

'I'm not having outsiders poking their noses in. You know what Auntie Hilda would think of that. It would take away all her dignity.'

'What dignity does she have, living as we found her today?'

'She's been under the weather, that's all. In fact, when I think about it she did seem to have a bit of a cold last Sunday. She'll be fine, now she's well again.'

Jan gave up. She knew she was getting nowhere, and that in a moment Keith would lose his temper – or come as near to losing it as he ever did; and if he didn't, then she would, without a doubt, which wouldn't have mattered if it could have achieved anything, but she knew it would not.

At home again, they found that they'd missed a telephone call. The number was not one Jan immediately recognized, but when she checked she found it had the code for Derby, where Melanie's hotel was situated. Jan was annoyed, but tried not to show it. She had been longing to hear how Mel was, and the silence was beginning to worry her. But it would not be fair – or not quite fair – to blame Keith for the missed call.

'Phone her back,' Keith said.

'It wasn't her own phone. I don't want to risk interrupting her at work. Besides, I suppose it might not have been Mel.' Though she did not believe that; she could only hope their daughter would phone again later.

It was in fact Fiona who rang as they sat in silence before the television that evening, though only to give a brief and not very satisfactory account of her weekend in Paris. Jan, who was the only one who spoke to her, sensed she was keeping a good deal back, and wondered whether that was a good or a bad sign. Fiona's voice gave nothing much away, though she claimed to have had a wonderful time – 'and useful too,' she added, as an afterthought.

When Fiona had rung off, Jan, weary of watching television, went in search of a book to read to fill the time before bed. In the corner of the lounge was a large bookcase, in which – forgotten, unread for many years now – were her student archaeology books. On impulse, she took down a volume covering the Saxon period and spent an agreeable hour skimming through it, reviving old memories, dredging up old knowledge, buried for years. The prospect of spending a weekend at Don Hadley's dig became more appealing by the minute, not because she was attracted to him, but simply for itself, as a means of reviving old enthusiasms. She was fifty-four, with her life at a turning point. From now on everything was going to be different, nothing taken for granted. All her life she had been a wife, a mother, devoted herself to her family and their needs. That would stay with her, of course, still be important to her (at least as far as the children were concerned), but the difference would be that from now on she would have space for herself, space to explore the parts of Jan St John which had been pushed aside when she took that step into marriage thirty-odd years ago. It was a time for taking stock and moving on into a new and exciting future.

She looked across the room at Keith, who had the paper folded so that he could do the crossword, but did not appear to be giving it much thought; at that moment he looked up and she caught his eye. 'I didn't tell you,' she said. 'Fee thinks I should go for the practice manager's job,' she said.

'I thought you didn't want to.'

'I don't. Oh, I can see her point of view, looking at it as a career. But I never have seen it as a career. It was only ever a stopgap that lasted rather longer than I thought. Now I want to let things run down gently, do a bit less, have a bit more time for a private life. Or,' she added on impulse, 'even do something quite different.'

'You seem to do all right.' There was just a faint hint of asperity in his voice, even sourness.

'Do you want me to go for the job?' she asked in surprise.

'Not if you don't want to. You might enjoy it, that's all.'

'But if I wasn't working full time I could do more in the garden – build that alpine garden we've never got round to. Go and visit the children, now they're all away. Maybe even do some further study of some sort. Oh, all kinds of things.'

'Then don't go for it. Whatever you want.' Indifference settled into his voice again. 'It's your life.'

She felt irritated at the lack of interest in his tone. 'It's your life, too. It would affect you. Maybe I could do a bit more for Auntie Hilda, for starters.' Though there are limits to what I can do or am prepared to do, she thought.

'If and when she needs it,' he added. 'As I say, you please yourself.'

'Of course,' Jan went on casually, 'if I went to that dig I told you about, it could be a first step towards taking up archaeology again. Who knows where that might lead, if I had more time to go into it properly?'

'Who knows?' he parroted, with the

faintest ironic inflection – or did she imagine it? He laid his paper aside. 'I'm going to bed. Are you coming?'

'In a bit. Shan't be long.' As usual these days, she felt the tension ease as he left the room, felt able to relax at last. She flicked the remote control, from channel to channel, found nothing she wanted to see (what a waste, when she could have watched without wondering if it was disturbing Keith!), went to put her book away. There were a number of books on Roman archaeology near the space where she had taken it from, some of which she could not remember at all. She took one out and opened it. On the flyleaf Keith's name had been written, in the rounded juvenile writing of the young man she had first met. She looked at it in bewilderment, and then she remembered. Of course! He'd been interested enough in the subject in those days to want to read further, though he had no training in archaeology. She wondered if he had ever got much further than the title page of this volume, which was rather a heavy work. It certainly didn't look well used.

She put it back, pondering the man he had been when they first met, a young trainee surveyor who had come, for some reason to do with his job, to the site where she had been working – a Roman site in Northumberland. Long after his task was done he had continued to come, in his spare time, partly from interest in the work being done, rather more from interest in her, an interest she had returned, though the feelings she had known then seemed very far away, irrecoverable perhaps, looked at from the perspective of where she now was.

'Goodnight!' said Mel, as she made her way towards the door that led into the staff quarters of the hotel.

'Goodnight, Mel.' Louise, left at reception to begin the night shift, yawned, and then laughed. Mel smiled faintly, then pushed the door open and found herself in the spotlessly bleak passage that led away from the public areas of the hotel.

When first offered the job she had been thrilled, not only by the responsibility it gave her, the trust they were placing in her, but also by the fact that her very own furnished flat was included, in an annexe in the hotel grounds. Now, as she reached the outer door and set out over the shadowy garden, she could no longer recall what that first euphoria felt like. It seemed to have a happened a long time ago to someone else. She tapped out her code on the outer door of the annexe, let herself in, walked up the stairs to her own front door, which she opened with her key. The building was very quiet – the downstairs flat was occupied by Louise, who worked odd shifts, so they were rarely at home at the same time. They met only in passing. It did not help that she sensed some jealousy on the part of the other girl. Louise had worked at this hotel for a year already, and Mel guessed that she had hoped to be given Mel's job. On the surface they got on well enough, but there was no warmth; though that might just have been because they did not see enough of one another to establish any kind of relationship.

It was a pleasant enough flat, Mel had to acknowledge, though with little in the way of personal touches as yet. There was a living room, large enough to take a bed settee, which was the first thing she was going to look for after her first payday; a bedroom with double bed and a shower room and a small kitchen, equipped with all one could possibly want. The rooms were decorated in much the same style as the hotel rooms – dark wood, inoffensively patterned wall-paper, matching curtains and bedspread, a few pallid watercolour prints hung on the walls. There was absolutely nothing to complain of in her surroundings.

Except that she was alone, with no one in the world to talk to, about anything. She enjoyed her work, dealing with the guests, sorting out their problems and requests, however bizarre; though as yet she still felt very new and untried when managing the hotel's staff. But once her office hours ended she spoke to no one at all, had nowhere to go and nothing to do, except wash clothes and hair, watch television or read. Today should have been a day off – she didn't often work at weekends, and almost never on Sundays – but she had chosen to fill in for one of the receptionists who was off sick, simply to give herself something to do, though the hotel, which catered mostly for business travellers, was almost empty, so that she did not find her usual pleasure in working either. On impulse, at one point, she had found herself trying to phone her twin, Simon (she had vowed never to abuse her position by making personal calls on the hotel phone, but somehow she felt too depressed to care), but he and the others who shared his house seemed all to be out. She had tried her mother instead, only to hear her father's voice reciting the answerphone message; she had simply slammed the receiver down again, without speaking. Then she remembered they would be at Auntie Hilda's house, as always on Sunday. That had only made things worse. All the recent unpleasantness of visits to the old woman's house was forgotten and she'd felt a sharp pang of nostalgia, a longing to be there with them all, to be part of a family again. I'll phone later, she told herself, but knew she was quite glad not to have spoken to her mother after all. She had been so excited about this job; it would be humiliating to admit that she was less than happy, now she was here.

Simon was different, of course. As her twin, he was the one person to whom she could confide everything and anything, knowing he would understand completely. Once she had closed the door of her flat against the world and made herself a cup of coffee, she sat down by the phone and tried Simon's number again. Someone called Steve answered. 'He's out. No, I don't know when he'll be back. Maybe late, maybe not tonight. Can I give him a message?'

'No, thank you. No message.' She rang off, feeling more depressed than ever. After a day clearing undergrowth, building hides, setting up bird boxes, Simon was usually too tired for more than a couple of cans of beer in front of the television. He rarely went out in the evening. But he was out tonight, and she did not know where, or – more to the point – who with; he was not, obviously, with his house mates. She sensed that there might be a girl. But if so he had said nothing of it to her, his twin, the person he was closest to in all the world – no hint of his hopes, of attraction to anyone, nothing about a meeting, still less of any response to an approach from himself. A sense of hurt, of being shut out, excluded, was added to her loneliness and homesickness, though she tried to tell herself she was being foolish – after all, she didn't *know* there was anyone.

She went into the kitchen, looking for food that was tempting but easy to prepare. She made a plate of cheese and pickle sandwiches, ate them in front of the television, and then made herself another coffee and drank it with a whole packet of chocolate finger biscuits. Then, feeling rather sick and not in the least tempted by anything on television, she went to bed.

At the nature reserve, Simon was on poacher watch with two others, Big Ken, who looked like an ageing hippy but was in fact a police wildlife officer, and Tamsin, a frail-looking blonde from the west country, who had come to work at the reserve only three weeks ago. Simon rather wished that he could have been on duty alone with her, but on the other hand, it might not have been safe without Big Ken, who was as gentle in nature as he was intimidating in appearance, but carried a gun and had a radio for communication with the local police station, who would provide back-up if need arose. Ken had warned him at the outset that poaching was not done by the wisecracking country characters of popular imagination, but by gangs of men from the towns, with lurcher dogs and lamps and powerful off-road vehicles; and guns, of course, which they would have few scruples about using, not only on deer, but on anyone who got in their way. There was a small but very lucrative market in venison, for those in the know.

The reserve covered just over two hundred acres of land, made up of disused gravelpits that formed lakes abundant with wildfowl, pasture, which was grazed by a small herd of Highland cattle and a flock of sheep, and mixed woodland, part of which was coppiced, its proceeds sold to bring in a small income. The three watchers (well protected with thornproof jackets, thick trousers and boots) had taken up their positions in a holly thicket in the place where the mixed woods of beech and oak, alder and scots pine gave way to the low, dense whippy growth of the coppiced hazel and willow. It was near here that, on two occasions last week, one of them had found the remains of a deer – the head, roughly severed, and some of the innards. There had been tyre tracks nearby, and considerable damage to the young saplings through which the poachers' vehicles had driven.

It was a dank night, moonless, with a thin drizzly rain and no wind. Odours of earth and trees, crushed undergrowth, the sharp sour smell of a fox that had recently passed this way, filled their nostrils. It was not particularly cold, but the dampness soon seeped into them where they crouched, chilling them to the bone. They kept close together, for warmth as much as ease of communication, but before long Simon felt Tamsin beginning to shiver; this part of Yorkshire was a long way north of the soft climate in which she had grown up. Should he put his arm around her? He thought she was interested in him. There had been some long thoughtful looks, and she had made a point of talking to him whenever they were together, even when there were others present, and seemed interested in his opinion on all kinds of subjects. But if he had misread the situation, a rash step now might only destroy any future chances he might have. He leaned a little closer to her and murmured, 'You OK?'

She must have smiled, for he caught a glimmer of white in the darkness. 'Bit cold, that's all,' she said.

He put a hand on her shoulder, hoping she would not feel how it trembled. 'Want an arm?'

Amazingly, gloriously, she snuggled against him. 'That would be nice.' He put his arm about her, holding her, and she laid her head on his shoulder. He felt scarcely able to breathe.

'When you two lovebirds have finished,' said Big Ken softly – he could sense what people (or animals) were doing even when it

117

was too dark to see them, 'something's happening. Back there – there was a light just now, headlight I'd say. They'll be getting ready to come in without lights.'

After that, while Ken murmured a message into his radio, there came a sudden crashing roar, a din that set the earth reverberating. What seemed like some giant monster exploded through the woods, past them, on and then halted. There was an equally sudden fall of silence, broken only by the lingering agitation of disturbed birds. They heard the soft opening of doors and their closing again, as just-discernible shadowy figures emerged into the wood, with lithe black shapes circling them. The scrunch of heavy but careful feet reached them, the odd snap of a twig, the panting of eager dogs. The three watchers stiffened, alert, ears and eyes strained. The new arrivals moved away from them, but not far. They knew, though they did not risk saying so, that the poachers had taken up their positions.

There came a prolonged silence, so that only those used to the night time sounds of the woods – as they were – could have guessed that anyone was hiding there. Simon, with his heart pounding, wondered if the poachers had any idea they were watched; presumably not, or they would probably have taken action, of a kind Simon preferred not to think about, remembering

Ken's stories. Instinctively, he felt his arm tighten still more about Tamsin; she was new to this, and a woman, and he would need to protect her, if things got nasty.

They were still for so long, all of them, that it began to seem tedious. It was almost as if that raucous invasion of the wood had never happened, as if they had simply been waiting here all night to no purpose. Even snuggled up to Tamsin, Simon felt cold, his limbs aching from crouching so long without moving. Could the poachers have crept away without their knowledge?

A deer walking through woodland made very little noise; to the inexperienced, none at all. But nearly all the watchers there that night were experienced to some degree and they sensed rather than heard her soft approach. Simon felt Ken's slight movement, and knew he had pressed the button on his mobile that sent a message to the waiting police, who should by now be in position on the wood's fringes, somewhere behind the poachers' vehicle. At the very same moment, the deer was suddenly caught, momentarily paralysed with terror, in a burst of light. Lurchers leapt out of the undergrowth, a muffled gun fired; the deer fell. Ken rose to his feet and stepped into the light, just as his waiting colleagues reached the clearing and ran out from the shelter of the Landrover to surround the poachers.

After that, it was all rather an anticlimax; no one fired or tried to resist arrest. The men, looking suddenly small and helpless, dropped their guns and gave themselves up without a murmur; the dogs were leashed and led away. Simon felt obscurely cheated, though he felt relieved too. They gave brief statements to a policeman, which would have to be enlarged upon at the police station on the following day, and then Big Ken gave them a lift back to the village in his Land-rover, stopping first outside the general store above which was Tamsin's tiny flat. 'Come up for a coffee?' she asked Simon.

It was foolish, for he at least had to be at work by eight the following morning (except that it was already the following morning), but he said, 'OK. Thanks. Don't mind if I do.' He followed her out of the Landrover, ignoring the wink from Big Ken.

The flat was tiny – a cramped living room with sofa bed, a small kitchen alcove and a bathroom in which there was scarcely room to turn round. The wallpaper was aggres-sively floral, and dark too, so that it made everything look even smaller than it was. 'Well, it was cheap,' Tamsin said, seeing the critical look in Simon's eyes as he looked about him. She filled the kettle and switched it on. 'I think I'll have camomile tea. Better to sleep on.'

'Me too, then, if that's all right,' said

Simon, who had never tasted the stuff and hoped it would be bearable. Now that he was in the flat, he no longer felt jubilant, only awkward and uncertain. But she *had* put her head on his shoulder, and accepted his arm about her. That must mean something.

He sat down, but on a hard chair, leaving the sofa bed to Tamsin. They sipped their drinks decorously, in silence. Simon did not much care for the camomile tea, but found it just about drinkable, so long as he gazed at Tamsin while he did so.

He finished it much too quickly, while she was still drinking, and wondered what on earth to do next. In the end, he simply stood up and said, 'I'll have to be going. Got to be up again in an hour or two.'

'Oh! Have you really?' She put her mug down and stood up too, very close in that cramped space. And then, wonderfully, he did not know how, they were kissing. 'You could stay,' she suggested, after a long interval.

Simon left the flat half an hour earlier than he usually set out for work, with only just enough time to run home, change and wash (no time for a shave) and then cycle the two and a half miles to the nature reserve – arriving a little late. He scarcely noticed how exhausted he was, for the events of the night kept him floating on a cloud of joy. On the other hand, he might as well have been incapacitated by exhaustion, since the euphoria that filled him cut him off just as effectively from everything around him. He went through the day in a daze, forgetting routine tasks, filling in forms with chaotic disregard for what they asked him, having time and again to go back and carry out some job he had forgotten earlier. He was glad in the afternoon when he was able to set to work on clearing a ditch in an isolated corner of the reserve. It took nearly three hours and was simple physical work that required no mental effort and allowed him to go over and over the previous night in his head without interruption from anyone. At first he had been disappointed that Tamsin had a day off today, but in fact he found it a relief to have some time to himself. Except that he found himself wondering if she too was going over the previous night and if, unlike him, she was now regretting every-thing that had happened.

Then, at the end of the day, having locked away his tools and washed the worst of the mud from his person, he wheeled his bicycle out of the shed where it had been stored through the day; and there in the paved yard beside the old buildings that had once been the headquarters of the gravel business and now housed offices and tearoom, came face to face with Tamsin. She looked both anxious and hopeful. 'I know you said you'd ring, but I couldn't wait.' Her eyes searched Simon's face – for what? Anger that she had taken the initiative, forced his hand? Or signs that he was glad to see her?

If it was the latter, then he was sure she must see them, for he felt delight suffuse him, along with hot colour. 'Hi!' Then: 'How did you get here?'

'Bus.' There were three buses that passed near the reserve during the day, none of them at any convenient time; there would be no more today, in either direction. 'But I can walk back.'

'I'll walk with you then,' he said.

They walked through the damp lanes (fortunately it was not actually raining), talking of anything and everything, reassured at every step that neither of them had the least regret about last night, that they both wanted what had begun then to continue.

It was clear though that Tamsin had one worry. 'There isn't anyone else is there? You wouldn't cheat on anyone?' Forcefully, he reassured her. 'It's just that when I first came, that first day, I saw you with a girl – not one who works here, or not that I know of. Tall, brown hair, pretty.'

'Mel,' he told her. 'That would be Mel, my twin. She came over to see where I work, just before starting her new job. She's in Derby now.'

It was clear from Tamsin's expression that

she had been more worried about the incident than her casual tone had implied. Now, she looked hugely relieved, her face full of unclouded happiness. 'Oh – what's it like being a twin? Is it very special? I've got two sisters, but that can't be quite the same. Do you always know when things go wrong, even when you're apart?'

'We haven't been apart that much, but no, I don't think so.' He tried to consider his relationship with Mel, but it wasn't easy. They were so close, she was so much a part of his life, that it was hard to look at it objectively. 'We're best friends, I suppose. We can always talk to one another – you know, we both know the other one will listen, if no one else does. We don't have any secrets.' But that wasn't quite true, or not any more. In coming to work here he had discovered something he had never realized until then and had certainly not confided in Mel – that it was a relief (a very small one, but a relief none the less) to set out on a life apart from his twin, his own individual life without her, of which she might, in a way, know all the details, but not the whole of it. More than that, he had begun, bit by bit, not to tell her things, and been glad that she did not know them. Most of all, he had not told her about Tamsin's arrival nor of his feelings for her, which seemed a bit like a betrayal yet gave him an odd sense of liberation.

'Does that mean she'll be jealous of me?'

'Oh no, that's different, quite different.' He spoke confidently, but he was not entirely sure about it. How would he feel if Mel were to ring him up and tell him she had a boy-friend? He really didn't know. There had been no one special in her life so far, only odd casual dates that had led nowhere, which was true for him too, until now. Perhaps in a way their close relationship had made it hard for either of them to look outwards, to other partners.

'Will I meet her some time?'

'Oh, sure to,' Simon said, hoping that the day would be a long way off; or at least, delayed until he had established something lasting with Tamsin, if that was going to happen.

'Do you want to come to my place again tonight? I can cook us a meal. Or there's a good Indian down the street.'

'Sounds fine to me,' said Simon. 'Just so long as I can get some sleep this time.'

She laughed. 'I might just let you, if you're good.'

Six

It rained all the way south, the drops running in uneven lines down the train windows, their monotony inducing drowsiness, inertia. But Jan stepped on to the platform at Oxford into sudden pristine sunlight and all her excitement and sense of adventure, even danger, sprang into life again. Don was waiting for her at the barrier, looking exactly as she remembered him, rumpled, relaxed, coming to greet her with such warmth in his smile and his eyes that she thought he was going to kiss her and was just the faintest bit disappointed when he didn't.

'Good journey?'

She nodded, unable to think what to say. For a moment he laid a hand on her shoulder, in what was almost a caress. She felt a shiver of excitement run through her, and anticipation; and then guilt. She was not here for that, of course she wasn't. She found some words, practical, sensible words, appropriate to what she was doing here. 'How's the dig going?'

There was a gleam in his eye now that she

knew had nothing to do with anything personal, but only with the work he was doing. 'Excellently. You've come at a good time. Just wait till I show you.' He glanced at her small suitcase. 'We'll drop this off at the hotel first, if that's OK with you.'

The hotel, in a small town about eight miles from Oxford, was uninviting, her room being cramped and dark and looking on to a damp yard, though it was at least clean. She reminded herself that in her student days she would probably have been sleeping in a tent or a dormitory. She left her case beside the single bed, glanced in the mirror over the washbasin (there was no en-suite bathroom) to tidy her hair, and then rejoined Don where he was waiting for her in his Fiesta in the hotel car park. It was, she thought, very much an archaeologist's car, untidy, with battered books randomly strewn on the back seat, among tools, pieces of string and odd fragments of bone. 'Modern sheep's bones, when we got them analyzed,' Don explained in answer to her query. 'Relic of a fruitless dig two years ago. I've just never got round to throwing them out.'

When they reached it, having parked the car at a drunken angle on a roadside verge, Jan saw that the excavation site was extensive, bordered by woods, and busy with students, in various stages of muddiness, at their painstaking work. Don led her first to the table where two young women were pot-washing – cleaning fragments of pottery, with infinite care. 'You've found all that already!' Jan exclaimed.

'I told you it had been a good day. And we'd only just begun to cut the evaluation trenches. Stupendous!'

He reached for this object and that, expounding on each one with the same infectious enthusiasm she recalled from the reunion. The pot-washers stopped what they were doing to listen to him, others abandoned their work on the site to gather round. She lost track of time, so absorbed was she in Don's exposition. It was not just a few fragments of old pots they saw before them or a couple of twisted belt buckles, but a whole world opening up, peopled and busy, troubled yet productive, a way of life long gone but very real and for a moment recreated for them in its entirety. The spell was not broken until a voice called from the far side of the site, from behind a screen over the top of which steam rose along with cooking smells. 'Grub's up!'

Don laughed, like a man waking from a pleasant dream, put down the fragment of Saxon pottery he had been discussing, looked round at the attentive group. 'I don't know about anyone else, but I'm starving.' Then, to Jan: 'I doubt dig food has improved with the years.'

'As I recall, we were always so hungry we didn't care what it was like.'

It was a spicy vegetarian stew, full of chick peas and vegetables and served with chunks of wholemeal bread. Everyone sat about where they could, on stools or (for the very fortunate, including the favoured Jan) folding chairs, or on the fallen tree trunks left by the men who had been felling trees when the site was discovered. Once the first silence of hungry eating was past, there was a good deal of laughter and teasing, of which Don received and gave a good deal. He was clearly a popular figure with his students. Watching them, hearing their talk, Jan was taken back once more to her own youth; except that there was then not quite this degree of informality, not quite the easy use of first names. It was the seventies that had broken down the final remains of those barriers of automatic respect, replacing them with only what was earned, whether of affection or respect.

After the meal, Jan declared a wish to get her hands dirty. Don led her to the corner where the first artefacts had been found and introduced her to a girl named Sarah; and then left her to rediscover long unused skills – and to renew the excitement of making finds, for there was still much to be uncovered – while he made a tour of the site. He returned often to her side, to see how she was getting on, to express his approval, to show her some newly unearthed artefact or explain what it was she had just found. For the rest of the time while they worked, Sarah chatted easily with her about work and her life, though she showed little curiosity about Jan. Perhaps, Jan thought with amusement, she thinks I'm too old to have anything interesting to talk about.

In the evening, Don took Jan to a nearby pub for a meal and a drink, though, recalling her student days, she was a little suprised that none of the rest of the team joined them. Perhaps they had not been invited. Jan did not know whether to be pleased or sorry.

'You've enjoyed today,' Don commented, his eyes on her face, as they waited for the food to arrive.

'Hugely!' she agreed. 'I'd forgotten what a sense of excitement there was in just exploring, hoping to find something – and then when you do...! There's nothing like it, nothing in this world.'

'Would you be feeling like that if it had been the usual story: hard slog and no finds?'

'Maybe not.' But she thought she would, as once she might not have done. There was the pleasure of young company, and not so young; the pleasure of laughter and talk and enthusiasm, all those things that now played so little part in her life. And, of course, the thing she could not acknowledge, or not openly, the added spice given to all she did by the undoubted physical attraction she felt for Don. Wary of it, she allowed herself only one glass of wine with her meal, but even then – what with the early start to her day and the subsequent hours in the fresh air – she felt light-headed by the time they returned to the hotel. She expected him to drop her off at the door and then drive on home to Oxford, where she knew he lived, but instead he parked the car and walked with her towards the hotel.

'I've booked myself in here for the weekend,' he said. 'Makes it easier to get an early start.'

She was not deceived. When she first phoned to arrange her visit he had offered to put her up at his house, but, fearful of trying to explain the arrangement to Keith, even more fearful perhaps of allowing herself to play with fire, she had asked him instead to book her into a cheap hotel; as he had indeed done, though this new twist rather invalidated her precaution.

In the dingy hallway, Don greeted the bored-looking receptionist (Jan hoped fervently that Mel's hotel was more prepossessing than this), then ushered Jan up the stairs. Their rooms faced one another across the same landing. He gestured towards his door. 'Coffee? My room's a bit larger than yours.'

Should she accept? No, definitely not, feeling as she did, with that flurry of excitement in her stomach, the catch in her breathing.

'Thank you. I'd love to.'

She followed him into the room, which was presumably what passed for a double room in this place, though it faced on to the street, directly opposite a noisy pub. At least there was a chair, so she did not have to sit on the bed, though she perched on its cane seat with all the awkwardness of a schoolgirl who knew she had no right to be where she was. She realized suddenly that Don was watching her; his reflective smile widened suddenly into a soft laugh.

'You know who you remind me of? That girl in the Victorian painting – what is it? *The Awakening* or something?'

She knew the painting quite well, with Holman Hunt's startled woman rising up from the knee of her lover, struck by a sudden realization of the sinfulness of her situation. Jan felt herself colouring uncomfortably.

Don came suddenly and took her hands in his. 'Don't look so guilty, for God's sake! I've only asked you in for coffee.' He paused, the little reflective smile back on his face. 'Unless you want something more, of course.'

'I'm a happily married woman,' she said with what sounded to her an intolerable primness.

Don sat down on the end of the bed, facing her. 'Are you? I wonder sometimes. I don't know much about happy marriages, but I'm very familiar with the signs of something going wrong.'

She coloured again (why did she keep blushing like a teenager?). 'Every marriage has its dry patches. That doesn't mean anything's fundamentally wrong.'

'No? All right, if you say so. You know best, I suppose.' He got up and began to pour water on to the instant coffee he'd put into two cups. 'Now for the really hard part – opening these things.' He handed her a cup and a sachet of milk; in the end she opened his as well as her own. 'I never was much good at the practical everyday things.'

'I thought archaeologists had to be practical.'

'Oh, give me a trench to dig or a pot to wash, and I know where I am. Household pots and gardens – they're another thing.'

'Maybe that's where your marriage went wrong.' She was immediately angry with herself for returning to that uncomfortable subject. 'Was your wife an academic?'

'Very,' he said drily. 'English literature. I think she looked on archaeology as a refuge for failed scientists – something of the kind. It took me a good few years to realize that she despised me at heart. That's when I decided I'd had enough. I'm happy with

133

myself. If she wasn't, that was her problem, but I wasn't going to stay around so she could look down her superior nose at me.' He paused a moment, as if considering his next remark carefully. 'I've a feeling you're not going to like this, but as I saw it she was one of those extreme feminists who despise men. We're all rapists at heart: you know the sort of stuff.'

Jan, who regarded herself as moderately feminist – like any reasonable person – had never in fact met any woman who held opinions of that kind and rather doubted if they really existed, except in the male imagination. But then she was not widely read in feminist literature; it was one of those things she had never quite got round to. 'Surely if she really felt like that she wouldn't have married you?' Or could he have given her cause to harden her views? It was difficult to believe of this agreeable charming man, but then first impressions could, she knew, be horribly wrong.

'She wanted children, I think. Having them without a husband wasn't so easy an option in those days.'

'But you had none?'

'No, they never happened. To be honest, I wasn't that bothered. But she was, more than she ever admitted, I think. Anyway, it's over and done with, in the past. No point in looking back.' He drank the rest of his coffee and put his cup down. 'Now, if I'm not going to be allowed to seduce you, I'm for bed. We have to be at the site by eight.'

She rose, put down her cup, smiled with what she hoped was a relaxed ease. 'On a Sunday morning! What a regime!' She found herself longing to kiss him – just a goodnight kiss, that was all, nothing more, nothing of significance – but instead she stood gazing at him for a moment, then said, 'I'll say goodnight then,' and left the room, turning her back on temptation.

In her own room she went to bed but did not sleep. Why did she not give in to her feelings? These days, surely, it was nothing, almost to be expected, that a wife should be unfaithful, at least once, if not more often. There need be no consequences, it would mean nothing, just a moment of happiness snatched in passing. For all she knew Keith had already been unfaithful to her – it was possible that this was the explanation for all those late nights, the odd moods.

For the first time, she gave serious consideration to the possibility, looking it full in the face, going over the minute details of the life she had left behind, wondered if it could indeed be true – and was aware both of a pain; and also a hope. For if it were true it would set her free to follow her own instinct, to seize her happiness where she could. But would the pain be worse than the freedom were she to find it were true? She couldn't tell. Without going through it, without knowing for sure, she would not know what she would feel. And if she were to find out, it would be too late to go back. You cannot unknow something, or only by losing all memory, like Auntie Hilda. The thought of Auntie Hilda brought her up short. It was, she recognized, that aspect of her life she would be most glad to leave behind, the knowledge that there was a responsibility to someone who had no claim on her, except through Keith, who meant nothing to her except as someone Keith loved and to whom he felt he owed a great debt of gratitude – but it was his love, his debt. If she were not bound up with him, if his actions should set her free, then she would be free too of any responsibility for the old woman. And free to have an affair with Don, if she so chose...

Then she found herself smiling with grim humour into the darkness (two cats were fighting somewhere). How arrogant of her, how smug, to assume that Don wanted an affair with her! It was so easy to misread the signs, so easy to jump to conclusions. Certainly he had spoken of seducing her, used the supposed difficulties of her marriage as an excuse, but he might simply have been joking, teasing her. She went over the evening in her mind, lingering on all that he had said and done, every expression on his face. No, she decided, she was not mistaken, not at all. She had only to make the slightest, the very slightest move towards him and they would be in bed together. She felt her body respond to the thought, knew how much she wanted it, she who had not only always been faithful to Keith, but had never in her life slept with any other man. How would she have felt afterwards, if she had got into that ungenerous double bed with Don this evening? There was something sordid about a furtive affair in a shabby hotel bedroom. That was what people did in the 1950s, when such things only happened between people of low morals and no principles; or the very desperate. If that was unfaithfulness, she wanted none of it.

Except that she did want it, and the hunger of her body kept her wakeful for a long time and ensured that when at last she slept it was to be troubled by erotic yet uneasy dreams.

Waking in the damp darkness of the autumn morning to the persistent beep of the alarm, it was easy to throw off the previous night's temptations. Jan's body now craved only sleep and warmth, neither of which she was in a position to offer it. As she made her way down to breakfast, she resolved that she would throw herself enthusiastically into the work at the dig and avoid Don's company when not at work. She was here to feed her interest in archaeology, not her need for rather more sex in her life. That last could be satisfied at home, if she only put her mind to it. She would, after all, be home again this evening, catching the last train in the day. It was not long to keep to her resolve.

It was not so easy to keep that resolution fresh in her mind when facing Don across the breakfast table. He was the perfect early-morning companion, reticent but good humoured; so different from Keith, who was quiet too, but grimly so, speaking – if he had to – only in snappy monosyllables. The face across the table this morning was calm, unfrowning, the mouth ready with a smile, the eyes bright and teasing, not the fixed scowl to which she had become grimly resigned.

By mid-morning the clouds had cleared; a warm day followed, one of those perfect late October days that sometimes make it hard to think of winter being so near. The students, infected by the brightness and the heat, broke now and then into song; the dig became a noisy and cheerful place. Jan spent the morning working alongside Sarah. She was surprised when, mid-morning, in response to some passing remark, the girl observed with studied casualness, 'It's good Don's seeing someone again.'

Again? Was this a frequent occurrence, that he should bring a woman with him to a dig?

Had there perhaps been students with whom he'd had affairs? It was a common enough phenomenon, the randy university lecturer with an eye on his students, though these days that sort of behaviour was fraught with danger, which might make him more likely to seek the company of women of his own age. Was Don a womaniser?

'Don't jump to conclusions,' Jan said. 'I'm just a friend – a happily married one at that.' The words sounded hollow, even to her ears. Catching the look of scepticism in Sarah's eyes, she went on quickly, 'Have there been many women in his life then?'

'Well, I wouldn't know for sure. But there's been no one anyone's known about since his wife died. There were a few before that, but not after. Guilt maybe.'

'He doesn't seem like a man haunted by guilt,' Jan observed, glancing across to where Don was talking to two students, his head bent over something they had brought to show him. A sudden burst of laughter ended the discussion, before he moved on to the next group. Would he show any sense of guilt if he should be instrumental in breaking up a marriage? Could you be held responsible for breaking up something that was already close to the rocks, in danger of shipwreck, perhaps even beyond help?

She threw off the uncomfortable reflection and was relieved when an exclamation from

Sarah alerted her to another find; a valid distraction.

By lunchtime it had grown so hot that most of the men on the site had thrown off their shirts, Don among them. (He was, Jan noticed, agreeably tanned – not with the unnatural colour studiously cultivated from vanity, but lightly, as any man would be who spent a good deal of time uncovered out of doors, as he was now.) By the time he sought her out, on her way back to the site from the chemical toilet at its edge, he had put on his checked shirt again.

'There's another place we can't get at for the moment, just over there.' He gestured towards a point where the woods covered a rising piece of ground. 'Like to take a look?'

She agreed enthusiastically and went with him. In a matter of moments they were alone in the screening trees, away from sight or sound of the students. They might have been miles from anywhere. She had a sudden suspicion that this might be a ruse on his part, a means of getting her to himself.

But the place he had mentioned was real enough, the signs on the ground, just visible here and there among the trees, indisputable.

'The only way to get at it would be by cutting down trees. You can see why they don't want to.'

Nor would she, in this lovely beechwood

with its mossy undergrowth, the occasional clusters of holly giving greater cover. They were close to one such now, in a tiny sunlit glade, warm and green, enclosing them. Don finished what he had been saying and fell silent, looking at her. She gazed back at him. This was not like the hotel room, sordid, squalid. It was magical, a lovely place. The heat roused her more than ever, and the look in Don's eyes. He reached out and gently caressed her cheek. She moved nearer, felt his arms close about her, moved her mouth to his, without any thought, instinct guiding her.

The sun on her head, around her, enclosing her, like his arms ... The sense that she was dissolving, her whole body melting in this moment – there had been another time like this in another wood in the far north, where Keith had held her, where once they had made love on the thin grass and moss of a woodland floor. Long ago, another time, another place, another man, who had loved her as passionately, as deeply as she had loved him; in that moment, then, she had known that she wanted to be with him for life, for ever.

She pulled herself free of Don's arms. 'No – No! I'm sorry, but we can't...'

Flushed, aroused, angry, he held her arms, tried to pull her back to him. 'For God's sake, why not? It's what we both want – it's why you came, isn't it?'

Was it? Could he be right? 'I came because I wanted to see the dig, that's all.'

'Don't give me that! You know it's not true!'

'All right, maybe it wasn't quite all, maybe yes, I fancied you, I do fancy you. But I'm married.'

It was as if what she said suddenly had a meaning he had not previously grasped. He stared at her. 'Let me get this right – you've never been unfaithful, never once strayed, in – what is it? – thirty years? My God!'

She wished she could get her breathing under control. 'Is it so unusual?'

'In my experience, yes.'

'Not in mine.'

'And you think he's never looked at anyone else either? You're deluding yourself, Jan.'

'I'm sure he hasn't.' Was she? Could one ever be sure? Last night, certainly, she had doubted his faithfulness. 'In any case, that's beside the point. It's me we're talking about. And I can't do it.'

He shook her gently, his gaze holding hers. 'Why not? Because your marriage is so good, so wonderful and happy? Then why are you here, here with me?'

'If it's not perfect, if it's going through a bad patch, then I won't make it better this way, only worse.'

'Why should he ever know? I'm certainly

not going to tell him.'

'We've never kept things from each other, not important things. I can't lie to him.' She was uneasily aware that though this might be true in a sense, in another way it was not at all. There was much of her life of which Keith knew nothing, even if that was largely because of his apparent indifference to it.

'Let yourself go now and you'll soon know if you want to save your marriage, if it's worth saving.'

She pulled herself completely free from his grasp. 'I can't, Don. I want to – dear knows I want to! But it wouldn't be right, not for me, not now.'

'Ah! Then you might be persuaded to change your mind, another time, in another place?'

'I doubt it. Besides, I'm leaving tonight.'

And she did, after an afternoon during which Don hardly spoke to her, beyond what was absolutely necessary, and dropped her off at the station still in the same mood of fury, resentment, frustration as had clearly been gnawing at him since the confrontation in the wood. Once on the train, weary, depressed, she found herself thinking, Why was I so stupid, so narrow-minded? Why didn't I give in, there in the wood? He's right – no one need ever know. A little adventure, that's all it would have been, a bit of fun and excitement – and goodness knows I need

143

some, if I'm going to cope with Keith again! It might even help me to coax him into letting a bit more excitement into our lives ... Or it might have shown me if things were worth saving, just as Don suggested.

She recalled what Fiona had said, at their recent meeting in London. 'A woman wants different things from the father of her children than she does later on. Why tie herself for ever to the ideal father, when there might be the perfect lover just round the corner?' Jan had brushed the words away as the probably fashionable views of an inexperienced girl, who had not yet learned to love, not yet come to understand commitment; views that would inevitably change as she matured.

Now she found herself wondering if Fiona had a point. In these days when everyone lived longer, when you could be expected to move through many different phases with many different needs, perhaps that view made sense. Was she now finding herself facing a new phase, with a need for another kind of man than Keith, who had been the perfect father, but was not the companion she would have chosen for the years that followed the growing of their children? Not that either of them had been perfect parents, she thought ruefully; like most parents, they had done the best they could, imperfect as it was. But it had been enough to help bring three children to a reasonably stable adulthood; and now that work was done. Was it time to move on?

I'm a fool! she thought. I had a perfect opportunity to taste a little more of life, to have some excitement – a moment or two of happiness, without commitment, without loss, just the sort of thing Fiona and her generation take for granted, don't waste a moment's regret on. Why didn't I take it? Now I'll never know what it's like. What chance is there it'll be offered to me again? I'm not exactly a beauty, I'm growing older. It's some sort of miracle even that an attractive man like Don should fancy me. The opportunities for meeting someone else like that in my life are very limited, back in Meadhope. Besides, it would be much harder to keep it secret, nearer to home.

She was shocked at what she found herself thinking, and yet a part of her mocked her old-fashioned moralising, her misplaced loyalty to a man who could now give her so little and did not even seem to wish to.

As arranged beforehand, she took a taxi home from the station, since she was back very late and Keith had to be up early for work in the morning. She was carried safely to Meadhope through darkness and rain by an uncommunicative taxi driver, and found Keith already in bed. He did not stir when she crept in beside him, did not even grunt or turn towards her. His breathing was quiet, shallow. He's awake, she thought; he knows I'm here, and can't even bring himself to ask if I've had a good time. And I can't make any approach to him, just in case he's asleep after all, not when he has work tomorrow.

She herself did not sleep for a long time. She lay on her back, full of resentment and hurt, hearing Keith's breathing slow and deepen into the familiar gentle snoring; and wondering what was the point of having scruples. If she had only been bold enough, she could have been lying here after a week-end of erotic pleasure (or so she supposed), instead of in her usual unsatisfied state, without even the compensations of companionship and affection.

Much later, she found herself thinking, I made my choice, for good or ill. I turned Don down and made him angry, so he's not an option any more. There's nothing for it now but to make the best of what I've got. Or try to, anyway, really try, as I haven't before. After all, we had something once, we must have done, even if I can't now remember precisely what it was.

She turned then in the dark and touched Keith's forehead with her lips, a kiss light enough not to disturb, but just perceptible if he should be awake. He did not stir, but it was, she felt, enough to seal her pledge, to mark the choice she had made.

Seven

Jan wanted to talk to Keith about her week-end, or the part of it that had to do solely with the dig. She wanted to share her enthusiasm, to try to rekindle in him his old interest in the subject – it was almost the only way she could think of to reach out to him. But he had never been a man for breakfast conversation, even in happier times. This morning, he threw a scowling glance in her direction, asked, 'Did you have a good time?' and paused only long enough to hear her 'Yes' in reply before bending his head again over his toast and marmalade. She was on the point of continuing, of telling him something of what had happened, but instinct held her back. This evening, per-haps, when he came home from work, she could tell him then, over supper. She began to consider what to cook this evening. She'd planned to take a casserole from the freezer, but now thought better of it. She would get some good frying steak from the butcher (she hoped he'd have something decent on a

Monday), serve it with chips and mushrooms and tomatoes; his favourite.

Keith put his breakfast dishes on the draining board (they were eating in the kitchen), went upstairs and a little later left the house, having planted a routine kiss on Jan's cheek. 'Bye.'

She unbent swiftly from loading the dishwasher and reached out to clasp him, to pull him nearer. 'Goodbye, love. Have a good day.' She had hoped he might respond with some warmth, but he merely shook himself free and left the house. She heard the car drive away.

The two surgeries were busy that day, as always on a Monday. On top of the usual number of patients with weekend sniffles and DIY injuries, there were a number of pensioners calling in for the flu jabs their doctors had recommended. Jan was kept busy directing them to the practice nurse's room along the corridor, in the intervals between answering the phone, making appointments, taking details for repeat prescriptions, going through the day's post (so much of it amounted to junk mail) and finalising the visiting list for the two doctors on call this morning.

About mid-morning, having just sat down again in front of her screen with a mug of coffee, she looked up to see an old man standing at the window – he must have come in quietly, for she had not heard him arrive. Once a big square-set man, he was bent now, shaking a little, his eyes tired in a face so lined there was no room for any further wrinkle in its surface. Jan's practised, routine, receptionist's smile gave way to something warmer, truly meant. 'Good morning, Mr Emerson. Have you come for your jab?'

'Dr Stephenson said I had to. Will it take long?'

Jan knew that there was a bedridden wife at home, who depended on old Jack Emerson for everything. She lowered her voice, thankful he wasn't hard of hearing. 'Just knock on the door. I've told Anne you're coming. She'll slip you in ahead of the rest.'

'I wouldn't want anyone saying I don't wait my turn.'

'To tell you the truth, most of them are glad to have a chance to catch up on gossip. They won't mind the wait.' She was glad he seemed reassured; and relieved when, not very much later, he left the surgery, with a wave and a smile of thanks in her direction, and no sound that she could hear of any noisy protest at his queue-jumping. Of course, most of those waiting knew his situation as well as she did.

On her way home, having successfully completed her shopping, she found herself passing the wall that enclosed the lovely old mansion that had once been the rectory, before smaller and more convenient accommodation was put up on the adjacent church meadow. Inevitably, perhaps, the Old Rectory Residential and Nursing Home had been established in the redundant building. Jan walked past it almost every day, but had never been inside. Now, suddenly, on impulse, she turned in between the high stone gateposts and walked up to the blue front door with its highly polished brass knocker. There was a bell, which she rang, and soon found herself ushered by a smiling woman in a blue overall into a spacious, brightly lit hall, full of flowers. She had expected the sour old-people smell that she recalled from her few previous visits to old peoples' homes, but there were simply the odours of polish, flowers (the lilies at least must be real), and freshly baked cakes.

'We're thinking of trying to find somewhere for our old auntie to live,' she found herself explaining. 'Nothing definite yet, but we have to consider the options. I wondered if I might have a look around.'

She was impressed; in the first place, the woman went, without hesitation, to bring the matron to her – a large friendly woman called Eileen Quigley – and a guided tour was immediately set in motion; clearly they had nothing to hide. Then, to her admittedly inexperienced eye, the place looked as comfortable and welcoming as any such home could be. The residents assembling for tea in the two small bright dining rooms seemed happy, talkative, enjoying the joking and laughter encouraged by the staff – mostly very young – who were supervising them. The sandwiches laid ready on the tables looked appetising, and pretty china cups and plates were set at each place. Further afield, the bedrooms – all single, mostly with en-suite facilities – were clean, full of each occupant's small personal belongings: photographs, ornaments, paintings contributed by small grandchildren or great grandchildren. There were several lounges with televisons, and one larger one with a piano. Jan, impressed, enquired about costs and was reassured to hear that those without many means of their own could be supported by social services (she knew Hilda had few savings).

She went on her way home feeling that here might be the solution to the old lady's difficulties. Surely even Keith would be impressed by this place and see its advantages for his aunt, especially as it was close enough to Mill House to enable them to visit often, every day if they wanted. They could easily bring her home for meals or take her for outings in the car, but they would know that she was safe and well cared for, that they need no longer worry as to how she was coping. It was a perfect solution. When the time was right, she would mention it to Keith and see what he thought. This weekend might have given him more time to consider his aunt's predicament, especially if things had been difficult again yesterday. She had tried to ask him at breakfast how his aunt was, but had known it was the wrong moment, and indeed Keith had simply told her irritably to stop hassling him, that everything was fine. Since it had been clear each weekend that Hilda's condition was worsening, Jan was certain that was untrue, but there was nothing she could do about it.

Keith was late home that evening, while Jan kept a restless eye on the clock, concerned that, once home again, he might be too impatient to wait while she cooked the meal; perhaps after all she should have defrosted the casserole. But he simply disappeared upstairs to change and had only just come down again when it was ready. She served the meal with a triumphant flourish, and was irritated when he started eating without any kind of comment. She bit back the angry words and began instead to tell him about her weekend. It had already begun to recede into memory and it was hard to rekindle the enthusiasm she could easily have mustered last night or even this morning, but she forced herself to do so, manufacturing a note of eagerness as she talked, watching his face (when he raised his head enough for her to see it at all) for any sign that she had kindled some answering excitement in him. There was none at all that she could detect, but she blundered on, sounding to her own ears more and more false as the words tumbled into the unresponding silence. 'Next time, you *must* come, Keith. You'd love it, you really would! You—'

He did lift his head at last and this time there was a response, but not in the least the one she might have hoped for or expected. 'Can't you shut up? I'm about to lose my job and all you can do is witter on about that bloody dig!' He threw down his table napkin, pushed back his chair and strode from the room. She heard him running upstairs.

For a moment, appalled, she sat where she was, frozen, trying to take in what he had said, trying to understand. Then she jumped up and ran after him. But he had locked himself in the bathroom and though she called through the door – 'Keith! I had no idea! When did this happen? Come out and tell me! Talk to me!' – there was no response. She had a sudden unpleasant recollection of times when something like this had happened with one of the children, some stormy moment ending in a locked door. But this was different, this was no teenage melodrama, no trivial tantrum that would blow over in a moment; she recognized that.

She banged a few more times on the door, until he shouted, 'Can't I even be left in peace in here?' at which she went downstairs again.

What should she do? What was the right way to respond? She had never been here before, never faced anything so serious. I'm about to lose my job, he had said, unmistakably, clearly. Yet how could that be, without her even having the slightest clue as to what was happening? And if it was so, why had he not urged her to go for the practice manager's job, instead of calmly accepting her reluctance to do so? Were they really so far apart as that, so estranged, that he could not tell her what he really thought, what he was feeling? She sat on the stiff-backed chair in the hall, listening for any sound from upstairs, while her thoughts went over and over the past weeks, searching for clues, markers, any indication of the crisis that had been fermenting beneath the apparently normal surface of their lives; though it had not been normal, of course. Except that she had taken it as if it was, as if Keith's gloomy silences, his moroseness, his unwillingness to talk, were the way he had always been. The fact that she could not recall when this had begun did not excuse her. She should never have accepted it, never have allowed it to go on. She should have pushed and nagged him for an explanation, forced him to confide in her. Yet then, surely, she would only have enraged him, driven him to outright anger? No man likes to be nagged. What then did it say about their marriage, that he had not felt able to confide in her about this supremely important thing? She felt hurt, guilty, bewildered, all at once; and angry too in her turn. But the guilt was the worst. She had put his moroseness down to lack of love, when in reality it had been due quite clearly to anxiety and simple misery. Simple, yet unrecognized. No wonder he had not confided in her! Yet he should have done, it was so much the obvious thing, to talk to his wife about something that must affect them both so crucially. If anyone had asked her, just a few months ago, she would have said they were the best of friends. But friendship would never have allowed a gulf like this to develop.

She heard the rush of water into the cistern, and the bathroom door open and close, steps on the landing. She went into the hall, so that she was waiting at the foot of the stairs when he came down. 'Keith, tell me about it, please!'

'There's nothing to tell,' he said, coming to a halt beside her. 'Early retirement, they call it. Not that I've any choice. There'll be some sort of lump sum, but not enough to live on, not while we've a mortgage to pay. And all this reorganization means fewer jobs, not more. They'll give them to the young men, not burnt out old cases like me.'

Ignoring the hostility, the rejection, in every line of his body, Jan laid a hand on his arm, reached up to stroke his cheek. 'You're not burnt out, love. Come and sit down. Let's talk about it.'

He pulled himself from her grasp, but did at least go with her into the sitting room and sit down near the fire she had lit on coming home. She perched on the end of the sofa, as near to him as possible. She wanted to touch him, hold his hand, but he sat hunched up, his hands in his pockets, pulled in on himself, his gaze not on her but on the fire. 'I don't see what point there is in talking. I've had two uses in this marriage – to father kids and to keep the roof over our heads. I finished with the one long since, and now I can't do the other. I don't see what's left, do you?' He did glance at her then, with eyes that were bleak with something beyond misery.

Jan felt herself shiver. She had wondered, following Fiona's lead, if the marriage that had brought three human beings to agreeable adulthood was enough to provide companionship in the years that lay ahead. She had asked herself if it could supply her needs. In a way, Keith was echoing that question, but not as she had, with excitement, with a sense of danger, with a hope of new possibilities, but despairingly, hopelessly, seeing only emptiness ahead, after years of exclusion. What kind of hollow thing had their marriage been, if this was what it had done to him, to them both? In a way they had reached the same conclusion as one another, but from very different angles, with very different results.

'We could try doing things together,' she suggested tentatively.

'I don't think so.'

'Why not? You'll have more time.'

'Thank you for reminding me! We've ten more years to go on the mortgage, remember.'

'Then I'll get another job – there's the practice manager's job. I'm almost certain to get it.'

'You decided not to.'

'But I didn't know what had happened, did I? Has it happened yet, by the way?'

'I've got a month. End of November.'

'That gives us time to work out what to do.'

'You do what you like. I know what I'm going to do.'

She studied his face, the grim line of his mouth, waiting for what he would say, instinctively dreading it.

'I'm moving in with Auntie Hilda. She needs someone to keep an eye on her.'

At least you admit that now, she thought, wondering what had happened in her absence to make him change his mind, but not quite daring to ask. This too was a symptom of what had gone so badly wrong with their marriage, that even now she feared to prod his anger into life. 'Keith,' she said gently, after a few moments of silence, 'please don't shut me out!'

She had done what she had hoped to avoid. He rose to his feet. 'Don't shut you out! What have you ever done but shut me out of your life, of the children's lives, of everything?' He began to stride towards the door. 'Well, you can have your way. I'm going.'

She followed him upstairs, to the bedroom, where he pulled a case from the top of the wardrobe and began randomly, furiously, to fling clothes into it. 'What are you doing?'

'Packing. I'm going, tonight, to Coldwell. You'll know where to find me if you need anything. But I don't suppose you will.'

In a way, his going made the silence seem less heavy, less oppressive. But it was not a relief, even so. Jan sat on the edge of the bed with the slam of the front door reverberating in her ears and shivered, though with what emotion she did not yet know.

Keith flung his bags in the back of the car, slammed the door shut on them, and got into the driver's seat. He turned the key in the ignition, reversed the car out of the drive and on to the track that led to the road, where he turned and drove on, too fast. There was rage in his head, rage and misery. He was leaving behind an enclosed world in which he had no place, had not had for a long time. Jan, Fiona, Melanie, Simon: they were a whole, complete, with no need for him any more – or not now, not when he was about to find himself redundant. Redundant: it was an accurate word, cruelly appropriate. That was precisely what he was, inside the home as well as outside it. In a few weeks he would have no function of any kind, not even that one single use he had still hung on to since the children grew up and left home and no longer had any need of a father's guidance: to keep the roof over their heads, his and the wife's who had become a stranger, with a life in which he had no part.

She had no idea what it had been like for him during the past months, while the reorganization was taking place; no idea of the hours during which he had lain awake, wondering what was going to happen; the strenuous efforts he had made to try and secure some sort of place for himself in the new order, the effort put into the way he dressed, the way he moved and spoke, the people he approached – or neglected – the meticulous care with which he approached every task, trying to miss nothing that might help him to keep some sort of job. It had been a joyless, anxious time, and in the end it had got him nowhere. He might as well not have bothered, he might as well have given up at the outset. The interview this morning had made that clear. 'Sorry, Keith, we're going to have to let you go.' That false reluctance, which convinced no one, the show of regret – he knew quite well what was unsaid: 'You're too old, we want young blood, eagerness, enthusiasm, new brooms for a new era.' Experience, maturity, all those years he had put into his work, they counted for nothing. But then he should have been used to it by now, able to accept it as the normal, inevitable course of things. In just the same way, all the work he had put into marriage and fatherhood counted for nothing. The children had turned away, made their own lives, as children always did, finding parents only an unnecessary embarrassment, an occasional duty, people from the past who might one day be an encumbrance but until then could be forgotten, most of the time. He supposed that was how it had to be. But that did not seem to be how it was with Jan. They still wanted her, needed her, talked to her for hours on the phone. On the rare occasions they spoke to him, it was awkwardly: 'Hi Dad, how's things?' A few more stilted words, and they would ask to speak to Mum again, or leave her some message and ring off.

Worst of all, with the children's growing, he had found he had lost Jan too. She had become a stranger with whom he seemed to have nothing in common, no point of contact. So long as he provided enough to pay the mortgage, then he supposed he had his uses, in her eyes. Otherwise, he seemed of no interest to her, no importance. All he did was provide the means to allow her to lead a busy productive life, to do a nice undemanding job that she was considering giving up, so as to spend more time absorbed in the many leisure activies which she alone was able to enjoy. Had they ever been friends, companions? Had they ever been anything to one another apart from parents, breadwinner and mother, bound in a useful partnership which was now as redundant as his job?

Through rain and wind he drove to Coldwell, to the one person who still needed him. Hilda had cared for him unselfishly, taken responsibility for him through all his orphaned childhood, made him happy, guided him to manhood. He – like his own children after him – had been guilty often of neglect since then, days, weeks, months even, when he had scarcely given her a thought, kept up only the most tenuous contact with her; times, too, when he had resented the Sunday lunch routine that had come to bind him to her again. Well, she was old now, could no longer cope; in that at least Jan had been right, though he had no intention of telling her so. He had finally been forced to acknowledge that fact on Saturday, when Hilda's neighbour had phoned, to report a fall. Hilda had been taken to hospital, where they declared her bruised and shaken, but otherwise unhurt. He had found her confused, bewildered, but longing to go home; only they would not allow her home unless she had someone to keep her company.

He had intended to discuss the problem with Jan, once she was home again, though he had dreaded her response, doubted whether she would have anything helpful to say. He knew she resented the increasing dependency of the old woman, suspected that she would say Hilda should go into a home, that she needed full-time professional care. 'There are good homes, you know,' she had said once. 'We could go and check them out.' Would he have been able to argue a different case, for Hilda to stay at home with help; even for her to come and live with them? He would never now know, because he had said nothing. There had been no one clear moment when he had decided not to tell Jan; it had just happened that way, once he knew for certain that he was going to lose his job. That was when he had known exactly what he must do, had even recognized a kind of rightness in his redundancy. Now he would be free to care for her, as once she had cared for him. It also gave him a way out of his marriage, a way of leaving Jan yet of continuing to be of real use to someone, now he was useless to her. There was no other good reason for walking out on her, no other love, no obvious incompatibility, just the dying of whatever they might once have had, the thing that he could not now remember, did not even try to remember; whatever it was that had brought them together in the first place. Biological instinct, he supposed. Something that no longer had any purpose in their lives.

He let himself into the house at Coldwell with his own key. He was glad that he'd made some attempt to clear the place up at the weekend, though the unpleasant smell still lingered and there was a good deal to do before it was fit to live in again. He would see to that tomorrow, once he'd visited the hospital and arranged for Hilda to come home; he'd phone in sick and take a day off – after all, he owed them nothing any more. Now, he went wearily upstairs, put down his bags in the spare room, made up the bed and got into it, exhausted, yet knowing he would not sleep.

Eight

He had gone. Packed his case and walked out of her life. She had heard the car drive away, and had done nothing, because there was nothing she could do. She simply sat for a long time with the silence of the house weighing on her, crushing her, so that she could not think, could not take it in.

After what seemed hours – but might have been only minutes – she got up slowly from where she sat on the edge of the bed (a position she had resumed after rushing to the window to watch the departing car, as if she could somehow have called it back with a glance). She walked downstairs with limbs that seemed to have become those of an old woman, aching too much to respond to what she wanted them to do.

The dining room looked frozen in time – in that moment when Keith had rushed from the table. His napkin lay where he'd left it, his plate, full of half-eaten food, already beginning to look dry and unappetising. Her own plate had rather less on it, but had a similar look. His chair, knocked over in the

164

rush, lay on the floor. She went to pick it up and then hesitated. What would she achieve by righting it? The moment had happened; she could not wipe it out. What she must do was to understand, to grasp what had happened.

She stood looking at the table, thinking of the silent meal, the estrangement that had lain between them; a meal like so many others, different only in its revelation of what lay beneath the surface. Yet that thing had lain there for a long time, had been beneath every one of those chilly meals they had lived through together. What she had thought was indifference had been something quite other; a sense of uselessness, a depression that had brought them to this.

In the end, her housewifely instincts made her move, mechanically, to set the chair tidily on its legs, to fold the napkins and put them away (or should she put them to the wash if Keith was not going to use his again for a time? But what would that make her admit?), to take the plates, scoop the uneaten food into the waste bin, stack the dishwasher. Or should she wash them by hand, assuming that it would be some time before she had enough dirty dishes to fill the dishwasher, now there was only one person to use them?

She was already allowing herself to think he would not come back. She must not do that. She who had so terribly misread the signs owed it to Keith to try and put things right, to reach out to him, to offer comfort and understanding, to make him feel wanted and loved. She had misjudged him, made assumptions about his feelings, about their relationship, because she had simply thought of it only from her point of view, making no allowance for what Keith might be feeling. How could she have been so self-centred, so self-absorbed? What was more, she had blamed him for failing to recognize how much Auntie Hilda had failed, where now it seemed that he had been aware of it all along, wanting through gratitude and love to do what he could to help. It was only too likely he recognized Jan's reluctance to be involved, her shameful resentment of the demands the old woman's needs might make upon them.

She closed the door of the dishwasher, tidied the kitchen, went into the sitting room and sat down and opened the *Sunday Times*, but the words seemed to blur and she could not take anything in. She was possessed by a sense that she should not be doing this, that she should be taking action to bring Keith back. But what could she do? Go to Coldwell after him? He had taken the car, and there was no easy way of getting there tonight – no way at all, probably. There was the phone, of course. But would he be there yet? And what if Auntie Hilda answered? Could she make her understand? Jan rather doubted it, and could not face the thought of having to try.

Suddenly she felt exhausted, drained. It was only nine o'clock, but she decided to go to bed, to curl up in the warmth under the duvet, perhaps read a bit until she felt sleepy.

There was a pair of socks on the bedroom floor, folded together, fallen where Keith had dropped them. She stared at them, and then felt a sudden unexpected flare of anger. After all, why should she feel guilty? She *had* known something was wrong. She had tried and tried to get Keith to talk. It was not her fault that he had shut her out, that he had taken it into his head to resent her comfortable life, her dependence on him. She had never seen it like that, she was not the one who had shut him out. Why should she feel responsible for his going, for his unhappiness?

If only it were as easy as that, to scour out her sense of guilt with anger. But even through the anger a small voice was asking if she had indeed done all she could, if she could have done more, could have done something differently, so that Keith would after all have told her what troubled him. As she got into bed conflicting voices clamoured in her head, and though she tried to read (*Captain Corelli's Mandolin*, which

Sheila Brandon had recommended to her) the words blurred on the page and made no sense. Yet she continued to lie against the pillows with her gaze on the open book; she knew she would find it impossible to sleep.

The bedside phone rang, suddenly, shrill in the silence. Keith! Saying he had arrived safely, checking she was all right, demonstrating that all was not over between them, that this was only one move, which would lead to another, perhaps of quite another kind – a tactic, perhaps, a means of forcing her to understand him without the necessity for him to make long difficult explanations. Men were so bad at finding the words for their feelings. She lifted the receiver, gave the number.

'Hi, there, Mum.' Fiona's voice, cool, untroubled, the daughter keeping in touch; the daughter who did not know that her father had just walked out into the night.

What do you say? *Your Dad's just left me?* She hardly heard what Fiona was saying; her mind was too confused for anything but what had just happened. After a while, her daughter must have realized that something was wrong, for Jan heard her repeating anxiously, 'Mum? Are you OK?'

Jan forced herself to concentrate. Fiona must not know; none of them must know. They were her children, hers and Keith's. She could not possibly tell them that their parents' relationship – the rock that had been the basis of a secure childhood, the model, as they saw it, of marital compatibility and stability – had suddenly cracked asunder, as easily and brutally as any ordinary marriage. From somewhere she found a note of cheerful normality. 'Of course. I'm fine. Everything's fine.' Had she carried it off? Was Fiona convinced? Or would she sense that her mother was protesting too much, so much that she would only be convinced that something was wrong?

'How was the dig? Has it whetted your appetite for more?'

It was a moment or two before Jan realized what her daughter was talking about. The weekend seemed lost in some distant past, almost beyond recall. She certainly did not want to try and recall it now, still less to talk about it, partly because the things that had made it enjoyable only served to underline her present sense of failure. They, too, had shut Keith out. But she forced herself to give a cheerful account of what had happened – of all those things that related to archeology, with no word of Don and what had passed between them.

It seemed that Fiona was satisfied, for she asked a few questions, listened with apparent interest, and then very soon moved on to events in her own life, amusing anecdotes from the office – but of her work only, Jan noticed; nothing of her private life. 'Have you heard anything of Sam?' she asked.

It was clearly a mistake. 'No,' said Fiona curtly. 'Thank goodness.' But she did not sound entirely pleased.

The call ended soon afterwards. Jan suspected there could have been few calls in which so little was said of what really mattered, in which so much was left unsaid, on both sides. Yet it was hardly reasonable of her to resent Fiona's lack of candour, when she was herself as guilty of the same offence.

She slept little that night. She lay wondering what to do; whether to phone Keith, to go and call on him; whether she should try to make this contact at once, or wait a little, in the hope that he might make the first move. In the end – sometime around four in the morning – she decided to wait, if only because time might make him realize that he wanted to be back at home with her, that the present situation was untenable.

She felt strange the next morning, setting out for work from the long silence of the house. She was exhausted from lack of sleep, dazed, but also felt as if something must mark her out as a wife who had failed, whose husband had left her. Surely everyone would see at once that something was seriously wrong.

She put on what she hoped was her most cheerful manner as she let herself into the surgery; it must have been convincing, for no one made any comment. The sense of shock, the persistent feelings of guilt and anger, seemed to leave no perceptible trace on the surface, though she was in tumult underneath. By the end of the day, if anyone had asked, she could not have picked out any incident, to recount what had happened in any detail. It had all been a blur. She had functioned on some automatic level, her work had been done efficiently enough, so that no one had noticed there was anything amiss; but she might as well have stayed at home for all the impression the day had made on her. After work, she went home to the empty house. Of course, it always had been empty at this time of day and often for many hours more. But this emptiness was different, a great echoing absence that added to the clamour in her head.

As the days passed, and she began to grow used to the silence and find some way of coping with the daily routine, Jan wondered how long it would be before people began to realize that Keith had gone and started asking questions; she tried to work out what she would say, how she would explain his going. But what shocked her most was to realize by the end of that long week that no one had noticed his absence at all. It was as if he were invisible, or nearly so, a figure glimpsed sometimes passing in his car on his way to or from work, a man who very occasionally met friends in a pub for a drink – but hardly ever; and now and then accompanied his wife to church – but only at Christmas or Easter or one of the other significant festivals. Otherwise he played no part in village life. She knew, uneasily, that if she were the one to disappear, her absence would be noticed immediately, and not simply because she had a high profile job at the village surgery.

On Wednesday afternoons the surgery was closed; and Jan as usual took the opportunity to go for a walk. This week in particular it seemed to offer her the opportunity to think over all that had happened, without distractions, to try and work out what she should do next. She took the well-worn footpath that led away from the village towards the hills. It crossed a meadow full of cows, passing a small railed area at the further side. Behind the rails a stone arch – about waist high – covered a low stone basin into which clear water bubbled, before tumbling into a little stream that ran along the side of the field. A bunch of late roses lay on the edge of the basin, with other flowers, faded beyond recognition, fallen on the ground beside it.

Jan halted and stood looking at it: the Holy Well, an ancient watering place sacred to the memory of some Celtic saint. When they first came to Meadhope it had been no more than a heap of rubble clogging the stream, the well itself a distant folk memory. It was Keith who had taken the trouble to search out all the records, going back to mediaeval times, to write them up and have them published in a glossy leaflet, and to set in motion a campaign for the well's restoration. He had been successful too, eventually, after much hard work. They had been good times, which had brought them many friends. Jan had been a stay-at-home mother then, her hands full with toddler Fiona and the infant twins; it was Keith who had invited their new friends to their home, who had spoken to local groups about the well, who had involved himself with enthusiasm in fund-raising events. At last, they had all gone as a family to join the celebration on that day twenty years ago when the restored well was blessed by the rector, who had processed there from the church with a cross-bearer going ahead and a surpliced choir following. If Keith had suddenly disappeared during those months – or was it years? – everyone would have noticed at once. They would have said, with concern, 'Where's Keith? We missed him last night. Is he all right?' But she knew that there had been no danger that he would have walked out of their lives in those days; he was too happy, too involved, had too significant a role to play for that.

173

Now, long afterwards, the procession to the well had become an annual summer event, which most people probably believed to have an ancient history, and Keith's leaflet was still available in the local library, as well as for sale (a little dog-eared now) in the two Meadhope newsagents. People still left flowers at the well, as they had begun to do immediately after its restoration, for the first time since the Middle Ages, or so Keith had maintained. It was only Keith himself who had faded from view, who had gradually, inexorably, relinquished his involvement in village life, as the demands of his job had pressed relentlessly in on his leisure time. And now that job, which had become the only significant thing in his life, had failed him too. No wonder he had felt marginalized, irrelevant.

She continued on her way, deep in thought. Surely if she now understood how Keith felt, then she could do something about it, help him to come to terms with what had happened and to move on, to make something of the very different life that lay ahead of him? But first, of course, they would have to talk. Without that, they could resolve nothing. And there, of course, was her difficulty. Every time she heard the phone ring, she would find herself thinking: it must be Keith, wanting to put things right. But so far he had not rung. She had phoned the house at Coldwell last night, but Hilda had answered and clearly had no idea who she was. Jan did not know whether or not Keith had been in the house at the time, but he had made no attempt to speak to her. Later, she had left a message on his mobile, but he had not returned the call. Now, she decided that telephoning was useless; it was too easy to ignore her calls. The only solution was to go to Coldwell in person. It was a complicated journey without a car, but she would do it, if Keith did not make any attempt to get in touch before the weekend.

He continued to ignore her calls, nor did he ring himself. The children did, all of them: Fiona again; Simon, briefly, but sounding overflowing with happiness, attributable, Jan supposed, to the Tamsin whose name peppered his account of his life; Mel, a long slow call in which she talked brightly about her new responsibilities, about difficult guests and (more rarely) grateful ones, and how she was decorating her flat, and then grumbled a little about her twin's failure to keep in touch. Jan suggested that this was due to the new girl in his life, but Mel said only, 'That's no excuse. He could at least phone. He always used to tell me things first, before anyone else.' So it looked as though he had not told Mel at all about Tamsin. Jan sensed her daughter's hurt, and tried to find some excuse for Simon, and, later, tried to phone him to tell him to get in touch with his twin, but there was no reply. It would have to wait.

Jan spoke to her mother too during that long week. She had been at a low point one evening and on impulse picked up the receiver, thinking she might even confide in her mother, tell her all that had happened. But Audrey Turner, assuming this was the usual sociable weekly call, went at once into a long account of all she had done since they last spoke (Jan's mother had a busy social life); and by the time there was an opportunity for her to speak at any length, Jan knew she could not plunge baldly into the subject of her marital difficulties. Instead, she approached the subject obliquely: 'Mum, when you married Eddy, did you look for a different sort of man than Father was – or is he like Father? What I mean is, you were older; maybe you wanted different things from your partner than you did when you married Father.'

'Oh, Jan, you've got me there. I've never really thought about it. You don't, do you? You just fall in love and that's it. Besides, we were so young when we married, your father and I – and we had so little time together. I suppose if he'd lived we'd both have changed, grown up together, done things together and got interested in them. As it was ... Of course, I met Eddy through a mutual interest. That's always a good start. And we set out wanting different things than if we'd been young. Oh, I don't know! What is this, anyway? Is something wrong?'

'No – no, of course not! It's just something Fiona said the other day; it set me wondering about you in particular. She thinks one man can't give a woman all she needs throughout her life. According to Fiona, we want one sort of man in the early days to be a good father, then, later, we're looking for companionship and shared interests. And in her view, you can't generally find that in the same man. She excepts me and Keith from that, of course,' Jan added hastily.

'Because you've taken the trouble to work at your marriage, to develop your relationship – and to see that men have needs too, come to that. Very unfashionable, I suppose. The trouble with Fiona's generation is that they think everything's disposable. If you don't like it, throw it out and start again. Any idea that they might work at it and turn it into something good and worthwhile – well! She's young, though. She'll learn. After all, she's had a good example to follow.'

Jan knew then that she could not tell her mother the truth; or not now, not yet, not until she had to.

On Saturday, Jan set out early to make the slow journey by public transport to Coldwell. She reached the town by lunchtime, and walked from the bus station to the ter- raced row – Hepburn Street – on the other side of town. She felt her heart thud pain- fully as she neared the place, and she was shaking as she reached out to ring the bell. She prayed Keith would be there, that he would answer the door; yet she was afraid of what his reaction would be.

She rang three times, each time waiting what she felt was a reasonable interval before pressing the bell again. The conviction grew on her that Keith was not there, that Auntie Hilda was alone in the house – or perhaps Keith had taken her out somewhere. Only it did not somehow feel as if the house was empty.

There came definite sounds of movement inside, a door closing, the shuffle of feet. The front door opened just a crack and the old woman's face – small, greyish, lined – appeared in the gap, the brown eyes – once bright and bird-like, now dull, uncompre- hending – gave her a vague look. Jan had no idea whether or not Auntie Hilda knew who she was, for there was no recognition in her eyes. But she did open the door wider, and stand back to indicate that she should come in.

There was still a dubious smell lingering in the house, together with a general mustiness. It felt cold too – it was a wet day – though

Keith had clearly done some cleaning since he moved in. 'Is Keith here?' she asked the old woman, who had now turned away and was shuffling along the hallway towards the back of the house. Jan could hear the sound of a tap running in the kitchen.

Hilda neither paused nor looked round, but continued on her shuffling way. Jan wondered if she had lost her hearing, though she could not recall any difficulties in the past. It was more likely a loss of understanding. She followed slowly behind the old woman, until they reached the kitchen. Jan had half-expected to find Keith there after all, but there was no one, only the hot tap running pointlessly into the cluttered sink, the table covered with a confusion of objects, that was almost, but not quite, the temporary untidiness of a not-very-orderly cook. There was a pastry cutter and a rolling pin, alongside a wooden spoon. In the centre of the table – encroaching on a small pile of envelopes, mostly bills by the look of them – was a heap of flour, dotted with sultanas and topped with long grain rice. The old woman went at once to the table and began to run her hands through the heap, spreading it further, over the uncovered part of the table, on to the floor, down the front of her green cardigan and black trousers.

Jan went first to turn off the tap and saw through the steaming water that filled the sink that the electric mixer lay there, not just the blades, but the whole of it, stand included and all the working parts – *once* working parts now, presumably. She tried to pull out the plug from the sink, but the water was too hot. She took a fork from the drawer and hooked it out, watching the water run away; then, aware of silence behind her, she looked round. Hilda had paused in her mixing and had now turned to look at her, almost accusingly, Jan thought. There was something very disturbing, almost frightening, about her behaviour, a sense that there was no knowing what she might do next. Nothing any longer was predictable. It was also unbearably sad. Auntie Hilda had been an intelligent woman, well-educated, highly principled, always smartly turned out, in an old-fashioned way. Jan had liked and respected her. But that woman, who had brought Keith up, helped to make him the man he was, welcomed Jan as Keith's wife, had now disappeared from the frail old lady staring across the kitchen at Jan as if she had never seen her before. This person here today was somehow not a person any longer but a husk, a shell with some sort of being still left in her, but nothing that could be called life or personality or intelligence.

And what of Keith? What was there left in him of the man Jan had thought she knew and once had loved? She had a sense of decay, of dissolution, all around her. She shivered. 'I'll put the kettle on and then we can have a cup of tea,' she said brightly, as if everything was absolutely normal. There was no point in asking again about Keith. She could see that it would mean nothing to the old woman, that she could hope for no coherent answer, or, probably, no answer at all.

She filled the kettle and plugged it in, and then brushed some of the flour from the old woman's clothes, disconcerted by Hilda's intent gaze on her face as she did so, and then steered her towards the sitting room. A fire had been lit, but no one had tended to it and it was almost out. Once Hilda was seated in one of the tapestried armchairs, Jan took coal from the scuttle (Keith had filled it, then, before he went out) and made up the fire. At that moment she heard the key turn in the front door, heard the sound of shoes scraping on the doormat, heard Keith call, 'I'm back, Auntie!', with all the cheerful matter-of-factness of someone returning to an entirely normal situation.

Jan placed the guard in front of the fire and went to meet him in the hallway. He had his hands full of shopping from the Co-op supermarket in Front Street; he was already making his way to the kitchen with them. Seeing her, he halted, and his expression – momentarily the open, friendly face of the man she had once known – closed down, cold, shutting her out. 'Oh – Jan! What are you doing here?'

'I thought we should talk.'

'I don't think we've got anything to talk about.' He moved on towards the kitchen.

'There's Auntie Hilda, for one thing.' It was not at all why she had come, but now she saw the urgency of the problem, more than ever.

'I don't think so. You've made your views plain enough. You know what I think.'

Following, she saw him halt momentarily in the kitchen doorway, as if struck by what he saw. Then he went on and laid the shopping bags on a chair, and started to put the shopping away.

'Look at this,' Jan said, gesturing towards the table. 'And I found this covered with water.' She indicated the food mixer. 'How long were you out?'

'I don't see what business that is of yours. Someone has to do the shopping. We have to eat.'

'I know that. And you have to go to work too. What happens while you're out during the day?'

'Nothing that can't be put right when I get in,' he said, his back to her as he stacked tins in the cupboard. 'In any case, in a few weeks I'll be here full time. She won't want for all the care she needs.'

'You'll still have to shop. You can't stay in all the time.'

He turned to face her. 'Leave me to do the caring. You made it clear enough you would not have anything to do with it.'

'Because it's not enough; because she needs full-time care; because she no longer knows who we are or where she is or what she's doing.'

'You haven't lived with her as I have; you know very little about it. If I can make it possible for her to hang on to her dignity and independence, then I shall do so, for as long as it takes. She's been alone too long, that's all. A few weeks of tender loving care and she'll be her old self again. Now, please go. There's no more to be said.'

Jan, hesitating, reaching for words that might make him change his mind, might make him consider talking things over with some hope of coming to an agreement, heard a shuffling sound behind her and turned to see Hilda making her way up the hall. She had a poker in her hand.

For just a moment Jan felt a surge of fear. Then Keith slid past Jan and went to Hilda and, very gently, took the poker from her hand. Jan, suddenly thinking of the fire (easy enough to remove the guard), ran to the front room. It looked just as it had when she had left Auntie Hilda there to wait for her cup of tea. She should have been relieved –

she *was* relieved – yet part of her was disappointed that there was nothing here to support her argument with Keith.

He had followed her into the room, to replace the poker. Hilda was following him, meekly. 'What did you expect?' he asked Jan. He looked round at Hilda, ran his hand along her arm. 'You get a bit muddled sometimes, don't you, Auntie? That's why I'm here to look after you.' The look the old woman fixed on his face was less vacant than anything Jan had seen so far, and she even smiled, faintly, for a moment. It seemed that she must at least know who Keith was and even understand something of what he said; unless she was simply responding to what she recognized as kindness.

Jan knew she had lost this particular argument, for the time being at least. She did not feel convinced, but the evidence had eluded her. She knew, too, that Keith was as far as ever from being willing to talk about their relationship; in any case, that subject seemed somehow to have become inextricably bound up with the other one, with Auntie Hilda and her needs. 'I'll go then,' said Jan wearily. 'You know where I am if you want me. In our home, yours and mine.'

Keith did not even reply. He was now returning Hilda to the kitchen, talking to her gently as they went, their backs turned uncompromisingly towards Jan. She watched them for a moment, despair crystallizing within her, then let herself out of the house into the damp freshness of the afternoon.

The bus journey home gave her ample opportunity to think, more opportunity than she welcomed. She had gone to Coldwell hoping to repair the rift between herself and Keith. Instead, she had found that it was all much more complicated than she had supposed, that it was not simply a question of depression brought on by impending unemployment, but that Auntie Hilda's condition was also a huge part of the problem, as much if not more than the lack of understanding between them. Except that her condition had also contributed to that lack of understanding. She had been so sure that she was right, that they should bring in help from social services for the old woman, who would, most likely, recommend a home for her – which, in her mental confusion, would be much the best solution for her and for all of them. Now she found herself wondering whether in fact Keith was right, that his aunt could still manage with family help. After all, he knew her better than anyone. Was Jan, then, the stumbling block? Should she have offered to bring Hilda to Meadhope, to live with them, so that they could care for her together? That would perhaps be a small return for all Hilda had done for Keith. Jan tried to imagine what that would mean for

185

life at Mill House. They had space, when she thought about it – four bedrooms upstairs, one of which could be turned into a study/sitting room, enabling them to use one of the downstairs rooms – the dining room perhaps – as a place for Hilda. When Keith came home again, there would be two of them to care for the old woman, so that they could each have some kind of life outside the house. And if Keith was right and with the right care Hilda would be less confused, less likely to do strange things, then they might even be able to build up some kind of life together again, the two of them. And Keith would no longer think her cold-hearted.

It was close to dusk when she reached Mill House. She put on the lights, took off her coat and walked about the house, trying to imagine how it would be with Auntie Hilda living there, with Keith back at home. Standing in the kitchen doorway, she suddenly saw her kitchen table – an old scrubbed oak table found in a saleroom years ago – covered as the table at Coldwell had been with a mess of ingredients; her food processor ruined with water. Keith had not left Hilda alone for long this morning, as far as she could gather, so the damage must have been done in that time. Was she prepared to have someone to live with them who would need watching every moment of the day? Keith would deny the necessity. He might be right, on the whole. Perhaps Auntie Hilda was just having a bad morning. Perhaps there was some other explanation. Perhaps she would behave normally for most of the time, and they would simply have to be prepared for the occasional moment of eccentricity. Perhaps indeed, with daily loving care, with stimulating company, she would regain much of her intellectual capacity.

I wish I knew what was right! Jan thought. And whether the cost would be too great, to bring Keith home. Would he come, if she agreed to those terms?

And then, another, fundamental question came into her mind. Did she want him home, on these or any other terms? Shocked that she should even think it, she switched off the kitchen lights and ran upstairs to change out of her outdoor clothes. She had just pulled on her slippers when the phone rang. Keith! she thought, with a longing to beg his forgiveness, to hear his voice soften towards her.

It was a man's voice at the other end, a deep husky voice, quite unlike Keith's. 'Don!' she said, disappointment thudding through her, and alarm. 'What do you want?'

Nine

Jan had not expected to hear from him again. She did not want to hear from him, not now. She had come home last weekend, the dutiful wife, putting temptation behind her; but all that effort, she now saw, had been a waste of time. She doubted if it would have meant anything to Keith if he had known all that had happened last weekend. He had taken himself from her life; she might as well have seized her moment of pleasure. Yet, at this moment, she had no sense of regret, of missed opportunities.

But what now? What should she tell Don, if anything? 'Jan!' he was saying urgently, uneasy at her silence, 'Jan! What's wrong?'

'Nothing,' she stammered. 'I didn't expect it to be you, that's all. Not after – well...'

'No, I don't suppose you did. I admit I didn't feel inclined to get in touch again. I was pretty angry. But maybe I was a bit un-reasonable. I've no experience of steady marriages to go on. I found myself thinking, why damage a good friendship, a good new friendship? So, I thought I'd give you a ring.'

She was quite sure that friendship was not what he had in mind, any more than it had been last weekend (was it really only last weekend?). She suspected that, like most men, he hated to admit defeat. If he had known how much things had changed since she had spurned him, he would, she was sure, be utterly confident of himself, convinced (if he wasn't already) that he had done right to phone her. And she no longer need have any conscience about betraying Keith, who had so baldly walked out on her. Yet some instinct told her that to confide in Don now would be to take another solid step away from Keith, away from any hope of salvaging her marriage. She was not yet ready for that. 'It's always nice to hear from a friend,' she said coolly, in a manner that she hoped would disappoint him if he hoped for any sign that she regretted her rejection of him. Though she was uncomfortably conscious that she did not want to go too far; that she did not want to push him irrevocably out of her life, just in case ... What? In case Keith never returned, in case her marriage was beyond repair, so she would not be left alone? It was a horribly calculating way of looking at things, if that was what it was. 'How's the dig going?' she asked quickly, fending off treacherous thoughts.

After that, there was little need to be on her guard. Don talked with all his old infectious enthusiasm, prompting further questions, until the call had lasted for nearly an hour. 'You'll have to come down again,' he said at the end.

'I might just do that,' she promised, and meant it. By the time he rang off, she felt exhausted and yet oddly exhilarated, as if the call had given her new self-confidence, a new capability; and ashamed that she should feel so. All these mixed emotions were an exhausting business.

But while a little long-distance flirtation might be fun, as were the subsequent fantasies about what it might lead to, the reality which flooded back after she returned the handset to its place was no fun at all. She was no nearer knowing what to do.

It was late on Sunday evening when Fiona's phone rang. She was already in bed, as she was due to catch the Eurostar to Paris again in the morning, but she still had the light on and the handset was beside the bed, just in case. She half-expected it to be Éric, altering the arrangements for tomorrow, but was surprised when her sister's voice came clearly to her. 'Mel? What's the matter?'

'Nothing,' said Mel. 'At least, I couldn't sleep ... I haven't woken you, have I? I know you don't go to bed early.'

'I wasn't asleep. What's keeping *you* awake then?'

'Something Mum said on the phone today. I rang her this afternoon, just for a chat, you know. She said they were thinking of having Auntie Hilda to live with them.'

'What, permanently? I know Mum was worried about her. She thought Dad didn't see how her mind was going. I suppose this means he must have admitted it now. I suppose they've got room.'

'Yes, but you haven't seen her lately; I have. I reckon she needs full-time care. Also, I'd doubt if she knows who she is or where she is any more. She'd be better off in a good home, with proper professional care. Otherwise, they'll have no lives of their own at all.'

She paused, and Fiona began, 'I don't see—'

But Mel broke in: 'It'll be horrible going home if she's there. It won't feel like home.' She sounded, astonishingly, almost tearful at the thought.

'I can't believe she's that bad,' said Fiona, beginning to feel irritated. This was hardly a matter of such crucial importance that she had to be kept awake discussing it. She didn't want to meet Éric with dark rings under her eyes.

'She was, and she'll be worse now. You don't get better from something like Alzheimer's, or whatever it is.'

'Anyway, nothing may come of it. You said they're only thinking of it. If Auntie Hilda is

191

that bad then I imagine Mum will put her foot down. At least it looks as if Dad's realized there's a problem. Don't worry about it, Mel.'

'Well, will you speak to Mum, just to find out what's going on?'

'Of course. In any case, I expect she'll tell me, when we're next in touch. Has she said anything to Simon?'

'The only thing in Simon's head is this girl he's moved in with.'

'What – Tamsin? Have they moved in together then?'

'Yes. Last week. He phoned to give me his address.'

'Good for him.' There was silence at the other end of the phone. 'Aren't you glad for him?' Simon had only ever had the most fleeting and unsatisfactory of relationships until now.

'Yes – yes, of course. But...' Mel's voice roughened. 'He hardly phones me at all these days.'

'Oh, you know what the first pangs of love are like. He'll cool down a bit, then things will be back to normal. Don't worry.' Fiona drew a deep breath. 'Now, I really must get some sleep or I'll never be on top of things tomorrow. I'm off to Paris first thing...' Mel rang off almost at once, full of apologies.

Fiona felt irritated at her sister's interruption. The physical effort of raising herself on one elbow, reaching out from the warmth of the duvet to lift the handset from the side table, sitting propped sideways while she talked, and then, afterwards, trying to find again the ideal snug nest in which she had been lying, half-awake, when the phone rang – that was bad enough. Worse was the mental disturbance. Dreamy thoughts of Éric had been shoved aside for her sister's concerns: for worries about her parents and Auntie Hilda. Memories came back of the last time she had seen the old woman, of how vague her expression was, how all her old incisiveness had gone, all the straightforward frankness, the firmness of opinion. This is old age, Fiona had thought, with a shudder of revulsion; I want none of it. She did not want to think – any more than Mel did – that her visits home would be shadowed by that disturbing presence. She did not want to think of it now, either. She wanted to reclaim her dreams, shut out the unpleasantness. She wanted the uncomplicated, agreeable, untroubled life which she had begun to find for herself; selfish perhaps, but exciting and pleasurable without making any demands on her at all. But Éric seemed to have vanished. She could not bring him in beyond the fringes of her mind. It was a very long time before she slept.

The surgery was busy on Monday. It always

was, after the weekend, but there was a heavy cold doing the rounds at present – 'flu', to most sufferers, many of whom sat coughing and sneezing and shivering in the waiting room, effectively spreading the virus. There were two large and colourful posters reminding patients that most viruses were impervious to antibiotics and giving them instructions about treating themselves at home, but Jan wondered if all the people who let their eyes wander over the notices and posters as they waited ever took in anything they saw. There were two patients this morning for whom a bad cold would be dangerous – old Mr Barlow, who was liable to severe attacks of bronchitis, and Kylie Bennet, a fifteen-year-old who was only seven months past a bone marrow transplant for leukaemia and still had a compromised immune system. Jan made sure they went in to their appointments ahead of the rest.

'Sometimes,' she said to Anne, who came to collect the cards for the nurse's clinic, 'I think we need one of those old-fashioned dragon receptionists here. You know, the sort who demands to know all the symptoms and then tells the patient whether or not they can have an appointment.'

'Maybe they should just have longer to wait for their appointments,' suggested Anne. 'I bet they don't have this trouble up at Dalehead surgery. You have to wait so long for an appointment there, I'm told, that you're either cured or dead by the time you get to see anyone.'

'I would guess some of that's just bad management.'

'Precisely why we need a good manager here,' said Anne slyly.

Jan pulled a rueful face but said nothing. In truth, she no longer dismissed the idea of applying for the job, though she did not want it any more than she had done before. After all, even if Keith came home again, someone would have to pay the mortgage, unless his redundancy payment was enough to pay it off, which of course at present she had no means of knowing; he clearly had not thought so. And if he did not come back, well, she would need something to live on, rather more than she was earning at present, if she was not to have a very restricted existence. After work, when everyone else had gone, she would look out a copy of the job specification and take it home to read. There was a lot of evening to fill without Keith.

At the end of the morning, Jan put away the patients' notes and sorted through the various papers awaiting attention on the counter. 'Hmm, Mr Emerson's not been in for his prescription. Hope he's all right.'

'Do you want me to take it round?' Anne offered. 'I pass his house on my way home.'

'I'll take it. I'll get it made up – that'll save him a journey.'

On her way home at the end of the day, Jan knocked on the trim front door of Mr Emerson's house in Front Street – painted in the traditional nondescript green which doors were usually painted when she was a child, as far as she recalled. She found herself wondering, in a desultory way, if that was due to a lack of imagination, an unwillingness to stand out from the crowd, or simply an indication of the cheapness of green paint as opposed to any other colour.

'Oh – Mrs Grey – that's kind of you. You'll come in and have a cup of tea?'

She didn't want a cup of tea, but she could not legitimately say she was in a hurry, so she went in and sat down while the old man put the kettle on.

It was a tiny house, with one main room downstairs and (presumably) the same upstairs, and a bathroom built over a small kitchen at the back, taking up most of the back yard. Mrs Emerson had long been unable to climb stairs, so a bed had been made up for her downstairs, with room left only for two chairs and a television. The little room was spotless, a fire burning gently in the hearth. The old woman lay propped on pillows, covered with blankets and a beautiful traditional quilt in red satin. She was sleeping noisily, her hands resting on the quilt, her face grey and lined and thin. Jan had found it hard to recall Auntie Hilda as she had once been, faced with the confused old lady at Coldwell. It was harder still to think of this person as a human being with normal thoughts and feelings; hard to imagine her as the strong large-boned woman in the wedding photograph on the mantelpiece.

Mr Emerson came in with the tea on a tray, which he set down on top of the nest of tables beside his wife's bed. 'That's a beautiful quilt,' said Jan.

'Aye. She made it herself, before we were wed. She was a great needlewoman, my Lily. Weren't you, love?' He touched her hand, as if she could hear and understand what he was saying; perhaps indeed she could, somewhere inside that apparently empty husk.

'Do you have any help looking after her?'

'There's a lass comes in to clean once a week. And meals on wheels. And we've good neighbours. We get by. We've been together sixty-three years. Fifty-six of those, she cared for me. It's the least I can do, to care for her for what time we have left.'

Jan left the house feeling humbled, ashamed even. All that devotion, all that love – for such it was, such it must be, in some sense unknown to most of those who talked glibly of love, who took its implications, its demands, so lightly. There was no sense here that the commitment made all those years ago was a finite thing, that it had its natural term, after which each could seek some other satisfaction. They had taken one another on for life, and that was it, plain and simple, except that it was not plain, not at all simple, but complex, demanding, profound. That care and love was not seen as something that could be given up, that could be done better by professional carers. And old Mr Emerson was a man – that often despised species, the ones who were seen as lacking in commitment, as helpless dependants who needed women to see them through life. This old man was as tender, as loving, as devoted as any woman could ever be. It all made so many everyday assumptions look trivial and superficial.

Jan walked home, deep in thought, picking up the post from the doormat as she stepped into the house. There were three letters for Keith, one a bill which she would have to deal with (she had always dealt with the bills anyway), the other two – well, what should she do? She put them to one side on the hall table, hoping that question would resolve itself. With luck he would be home soon to open them for himself. She went to the kitchen, intending to heat through a chicken casserole she had taken from the freezer last night, but on impulse went instead to the phone and dialled Hilda's number. She was relieved (yet apprehensive) when Keith answered it.

'Oh, hello,' he said, repelling her by his tone.

She forced herself to sound positive, impervious to hurt. 'Keith, I've been thinking.' She had been going to say a good deal first about how she was sorry for the misunderstandings between them, for her part in their estrangement. But she thought better of it. She thought it only too likely he would simply ring off before she had finished, without waiting to hear the proposal she had to make, or even knowing that she had one in mind. She had to get to the point quickly. 'I've been thinking about Auntie Hilda. It seems obvious to me now. She should come and live with us here. There's plenty of room.'

'You've changed your tune,' said Keith, just as if the matter had often been discussed between them, which it had not.

Jan suppressed her impatience and, with great difficulty, resisted making any comment. She had to be unfailingly emollient if she was to get anywhere with Keith in his present mood. Later, when he was back here, there would be time enough to talk things out, thoroughly. 'Whatever,' she said. 'What do you think? It makes sense, doesn't it?'

'Not really,' he said. 'In fact, I don't see

how it would help at all. Auntie needs familiar things about her. Take her away from them and she'll go to pieces completely. No, she stays here and I stay with her.'

Jan felt exasperated almost beyond words. Was he asking her to come and live at Coldwell? No, he could not be, for Hilda's tiny spare bedroom only had space for a single bed. 'Then what do you want me to do?'

'Nothing. Get on with your life. I'm not stupid enough to imagine my absence makes any difference to that.' Then he rang off.

Jan was shaking as she replaced the handset. She did not know what she had expected from her approach to Keith, but it had not been this complete rejection, this refusal even to consider what she said or to acknowledge that they had anything to discuss. She stood where she was in the hallway, staring at the letters on the table – Keith's letters, which she would now have to forward. She felt numb and yet miserable.

There was, suddenly, the sound of a car on the gravel outside. Well, she knew it couldn't be Keith. A delivery then, she supposed, though she could not think of anything she might have ordered. She opened the front door.

There was no delivery van, just a small blue Fiat from which, a moment later, a

200

young man emerged, stretching as if he had been cooped up for a long time. She watched him come towards her, saw an open boyish face and clear blue eyes. 'Hope this isn't a bad time. I should have phoned ahead, I know.'

'Sam!' What on earth was he doing here? She watched the young man they had all known for the past five years as Fiona's partner, who had first come home with her during a university vacation and whose life had been linked with hers ever since, irrevocably they had thought. Now, no longer part of her life, he was here in the Mill House driveway, as if nothing had changed. Jan did not exactly welcome the intrusion, but she thought that if she had to cope with a visitor, it was better this one than almost any other. She looked at his face, trying to gauge his mood, but he was simply smiling in his old friendly way. She kissed him. 'What brings you here?'

'Oh, just passing,' he said. 'I'm on my way to Scotland, to look at a house.'

'A house? For you? Have you got a new job then?' She looked up at his face and suddenly laughed. 'I'm sorry – I shouldn't be interrogating you out here in the cold. Come inside. You'd like a meal, I expect.'

'Well, I...'

'Of course you would!' She led the way inside, recalling suddenly that Sam would expect Keith to come home from work, to join them for the evening meal, as had always happened in the past when Sam had come to stay. What should she do? Invent a late meeting? Or a conference in some far-away place? It would sound entirely plausible. She pushed the questions aside for later, when she would have to answer them.

Sam hung his coat in the hall, in its usual place. 'Feel as if I've never been away,' he said. Then added ruefully, 'At least, I could almost believe nothing's changed.'

Little did he know how much had changed! 'I was sorry about you and Fee.'

'These things happen.' There was a raw edge to his voice, for a moment. Then he said more cheerfully, 'But you have to move on.' She led the way to the kitchen and he sat by the table while she opened a bottle of Chilean cabernet and poured them each a glass. 'That's why I'm thinking of Scotland. I've decided to go freelance, so I can base myself wherever I choose.'

'But won't it be difficult so far from London – to find work, I mean?'

'Oh, there'll be work – maybe not so well paid. Certainly not so well paid. But I've only myself to think of and I'm going to do what I want to do. See how it goes anyway.'

'Good for you!' Jan raised her glass. 'Here's to you and the future!' She felt as if she were toasting her own future too, that unknown and rather frightening time that faced her now. 'I've got a chicken casserole out of the freezer. I was just going to heat it in the microwave. There's enough for two, if that suits you. Or I can do fish fingers. If you're anything like our three that would go down just as well.'

'Chicken casserole's fine for me. But what about Keith?'

'Oh, he'll not be here for supper.' She heard the words come out, casual, matter-of-fact. She had not even had to think about what to say. It was entirely true too, as far as it went.

'How is he? Overworking still?'

So that was how Sam saw him, a man who was overworking! It was true, of course, but she had not realized it was so obvious to everyone else. 'Yes, 'fraid so,' she said. To her ears her voice sounded forced, even nervous. She turned away from the table and busied herself with putting the casserole in the microwave, and then with setting the table. 'I know you won't mind eating in here.'

'Like old times,' he said. 'Almost.'

Two people suffering the pain of a broken relationship, but only one of them knew it ... Should she tell him? Suddenly she wanted to, very much. But she held back. After all, so far she and Keith were the only people who knew, or so she supposed. Auntie Hilda did not count, because Jan was quite sure she understood nothing, even if Keith had tried to tell her. It was not right for Sam to know the truth before those who were closer to her. In any case, with luck, there would be no need for anyone to know, so long as Keith came home soon.

They ate companionably, talking easily of old times and future plans – Sam's future plans, at least. Jan was relieved to find that he seemed over the worst shock and pain of the separation, finding solace in the future he planned for himself. But the pain was real enough, for it showed through now and then. 'I'm thirty-one,' he said. 'I thought I was ready to settle down. But – hey, who's to say this isn't for the best?'

'I'm sure it is,' she said, reflecting as she spoke how banal and silly the words sounded. How could she possibly know? What a lot of time was wasted on trite, meaningless phrases of reassurance, which did nothing to reassure and seemed to serve no useful purpose at all. 'Why Scotland?'

'Oh, there was somewhere I stayed once on holiday, years ago, near Moffatt. I've always had a hankering to go back. So I got in touch with a local estate agent and this place came up. Sounds just what I'm looking for, though that's not to say it will be, when I see it. But it's a start. I can have a good look around the area while I'm there. I'd some holiday due from work, so I've taken that. Not that they know I'll be leaving for good.'

'Have you got anywhere to stay tonight?'

'I was making for Tyneside. I'll find some-where there easily enough.'

'Then stay here. There's plenty of room. You'd be very welcome.'

He put up only a very token protest, so after the meal, eaten in the kitchen, she made up the bed in the smaller bedroom, next to the bathroom (she didn't want to rub salt into his wounds by putting him in the double room he had shared with Fiona last time he was here). Then they sat by the sitting-room fire with the last of the wine. 'What time do you expect Keith home?'

'Oh, he's away at the moment,' Jan said, trying to sound casual. It was perfectly true, of course, in its way. Why did one's mind go blank when something urgently needed to be said to change the subject? She could think only of the one thing that was true but very near to dangerous ground. 'He's losing his job.' I shouldn't have said that, she thought; I haven't even told the family yet.

'Oh, I'm sorry. Will he look for something else?'

'I expect so.' She thought of another topic at last, though it was, she felt, only too obviously a conversation filler: 'When did you leave London?'

'This morning.' A pause, and she was

afraid that he was about to bring up the subject of Keith again. Instead, he said, 'Tell me, when you saw me, did you think I'd come to get you to speak to Fee for me?'

'I suppose it crossed my mind. I gather you were pretty desperate at first.'

'I was. Then I saw I was making a complete fool of myself. I thought, if she doesn't want me any more, the only dignified thing is to make the best of it. Time to move on.'

Jan smiled. 'In every sense.'

'Exactly.' He turned the glass in his hand, gazing at it intently as he did so. 'Which isn't to say I wouldn't take her back without a second's thought, if that was what she wanted.' He looked up then and grinned ruefully. 'I'm not angling to know what my chances are. I know Fee better than that.'

'Better than I do, probably. Or at least as well. I'm sorry it's come to this, but it sounds as if you're doing the right thing. I wish you every success.'

In bed that night, Jan set herself to read through the job description for the practice manager, though her mind kept wandering. Sam was wise. He'd taken what was certainly a loss and turned it into an opportunity. He now had something to look forward to, to plan for. Should she not be doing the same? But it was not a comparable situation, not entirely. For one thing, it had only just happened to her; Keith had not gone long, and their lives were still inextricably tangled together – not perhaps ultimately or eternally, for they might reach the point where they had somehow to disentangle all those twisted threads – but for now they had only gone a short way down the road. To unwind their lives one from another would take time and painful effort. Even if they were to separate in every way they could, there would still be the children, the things they'd all shared over the years. And in any case it had not yet come to that, not at all. Nor, she thought, did she really want it to. Or not yet. Time enough if it did, if the moment came when she knew Keith would not come back, not ever – time enough then for her to follow Sam's example and move on, alone, to a new phase of her life.

Ten

Fiona hurried thorough blustery rain towards the Charlotte Street restaurant where she was to meet a client for lunch. It was further from the office than she had wanted, but it was convenient for him, so she could hardly argue the point. She had her head bent and her umbrella clutched tight at an angle designed to stop it blowing inside out (it had already done so once since she left the office), so that she did not see the man she collided with until he exclaimed and then, through her stammered apology, spoke her name. 'Fee!'

She lowered the umbrella and the apology evaporated as if blown away by the wind. She was annoyed to find how deeply she blushed. 'Sam!'

For a few painful moments they stood looking at one another and saying nothing. To her surprise, Sam was the one who found his voice first, asking with near nonchalance, 'How are you, Fee? You're looking well.'

'So are you.' She struggled to shut her umbrella, not because the rain had eased at all but to avoid looking at Sam, to cover her awkwardness. 'Mum said she'd seen you. She said you were moving to Scotland. Or planning to anyway. You were going to look at a house, she said.'

'I bought it. Go in two weeks. Can't wait.' It was his turn to pause. 'I'm sorry about your father's job.' He must have seen the blankness in her expression, but apparently put it down to her having her mind on other things. 'Losing it like that. It must be hard at his age – though maybe he doesn't mind. I didn't see him of course, as he was away.'

Away? thought Fiona; my father never goes away – besides, Mum said nothing about it. She hoped Sam could not see the surprise she felt, though he knew her too well for her to be able to conceal much from him.

'Fee,' he said after another silence. 'I couldn't help noticing. When I came down in the morning, at your parents' house, your mother was readdressing some letters to your father. As soon as she saw me coming, she pushed them away, out of sight. She didn't say anything. Perhaps she thought I hadn't seen. Has something happened?'

'I expect it was something he needed urgently,' said Fiona briskly, 'to do with his work.' She made a show of glancing at her watch and exclaiming at the time – any excuse to avoid further pressing questions, which she had no idea how to answer. 'Got to go – sorry! Hope your move goes well.'

She went on her way, without looking back.

What was going on? Had Sam imagined it all? Yet he seemed sure enough, at least with regard to her father's redundancy and his absence. Why then had her mother said nothing of either event to any of them? It was so unlike her, not to have mentioned something that must be of huge significance to both her parents. And forwarding letters? There was probably some simple explanation for that, the most likely one being that Sam had misunderstood what he saw; but taken with the other things it made her feel uneasy, to say the least. One moment her mother was looking into the possibility of having Auntie Hilda to live with them; the next, she was apparently alone in the house.

That evening Fiona telephoned her mother as soon as she returned from work. She decided that the casual, no-suspicion-of-anything-wrong approach was better than tackling the matter head-on – at least to begin with. 'How's things? Any more thoughts about Auntie Hilda coming to live with you?'

'Your father thinks she'd only be more confused by it. I expect he's right.'

'How is Dad?'

'Fine. We both are.'

'I saw Sam today. Just bumped into him in the street.'

Jan began to ask after him, with suspicious haste, Fiona thought. It was some time before there was an opportunity for her to say, 'Is Dad there? Put him on, if he is. Seems ages since we had a chat.'

'He's not home yet.'

Time, Fiona thought, to stop circling the subject. 'He's still got a job then, for the moment?'

There was a silence, then Jan said, 'Sam, I suppose. Yes, he's still got a few weeks to go, until the end of the month.'

'Why didn't you tell us? Surely that's something we should know?'

'I left it to your father. It's for him to do.'

'Sam said he was away. Sam thought there was something more wrong.'

This time the silence seemed to go on and on, until Fiona at last broke in: 'Mum?'

'I'm sorry. I didn't want to tell you. I hoped there'd be no need, that it would resolve itself. Your father's gone to Coldwell. He's moved in with Auntie Hilda. I – I'm still not entirely sure why. Except that Hilda's worse, much worse, and he can care for her better there.'

'Let's get this straight – Dad's moved out? Moved out as in gone to help Auntie Hilda? Or moved out as in – as, like, when I moved out on Sam?'

'Yes, like that. I think.' This time Jan seemed to be swallowing hard, trying to control the pain in her voice. 'No, it was like that.'

'But why? You and Dad! You're the last

people...! Anyone else, yes. It happens all the time. But not you. What on earth's going on?'

'Oh, it's lots of things, I think. Especially losing his job. He's depressed, I think – no, I know he is, quite seriously I think. More than I realized.'

'But why should that make him walk out? Lots of people get depressed. Stress – it's the modern disease.'

'I suppose,' said Jan slowly, 'you get in the way of not talking, except about the family. So you don't realize what's going on. And your father never was much of a talker.'

'That's men all over! But I still don't see...'

'Nor do I, altogether. Maybe he wouldn't have gone if Auntie Hilda hadn't provided the excuse. I don't know.'

'Have you tried to talk to him – since he left, I mean?'

'Of course. He won't talk. Not so far, any-way.'

Fiona pondered the enormity of it, tried to understand how her parents, those people who seemed to live on some plane above the mundane messiness of most people's lives, suddenly found themselves down there with everyone else, behaving like ordinary mor-tals. 'Would you like me to talk to him?'

'You can try if you want. But if you do, I don't take any responsibility for it. It has to be your initiative.'

'Do you think he might be really seriously depressed? Clinically depressed, I mean, needing medical help?'

'I honestly don't know. It's possible.' Jan considered the matter a moment longer, then said, with sudden alarm, 'Are you suggesting he might be suicidal? God, I hope not! But no, when I think about it, he feels Auntie Hilda needs him. That's—'

'Then couldn't that just be why he's gone? Nothing to do with you at all?'

'No, no I don't think so. Otherwise he wouldn't have shut me out, not like this.' Then a sudden cry from the heart, 'Oh, Fee, I don't know, I really don't know!' She sounded weary and close to tears.

'Oh Mum!' On a sudden impulse, regretted almost as soon as it was acted upon, Fiona added, 'Shall I come and stay for a bit? Would that help?'

Rather to her relief, Jan sounded amused rather than delighted; though touched too. 'That's very sweet of you, darling, but no, I'm fine. Don't worry. Things will sort themselves out, I'm sure they will.' Then: 'Oh, by the way, I've put in for that job – the practice manager.'

Later that evening, Fiona made four telephone calls, three to Simon (it took her some time to get an answer from him) and one to Mel. 'Can you book two rooms?' she asked her sister. 'Singles – one for me and one for Simon. For next weekend – Friday night.'

'What is this?' Mel sounded utterly baffled.

'Family conference,' Fiona said. 'What to do about Mum and Dad.'

'What do you mean, what to do about them?'

Fiona told her, and into the appalled silence that followed, said, 'Here's what you have to do before next weekend: phone both Mum and Dad and get all the information you can. Simon's doing the same, and so am I. We'll compare notes when we meet. Have you got two rooms, then?'

'Yes – yes, it's a quiet time of year. Special rate at weekends, even for singles.' They discussed the details of the bookings, but said little more then about the reason for them.

On Friday evening Fiona's train was delayed by mechanical failure and Mel had been waiting at the station for an hour by the time she stepped, exhausted, on to the platform. They hugged, and then Mel took her bag and led her out to the taxi rank. 'I've promised myself to get a car,' she said, as they climbed into the vehicle and gave directions to the hotel. 'But I just don't seem to get round to it. And it's such an expense too. But it's such a long way out.'

They were passing through unprepossessing streets, lit by the yellow glow of street lights. It all seemed, to Fiona, slightly depressing. 'Has Simon arrived yet?'

'He's going to be very late.' Mel said; she sounded almost tearful with disappointment. 'He rang my mobile to say he couldn't get away as early as he'd hoped. He's getting a lift with someone, so he's dependant on them, I suppose.'

The hotel, when eventually they reached it, looked pleasant enough; a solid Victorian mansion softly lit among well grouped trees. In the hallway – careful flower arrangements, a reproduction stone nymph, a water feature – the young receptionist greeted them with the extra warmth that Fiona would have expected from someone attending to a relative of the boss, and then Mel gathered up the room keys and led the way to the lift.

'So this is your kingdom,' Fiona said when they were alone. 'Very nice.' It was, she thought, as they stepped out of the lift and walked along carpeted passageways, exactly like hundreds of other hotels she had stayed in, a comfortable bland place catering mainly for businessmen. Now, on a Friday night, it seemed almost empty. 'Do you get weddings and things at weekends?'

'Sometimes. Not often. It's a bit out of the way, without being anything special.'

As Fiona had already anticipated, her room was unmemorably acceptable, though it was at least quiet, looking on to the hotel's small garden. 'What's the food like?'

'You're about to find out,' said Mel guardedly.

Simon arrived, full of apologies, when they were halfway through a meal that was as inoffensive but uninspiring as the rest of the place. Her brother looked well, Fiona thought, with a new glow about him, a new sparkle in his eyes. It only threw further into contrast how subdued his twin was, how silent and preoccupied. Until then Fiona had not been sure. Now she was; something was wrong with Mel. Part of it was clearly resentment at something her twin had done (or not done), for she greeted him with less than her usual warmth, with nothing like the effusive – indeed almost suffocating – hug with which she had greeted Fiona. It was only when Simon stood beside her and said, 'Don't I get a hug then?' that his twin got up and put her arms about him. 'More than you deserve!' Mel said afterwards. 'I'm surprised you've remembered I exist.'

They moved to the hotel's lounge for coffee after the meal. The room was empty, which might have been daunting had they been here as ordinary guests, but tonight had the advantage not only that they were able to occupy the most comfortable seats about the log fire, but that they could talk wihout interruption or embarrassment.

216

'This is better!' said Fiona. The twins were talking together now, and she watched them, seeing how Mel seemed to come to life, but in a brittle way that had almost an edge of hysteria to it.

'How much say do you get in the way things are run here?' Fiona asked.

'Not as much as I'd like. But I'm working on it. Mostly, when I suggest anything they say, "Oh, that won't work, not with our clients. We know what works." You can imagine the kind of thing. When I've been here a bit longer I'll have a better idea of what might work, then I'll be in a stronger position to suggest things and try them out. I came here with all these grand ideas, but you have to work with what there is, I suppose.'

'But you like the work?'

'Oh yes, of course.'

She sounded, Fiona thought, less than convincing – or indeed convinced. But before she could say anything, Mel had changed the subject.

'Anyway, let's get down to why we're here: Mum and Dad. I can't believe things are that bad between them. Not Mum and Dad.'

'I know what you mean,' said Simon. 'Other people, yes. But they're different. Anyway, I didn't get very far talking to them. I did phone, but Mum was about to go out and couldn't talk long and when I tried phoning Dad I just got Auntie Hilda and she babbled on about how the postman was opening all her letters or something. I don't think she had any idea who I was. I was going to try again, but I didn't have time.'

'Oh yes!' said Mel. 'You mean you had better things to do. Like chatting up this Tamsin person.' Mel was smiling, but the words sounded more accusatory than teasing.

Simon coloured slightly. 'We have to work shifts at the reserve these days, because of the poachers. I don't get a lot of spare time. Anyway, I thought Mum sounded completely normal. I can't really believe there's anything much wrong between her and Dad.'

'Maybe that's only because we've never seen them as ordinary people,' suggested Fiona. 'Maybe you never do with your parents, not quite. But they are. If we're going to do anything we have to understand what's happening. I did speak to Dad last week,' she added. The other two looked at her expectantly. 'Mum's right, he won't talk about it. He just said Auntie Hilda needed a bit more care so he'd moved in with her.'

'Maybe that *is* all there is to it then,' said Mel. 'He said the same sort of thing to me. But when I tried to ask him about him and Mum he said Auntie Hilda was calling and he had to go. Did he have any more to say to you, Fee?'

'Only when I asked him, what about Mum? He just said she was fine and Auntie Hilda needed him more. And when I asked about his job, he said, yes he was being made redundant, but he wasn't the only one and he'd get by somehow. And that was all he'd say about himself.'

'I was going to ask when he'd be moving back home, if I'd got a chance,' said Mel.

'I did ask him. That was one of the questions he wouldn't answer. He said he hadn't made any plans about anything – something of the sort. I also asked if he didn't think Auntie Hilda would be better off in a home.'

'What did he say to that?' Mel asked.

'He said I'd obviously been listening to my mother, and that he was a better judge of what Auntie Hilda needed than anyone else. He was about as near as I've known him to being angry, I think.'

'Do you think,' Simon suggested after a moment, 'that we're a bit ready to look at things from Mum's point of view? Maybe Dad's right – about Auntie Hilda, I mean – and maybe that's the main reason they've disagreed; maybe the only reason. Perhaps one of us should go up there and see for ourselves.'

'I'd go, if I had a car,' said Mel. 'But it's such a hassle on the train. I suppose I could do it though. I have got next weekend off.'

'If you don't mind, it's a good idea,' Fiona encouraged her. 'Worth a try anyway. See them both, try and find out exactly what's going on; bang their heads together if necessary. We can't have our parents falling out – if that is what's happening.'

Mel shook her head. 'Definitely not. We need to know they're there, just the same as always.'

Again, Fiona detected that rough edge to her voice, the closeness of tears. When, soon afterwards, Simon left them to go to the gents, she said to Mel, 'What's the matter, Mel? You wanted this job so much. Something's gone wrong, hasn't it?'

'No – no, not at all. Not with the job. The job's fine.' She swallowed hard. 'It's just – well, all my friends, everyone, they're a long way off.' Her voice was growing increasingly rough. 'When I'm not working, there isn't ... well, this place is a long way out; there's no transport; I don't know anyone.'

'I thought you'd have made friends here. That girl on reception seemed nice.'

'She is, but I'm her boss, sort of.'

'So what? It's not as if you're a multi-millionaire managing director!'

'It wouldn't matter to me, but it does to her. Especially as she wanted my job. It's the same with all of them.'

Fiona gave her a hug. 'Poor Mel! You'd better get yourself that car, asap. But even without it there must be a way to make friends, to have a social life. You don't work shifts, do you?'

'Not usually.' She paused, swallowing hard. 'I wouldn't mind if Simon – well, I've hardly heard from him for weeks, especially not since he met Tamsin. He didn't even tell me about her until...' She fell silent as Simon reappeared at the far side of the room.

'Talking about me, then?' he asked as he rejoined them. 'There's a suspicious silence.'

'We're just saying how hopeless you are at keeping in touch,' Fiona said, unsmiling, so that he should know she wasn't joking. 'Your twin's feeling neglected.'

Later, after they'd said goodnight to Mel and were making their way without her back to their rooms, Fiona said to Simon, 'Mel's desperately lonely here.'

'Is she?' He looked genuinely surprised. 'But she always has lots of friends.'

'She left them all behind when she came here. And then you go and neglect her too. Think how terrible that must make her feel!'

Simon considered the matter. 'You maybe have a point. OK, I'll keep in touch better. That satisfy you?'

'It's not me you have to satisfy. I can't understand what's going on anyway. I know you've just met the love of your life, but you and Mel always used to be so close. You told each other everything, even things you'd tell no one else. You never had secrets.'

'I think,' said Simon slowly, shamefaced, 'I just found I liked having a life of my own, just for me. It was the first time I'd ever been away from Mel, so I hadn't known anything different till then.'

'Well, now you've had a taste of freedom, perhaps the novelty will have worn off. I'm sure you don't want to shut Mel out for good.'

'Of course not!' He halted outside the door of his room. 'I wish I'd thought about it before. I wouldn't hurt Mel for the world.'

'Of course you wouldn't,' said Fiona. Then her tone lightened. 'When do we get to meet Tamsin then?' She watched his colour rise and thought how young he looked and how innocent. It was a long time since she had experienced the consuming chaos of new love, and she felt a sudden pang of regret and loss. This business with Éric was a much more calculated thing.

Jan was surprised when Mel phoned to say she was coming to stay the following weekend, though pleased too, both for herself and for Mel. For once, her daughter sounded reasonably happy. Simon had visited last weekend, she said, and on Saturday morning had gone with her to choose a car. She would be driving herself home in this new vehicle, a second-hand Renault Clio bought on loan. But Jan found she was glad too that she would have company for a time. The weekends in particular seemed very long. Though she had plenty to occupy herself, she was reminded often that the weekend was a time when couples and families were together, for good or ill. Solitude might be pleasant enough now and then, but full-time and without any choice in the matter was much less agreeable.

She had tried several times more to make contact with Keith, and had even got through to him once, but as soon as he heard her voice on the other end of the phone he had rung off. She thought that had been the lowest point so far; the rejection had felt complete. Yet they would have to talk in the end, at some level, if only to sort out financial arrangements for their separate lives. Perhaps she would write to him about it, in the hope that he would at least read the letter. On the other hand, to do so would be to admit that their lives were to remain separate, and that she was still not ready to do, however likely it was beginning to seem. She tried to put from her mind that Christmas was not so very far away. Were they to spend that time apart too?

Mel arrived on Friday night. It became clear almost at once that she had come on a reconnaissance mission, with the knowledge and agreement of her brother and sister. She interrogated Jan as they ate and afterwards as they sat by the sitting-room fire, asking for every detail about how the rift had occurred, what had been said and done, what had happened since, what events had led up to it, what feelings and actions might have brought it about. The fact that Jan was not herself sure about the answers to most of the questions did not seem to deter her daughter. She was so relentlessly persistent that in the end Jan burst out laughing. 'Mel, you're remorseless! Are you going to stay up all night after this, composing a written report for the others?'

Mel grinned sheepishly. 'We're just worried about you, Mum. Both of you.'

'We're fully grown adults. I think you have to let us work things out for ourselves.'

'Hasn't it occurred to you that someone outside the situation, a third person, might see how things can be put right where you can't?'

'I'm sure that's true, but I'm not convinced you three are outside the situation. After all, isn't that why you're so concerned? Because we're your parents and parents are supposed to be perfect?'

'Oh, we know that's not true! We're adults too, remember.'

'Well, let's see how you feel when you've seen your father – I presume that's part of the plan for the weekend?' She saw Mel nod.

'Right, now let's talk about something else. You haven't said much about your job. I want to hear all about it.'

Later, in her room – the room looking over the stream that had been hers since childhood – Mel did find herself, rather self-consciously, writing down her impressions of the situation, as seen from her mother's eyes, though she did so only in note form, and she hid the notebook in the bottom of her suitcase before she got into bed, in case her mother should happen to come into the room and see it.

She could see now that there was more to the rift between her parents than a simple disagreement about how Auntie Hilda should best be looked after, even though that had played a large part in the disagreement. She was also sure, in spite of the fact that her mother had said little about it and seemed cheerful enough, that Jan was missing Keith more than she would ever admit. Tomorrow, she resolved, she would do all in her power to work for a resolution.

She had telephoned her father before coming north and arranged to go to Coldwell on Saturday afternoon. He seemed pleased enough to see her, but she quickly found that there was no hope of questioning him as she had her mother. Keith was not remotely prepared to discuss what had happened or why, still less analyse his feelings or the events that led up to his leaving home. 'That's between me and your mother,' was all he would say.

They walked through Coldwell's shabby little park, taking Auntie Hilda with them, but their conversation largely involved pointing out sights of interest to the confused old lady. Keith did not even ask Mel much about her job, as if that were a way of underlining that they lived separate and private lives, to which no one else had any right to be admitted. Nor would he discuss the related matter of the care of the old lady. Mel saw a considerable change for the worse even in the relatively short time since she had left home: Hilda was more confused, seemed now to have no idea who Mel was and, Mel suspected, did not really know Keith either. But when she tried to say this, Mel found her father entirely unprepared to listen. 'I'm with her every day. I'm the best judge of her condition,' he said, dismissing the subject along with everything else of a personal nature.

Mel was relieved when the time came for her to return to Meadhope, where she spent the Sunday peacefully with her mother, before returning – with sinking heart – to the hotel. She had told Jan how the meeting with Keith had gone, conscious of the 'I told you so', that lay just beneath the surface of her mother's attentive silence, but thankful at least that it was not put into words. She knew that Jan blamed Keith for his unwillingness to talk things over with anyone, that she was angry with him about it; but Mel could only feel sadness that he was so entangled in his own problems and emotions that he was unable to see them clearly, give them expression or see any way out.

Once back in her solitary flat, she telephoned Fiona, but got only the answerphone; she recalled then that her sister was in Paris again this weekend. She felt a faint stir of disapproval. Fiona had not told them a great deal, but she knew there was a married man involved somewhere. Yet she could not help feeling just a little envious too, at her sister's nonchalant worldliness. There was something so splendidly decadent and sophisticated about being the mistress of a (presumably) attractive Frenchman.

She tried Simon then, not expecting an answer, and was startled close to tears when, after just four rings, his dear familiar voice came clearly to her. 'Hi! Simon here.'

They talked for a long time, not simply about their parents but about themselves, their lives and thoughts and feelings, talking as they had not done for a long time, as they always used to do, openly, easily, knowing that they were understood and there was no need for every thought and feeling to be underlined. At the end of the call, Mel might have felt that they were no nearer resolving the problem of what to do about their parents – or even knowing what the problem was precisely – but she did feel hugely comforted, happier than she had for a long time. She went to bed and fell into a profound sleep that lasted, undisturbed, until the alarm roused her for work at seven the next morning. 'I'm going to get through this,' she told herself as she dressed. 'It's going to work out all right.'

The post on that Monday morning brought Jan a letter addressed in a not-quite-un-familiar hand, which yet stirred something in her memory. She peered at the smudged postmark: London somewhere, she thought, though she couldn't be sure; it didn't really help very much. She slid her finger under the flap and edged the envelope open, pulling out the folded sheet inside. Of course! Rosemary Chawton! Who else had that elegant italic script? So she had written after all; though not at any great length, nor with much to say for herself, except that she was going to Scotland to a conference in early December, and would like to spend a night or two with Jan on her way north. 'You can show me what it is to be a smug married,' she ended. 'Look forward to meeting your paragon of a husband.'

Jan felt a knot of something approaching

panic twist inside her. How was she going to conceal the situation from Rosemary? She folded the letter again and pushed it back into its envelope, staring at herself in the mirror over the hall table, seeing wide frightened eyes looking back at her. This is ridiculous, she thought; why should I need to pretend? This is a common enough situation, for goodness sake! Rosemary's been through it herself; she'll understand, well enough.

Only she wouldn't, because for her the ending of a marriage was a trivial, commonplace thing, a long marriage something unknown, probably incomprehensible; the extent of this blow coming after so long, after so much apparent security, all the harder to understand.

Jan glanced at the calendar hanging nearby. They were already halfway through November. That gave her about three weeks to put things right, to persuade Keith to come home, with or without his aunt. She went into the sitting room, opened her desk and began to compose a letter to her husband, the first she had written to him in the whole of their married life, and a letter that she prayed would make sure that they still shared one.

Eleven

Jan felt that she had put everything into the letter, her heart and soul, her very lifeblood. It had taken her three days, sitting at her desk for every hour after work, to get it right – or at least as near to right as it was ever likely to be. By then, she had to accept that she was never going to find precisely the right words to express what she wanted to say. How did one say everything, with words alone; even with words emphasized and underlined by gestures, caresses, the help of expression of eye and mouth, none of which in any case she had available to her?

It would perhaps have helped if she had been sure precisely what she wanted to say, what she was trying to achieve, beyond the obvious aim of trying to persuade Keith to come home. Even with so apparently limited a goal as that, choosing the right words was very hard, for she had no idea what might make him reconsider his apparent determination to shut her out. At first, she kept it simple, telling him how much she missed him and reminding him that whatever happened in the future they needed to talk things over, to make arrangements. But, reading the words through, she saw only how cold they seemed, how they even implied an acceptance that the marriage might end, even if she hoped it would not. They would not do at all.

She tore that letter up and started again, this time using the computer in the study upstairs, trying to order and reorder the words, to get them right. She would not, of course, send Keith a printed letter, but would copy out the words in her own handwriting, so that it was more essentially a part of herself.

She told him how deeply she loved him, how sorry she was that she had taken him for granted, inadvertently shutting him out of her life and that of his children, how much she wanted to put that right, to include him. She assured him that she was now willing to listen to all he had to say about his aunt, without prejudging the situation, in the conviction that they could somehow find a solution, together, as to how best to care for her, one that would take into account all their needs. She promised him that she ruled nothing out. They could even continue to live apart for the time being, so long as the separation was only a physical one, for Hilda's sake, and that in every other sense they remained man and wife, sharing

231

thoughts and fears and hopes as she admitted they had often failed to do in the past; so long as they both knew this was a temporary arrangement, made necessary by Hilda's condition, which would end when the need for it was no longer there, so long as they shared telephone calls, meals, chores that had to be done, like shopping and taking the old lady for outings in the car or on foot; so long as, sometimes, they still shared a bed. She ended the letter with the most erotically tender thoughts she had ever openly expressed, words such as she had only used before when they were in bed together and then not for a very long time, not since their lovemaking (if such it could still be called) had become a matter of habit and routine. 'Get in touch soon, my darling,' she had concluded. 'I love you and need you so much.'

Then, on her way to work on Thursday morning she'd posted it in the box on the corner of the street. She'd tried to put it out of her head after that, for today she was to be interviewed for the practice manager's job. She had been led to believe the outcome was a foregone conclusion, that she could consider the job hers already, though they had to go through the motions of throwing the appointment open to anyone who was interested and interviewing them – especially as Jan had not indicated before it was advertised that she was intending to apply. But Jan knew that nothing was quite a foregone conclusion, that some extraordinarily well-qualified candidate might have applied for the job, unknown to her. She was nervous about the interview and had dressed with care this morning, in an elegantly cut charcoal trouser suit, and given extra attention to her make-up, flattering but understated. She knew she would feel humiliated and hurt if she failed to get the job; yet a part of her hoped that she would be rejected. She needed the job, whatever happened between her and Keith, but she did not want to continue to work full time at something that, however interesting and worthwhile, was not what passionately interested her. A part of her still thought, 'If I don't get this, perhaps I can take up archaeology again, properly.'

On Friday, she received the letter officially appointing her to the job as practice manager for the Meadhope group practice; the speed of the response made it clear that the result had indeed been a foregone conclusion. She was to take up her position on January 1st, when the present manager, who had long struggled with the increasing demands of the job, was due to retire. There were no other letters for her that day. It was too soon as yet for there to be any reply from Keith or not by post; he would only have received her letter this morning. No one had tried to phone her in her absence, but then he would have known she was at work. He also knew quite well when she usually returned from work.

Jan cooked herself a meal, read the paper, watched the television news and *EastEnders* (miserable, unpleasant lot, she thought afterwards, why do I watch it?); and all the time her hearing was strained to catch the sound of the phone. She hardly dared to go to the toilet or out to the dustbin in case she failed to hear it ring. Yet when it did, around eight thirty, she heard it at once, jumping up at the first ring.

It was Anne, the practice nurse, congratulating her on her appointment. It was kind of her and she was clearly delighted to be doing so, but Jan felt impatient, felt like telling her to get off the line, in case Keith should ring and give up at the first difficulty.

Keith did not ring, and she went to bed feeling restless and anxious. Had the letter not reached him, through delay or some more serious failure of the post? Worse than that, had he decided not to open it? She could not bear the thought that all her hours of effort should go for nothing. Surely, if nothing else, curiosity would get the better of him? She knew she would never be able to leave a letter unopened, whoever had sent it, however angry she might be with the sender.

She lay awake for much of the night

wondering what she should do if she heard nothing from Keith over the weekend. Should she phone him? Write again? Try to be patient and wait for him to make contact?

By the end of Sunday she'd heard nothing, even though she had failed to make her usual calls to the children, not wanting to risk blocking the line in case Keith should call. More than once she went to the phone and reached out to lift the handset. Each time she thought better of it. If he'd only received the letter yesterday, he probably needed time to consider its contents and decide what his answer should be. It was quite possible that he would reply by letter rather than phoning. She must leave it to him to make the first move, at least for a little longer. She drew a deep breath and phoned each of the children in turn, speaking cheerfully, saying nothing of what she had done, but assuring them in answer to their inevitable questions that she was confident everything would soon be resolved for the best.

On Monday evening, before switching on the late BBC news, she allowed herself to pick up the phone and dial the Coldwell number. Keith answered almost at once. 'This is a bit late,' he said abruptly.

She felt her heart thud. 'Did you get my letter?' Surely he couldn't have done, or he wouldn't have spoken in quite that way?

'Of course. I don't know why you bothered. It doesn't make any difference. What are you ringing for this late?'

She felt as if a huge obstruction had suddenly formed in her chest and swelled up into her throat. 'Only that,' she said in a flat, raw voice. 'To see if you'd got it, and what you thought.'

'Well, now you know. Goodnight.'

She stood with the receiver in her hand listening disbelievingly to the dialling tone. There were tears in her eyes, which she brushed away in a sudden surge of anger. All she had put into that letter, all of herself, her deepest feelings, and he dismissed it in a few curt words! Had he read it at all? Surely if he had he could not have dismissed it so brutally? Yet nothing he said had implied that he'd not read it – in which case all her hours of thought and feeling, all those words dragged agonisingly from her on to the page had gone for absolutely nothing. She might as well have saved herself the trouble, for they were no further forward at all, not one step. Keith was shutting her out as adamantly as ever.

How dare he! How could he be so cruel, so stupid, so blind? Did she deserve such treatment? Had she been anything worse than heedless, a little insensitive? Surely not – and above all she was ready to move on, to start again, to put the past behind her. She deserved forgiveness, a second chance, at the very least. This punishment that Keith was inflicting on her was beyond anything she merited. Worse, it was beyond forgiveness on her part. If nothing else, it said more clearly than anything that had gone before that this was the end, their marriage was over; they no longer had any life together, or hope of such a life.

That's it! she thought; I see a solicitor next week. If he won't talk about the future, then I'll have to get it sorted out this way. I want him out of my life, out of my head. If I can't start again with him, then I'll start again by myself – or with someone else, if that seems right.

She thought of Don, though she knew she did not see him as an alternative to Keith, still less a substitute – certainly not as things were at present. Fiona had talked of casual relationships, which offered pleasure, but nothing more. If that was acceptable for the young, why not for her too? There would be excitement in a life lived on several parallel tracks – the one where the children were, where her deepest affections were most closely involved; the one here at home in Meadhope, where she was an essential part of the community, manager of the group practice, member of local organizations, flower arranger, surrounded by friends; and, now, possibly, a quite separate, even secret, erotic life, which she could visit or leave alone as she chose, as her desires invited her to do. If men had, in some societies, traditionally had a mistress they kept secret from wives and families and some friends, then why should a woman not do exactly the same, especially once her children were grown and her childbearing days were done?

Don had phoned her several times since that first call, and had invited her pressingly to visit the dig again one weekend. 'Better still, come away with me somewhere else for the weekend – Bath, say, somewhere with a lot of history and good restaurants. A feast for the senses. I know a really good hotel that's not expensive.'

Jan glanced at the clock. It was half past ten – all that rage had already wasted half an hour of her life! Too late now to risk phoning him, for she knew he had to be up early, and she wanted to catch him in a good mood. She would spend the weekend with him, either at the site or (more dangerously, more irrevocably) in Bath, and this time she would not be coy, she would leave behind all trace of the dutiful wife. Why be dutiful when her husband no longer wanted to play the husband?

She went to bed herself then, taking from the bedside a book she had borrowed from the library following her weekend at the dig, but never read because of pangs of conscience about what had happened between her and Don. Now she opened it and began to read about the background to the world in which that Anglo-Saxon settlement had developed. Erotic imaginings became entwined with dreams of reviving her embryonic archaeological career. Perhaps the two fields of sexual satisfaction and work need not after all be kept separate, perhaps the one would lead naturally and easily and entirely pleasurably into the other. People talked of a Third Age, which she had always taken to mean the age of slippers by the fire, geriatric ambles on level roads, daytime television, evening classes. But why should not the time of youth and learning, the time of parenting and work, lead into something more fulfilling, more productive than either, because now she would only have herself to please? She could put aside her anger with Keith, even feel a kind of sour gratitude towards him, who had made this possible. It was not quite that yet, of course; the hurt was too raw, the anger too recent, to be put aside as if they had never been. But she could now see that nothing was over, apart from a marriage that had been moribund for years; that in its place all kinds of possibilities lay before her.

She had planned to phone Don the following evening, as soon as she returned from work – she had his mobile number, in case he was still at the site. But by the end of the evening she suddenly recalled that she had not done so, when, once again, it was too late. How could I have forgotten something so important? she asked herself, and wrote a note to remind herself to do it tomorrow – Wednesday – evening. That day she came in from work to find a letter – a letter, not a phone call! – from Fiona, which, when opened, turned out to be (so Fiona claimed) written on behalf of all three of her children. They were intending, Fiona said, to come home for Christmas, all three of them, and very likely Tamsin as well, since she and Simon were now an item; and they hoped, even expected, that their father would be there too; they were writing to him to say the same, in the hope that it would persuade him to a reconciliation.

Jan stood gazing at the letter with feelings that mingled love and exasperation in equal measure. They cared so much, and she understood why they did, but she did wish they would stop interfering in something they really didn't understand. How could they, when she didn't entirely understand it herself? In any case, she wanted to move on, to step into the next stage of her life, but here they were doing everything in their power to hold her back. What was she to do?

She went to the phone and dialled Don's number. 'You know that weekend you suggested – the one in Bath? I thought I'd come down the weekend after next,' she told him. As they made their arrangements, she wished he didn't sound so smugly delighted about it.

Then she sat down and wrote to Rosemary Chawton, to say that she was very sorry, but she would be away the weekend her friend was coming north. 'Next time, I hope we can manage to coincide,' she added, while wondering what her life would be like by 'next time'. Would the coming weekend mark a turning point, or prove to be no more than an aberration?

It was a dark morning, the rain lashing on the windows of the little flat, so that Mel left it to the last moment to pull back the curtains and let in what daylight there was. Dressed in the dark suit that marked her out as 'management', against the charcoal skirts and grey checked shirts of the other visible staff, she finished her coffee and then set out across the garden (running, her umbrella open) and along the corridors to work. She found herself wishing once again that she had a bus journey to carry her to work, or even a long walk in the fresh air; that at least might have made her feel that she had a life separate from that of the hotel. Certainly, since Simon had begun to keep in touch with her again, she felt much happier – or, rather, the despair had gone and she was merely a bit miserable for much of the time, and very lonely. The real difference was that she thought she could endure it – just about, most of the time. This morning was not, however, one of the better days, and the weather didn't help.

As she entered the foyer she heard a gentle humming from behind the reception desk, something that sounded like a hymn tune, a melody dimly recollected from childhood. In spite of everything, she smiled to herself: Tracey was on duty – she'd omitted to check the rota before she left the flat, though it was somewhere in the bunch of papers under her arm. Of all the receptionists, Tracey was the one she liked best. So did the guests come to that, because she was not only unfailingly courteous (they were all expected to be that, at the very least), but also warm and friendly, as if each person she came across were the one person in all the world who, at that moment, she wished to be with. More to the point, from Mel's point of view, if she had ever had designs on Mel's job, she gave no sign of it. Mel doubted if she had an enemy in the world, or anyone she even remotely disliked.

Tracey, who had been bent behind the desk, appeared again above it, neat in her uniform, her broad rosy face smiling under a just-controlled mop of fair curly hair. The humming stopped. 'Good morning, Mel.'

Mel smiled. 'You sound happy.'

'Why not? God is good!' Before Mel could wonder quite what she meant by that casually matter-of-fact remark, or begin to feel embarrassed by it, Tracey went on: 'There's a problem with room 32. The shower's not working and the window won't close properly. I moved Mr Ahmed to 22 and I said we'd knock ten per cent off the cost of last night, since he was inconvenienced. That was right, wasn't it?'

'Of course. I'll go and have a look at it now and get it seen to. Is there anything else?'

'Don't think so.' Then, as Mel began to move away, she said, 'Mel! Would you fancy coming to a social tonight, at my church?'

Mel halted, startled, and suddenly very wary. 'What sort of a social?'

'Oh, just a friendly get-together, a way of meeting people. Nothing religious, though I expect they'll say grace. There'll be food – they do a good spread. They said bring a friend, and well, I know you're my boss, but I don't know that many people here and I do know what some of them would say if I asked. You know, it would look good if I could bring someone along. If you hate it, you don't ever have to come along again.'

Mel was on the point of finding an excuse,

which was not easy, as she never had any alternative activity laid on and saying she wanted to stay in to watch a television programme or wash her hair would sound pathetic in the extreme. But a church social was hardly an enticing prospect; even at home in Meadhope she would probably have avoided an invitation to the harvest supper or the summer ceilidh – and Meadhope was a normal church. She had a suspicion that Tracey's church might be one of those fundamentalist, happy-clappy places that were close to being cults. It might explain Tracey's constant cheerfulness. On the other hand, she liked Tracey and she had no friends here and there was nothing lost, really, if she hated the evening. She was pretty sure that Tracey's good nature would be proof against such a disappointment. She would probably pray for her instead, but Mel supposed she could cope with that. 'All right then,' she said. 'I'll come along – but just this once!' she added warningly.

Tracey was wrong about one thing – the social in the crowded hall at the back of the old brick chapel began and ended with a hymn, enthusiastically and joyfully sung, at least by the chapel's regulars; and that was in addition to the lengthy extempore grace that signalled the readiness of what was indeed a magnificent spread of traditional chapel food. But there were many like herself who were clearly visitors, and wary with it. Like her, they appeared to be speedily disarmed by the unaffected warmth of the welcome that greeted them. It was not just Tracey who treated her as if she were the most important person in the world to them; many of Tracey's friends came to talk to her, showing what seemed a genuine interest in her. There were silly party games, but no one seemed to mind if you did not choose to join in just then, though the enthusiasm was infectious; and there was some dancing to a rather temperamental and not always audible CD player. There seemed, too, to be rather more than the average number of fresh-faced youths among the chapel members, one or two of them definitely on the attractive side. After all the weeks of loneliness, Mel felt almost emotionally overwhelmed by the warmth and cheerfulness, by the sense that she was surrounded by light and colour and happiness, which was ready to enfold her and catch her up and make her an integral part of it.

Much later, as she drove the two miles back to the hotel in her car, she agreed that, yes, she had enjoyed the evening. 'Thanks for inviting me.'

'If you want,' said Tracey a little warily, 'you could come along on Sunday morning. You'd be very welcome.'

I'm sure I should, thought Mel, but I don't

know that I'm ready for that. Aloud, she said, 'I'll think about it. In any case, I think I'm working this weekend.'

'Oh well, the one after then,' said Tracey easily, and then – to Mel's relief – changed the subject.

Later, as she got into bed, Mel wondered what she would say to her twin about this evening, when next she spoke to him; or if indeed she would say anything at all.

Simon and Tamsin sat slumped against one another on the sofa. The television was on, but neither of them, if asked, could have said what they were supposed to be watching. It had been a long wet day, spent planting young trees in one of the most exposed parts of the reserve, so they had come back to the flat together in a state of exhaustion, to race one another to the bathroom for a hot bath (they were much too tired this evening to find enjoyment in the cramped excitements of a shared bath, especially as the tub was on the small side). Afterwards, they'd rung out for pizzas, which they'd eaten where they now sat, two hours later, the containers still lying where they had been left to fall on the floor near their feet. Now and then one of them would doze off, to be jolted awake by some question or comment from the other, requiring a slow and sleepy answer. 'I suppose we could go to bed,' Simon said eventually.

'It's cold in there. Though I have got a hot-water bottle.'

Simon chortled at the very idea. 'You'd have to get up to fill it.'

'Oh, and there I was thinking you were the gentlemanly sort who'd fill a girl's hot-water bottle for her! And get the bed warmed up.'

'Oh, I'd get it warmed up all right – when we're both in it.' He shifted his position slightly, so as put his arm right round her and draw her nearer still. He might be tired to the point of exhaustion, but he was happy beyond words, to be relaxed against the body of this girl he loved so much, so that they were almost one body, wholly at ease with one another. 'Have you put in for leave over Christmas yet?'

'I'm thinking about it. My parents are going skiing. I don't really want to go with them.'

'Why ever not? I'd love to go skiing!'

'Oh, it's not the skiing I mind, it's the whole pretentious set-up. I'd rather stay here with you.'

'What if I go home?' said Simon, introducing the subject with care; he'd been trying to find the right moment, ever since Fiona and Mel told him of their plan and his proposed part in it. 'Would you come with me?'

'What, to your family, for Christmas, when I've not even met them? That doesn't seem quite right.'

'They wouldn't mind, not at all. Mel's dying to meet you, and my mo– parents too. They're nice; you'd like them.' So long as they're not fighting, or apart and miserable, Simon thought, and so long as Auntie Hilda isn't living at home. He found himself rather hoping Tamsin would turn the suggestion down flat, since the potential for disaster seemed huge. Also, he would, he supposed, have to explain something of his parents' situation to Tamsin before she went home with him, and he did not know where to begin. The fact that her parents still apparently had an intact if not particularly happy marriage did not make it easier.

'If that's what you really want, I might then,' said Tamsin. She exerted herself enough to kiss him.

Oh well, thought Simon, all I can do now is hope Fiona's idea works and Mum and Dad get together again, rather than condemn us to a miserable Christmas. He still rather doubted that it was an argument likely to have much effect on mature parents of adult children, but maybe women knew better about these things.

Twelve

Keith peered at the clock again; he could just make out the numbers by the light of the inadequate street lamp in the alley behind the terrace. Five o'clock. Only an hour to go now until he had to get up. He knew he had no hope of getting to sleep again and simply wanted the night to be over, without being sufficiently rested to get out of bed so early as this; he could only have slept for two hours, at the very most. Besides, if he were to get up now, he would almost certainly wake Auntie Hilda, which would only make life more difficult for both of them. His spirit shrank from the thought of facing her; though better her than anyone else, like the colleagues at work he would have to cope with later in the day. Best of all would be complete solitude, an anonymous, hermit-life without companions of any kind. He turned his face to the wall, away from the grey rectangle of the window, patterned with darker splodges where blowsy roses decorated the curtains, away from the clock relentlessly dragging its way towards day and work and life. He closed his eyes and did, for a time, drift off into a troubled sleep.

In the end, it was the alarm that woke him, beeping into a too-vivid dream, dragging him violently back into wakefulness, so that he reached out for the clock in a rage, hammering it into silence. Then, hearing the sound of Hilda moving about in the next room (the partition wall was paper-thin), he leapt out of bed, banging his head on the opposite wall and his toe on the open suit-case by the bed as he reached for the shirt he had left crumpled on the cane-bottomed chair that was the only furniture in the room apart from the narrow single bed – there was no room for anything else. He rubbed his head as he fastened those of the buttons that had come undone when he pulled the shirt off last night, then reached for underwear (some of it under rather than on the chair), trousers, shoes. He felt his chin, and thought it might pass without a shave today; he would clean his teeth after breakfast.

By the time he reached the tiny landing, the old woman was standing at the top of the stairs, barefoot, wearing a flowery summer dress over her nightdress. Perhaps she was recalling, somewhere in her confused old brain, that he had warned her not to try walking downstairs by herself. It was not so much that she was frail and unsteady on her feet, but that she could no longer concentrate on what she was doing, that she had somehow lost all the instincts that kept her safe. She had already had several falls since he came here, though mercifully none of them had been serious. He made another mental note to see about having a stair lift installed, though he was not sure she could be made to understand how to use it. He took her arm and steered her back towards the bedroom. 'Come now, Auntie, let's get you dressed properly.' She turned to look at him with those eyes that saw nothing familiar, and he caught the sour fishy smell that hung about her. There'd be wet sheets again too then.

With a patience fiercely imposed, he helped her wash and dress and guided her down the stairs. In the kitchen, he directed her to one of the chairs while he made breakfast for them both – tea and toast – which he laid on the table before her. She watched him all the time as he worked, with that vacant yet penetrating stare. Sometimes, momentarily, he would think he saw something else there, some gleam that reminded him of the old lady she had been, something that looked like recognition or even affection. More often, any hint of intelligent light had a sly and crafty look to it. How could a human personality be so overturned, so wiped out, while the body remained almost unchanged, its infirmities almost wholly attributable to the mind's deficiences? As he tried to chew his way through a slice of toast, he watched the old lady, thinking, This is what we come to. This is the human condition. Nothing; meaningless. Then: Why go on, what is there of life left for either of us, what is there to keep going for; what is the point of pretending?

Then, with a kind of additional horror, he realized what he had come close to thinking, stood up, threw the uneaten piece of toast into the bin (he seemed to have no appetite these days), gulped down his tea, turned away from her to wash his plate and cup. He was appalled to find that he was fighting back tears. Tears – for what? That would achieve nothing.

During the next three quarters of an hour he finished clearing the breakfast dishes, washed and put them away, changed the sheets on Hilda's bed and put the soiled ones in the washing machine, sat the old woman down in front of whatever was on the television (he felt bad about that, since it was hardly the stimulation he felt she needed, but it would be less than a week now until he was able to be with her all the time), made up the fire and secured the newly-acquired nursery fireguard round it, and hoped she understood when he told her that he would be back at lunchtime to prepare a meal for her. It would, as usual, take a large chunk from his working day, but he no longer cared what they thought of him at work and it was the only way of ensuring that Auntie Hilda ate properly. Meanwhile, Mrs Kelly from next door would look in mid-morning and mid-afternoon to make sure all was well, as she had done for some time now.

He kissed Hilda, went upstairs to collect his briefcase and then let himself out to where he had parked his car in the street. Once in the driver's seat, he made no move to start the engine, but simply sat for a long time, staring into space. He felt weary, with a strange debilitating weariness, as if all the willpower that had taken him through the morning's tasks had gone now, melted away, leaving nothing behind, only emptiness. He had a longing for sleep, a deep, long, dream-less sleep, which would take him clear away from all the demands that life, and other people, thrust upon him; from the dark pit into which, without knowing how or why, he had somehow fallen and from which there seemed to be no escape. How long he had sat there, how much longer he would have done so, he had no idea, for there came a tapping on the passenger window, which gradually reached him and caused him to look round. It was Ida Kelly, the neighbour, looking anxious. He wound down the window. 'Is something wrong?'

'That's what I was going to ask,' she said. 'I

saw you sitting there. You don't look well, Mr Grey. Is there anything I can do?'

He forced something approaching a smile. 'No – no, thank you. I'm fine. Just thinking, that's all.'

'Oh well, that's all right then.' She still looked a little doubtful. 'I'll be sure and look in on Hilda. You don't need worry about her.'

He thanked her and closed the window and drove off before she could think of anything else to say or any more questions to ask.

That morning, Fiona was returning by Eurostar from yet another trip to Paris. The work aspect had been settled entirely satisfactorily, and she had spent the nights, as usual, with Éric, who had treated her with his customary charm and consideration. But this time the trip had left her feeling oddly discontented, even uneasy. She had thought being a mistress – no ties, no demands, no expectations – was an ideal situation, putting the emotional, erotic part of her life into a neat and manageable compartment. But it was not proving as simple as that. She did not think it was because she was developing any sort of grand passion for Éric or wanted any more from him than he was prepared to give. Nor was it because of any moral qualms about his married state. Yet, when she considered the matter, the fact that he was married *was* part of it; that he had a wife and children who were integral to his happiness. Even if his wife knew there was a mistress somewhere, she would also know that the mistress was peripheral, an entertainment and no more. And that was the trouble. Fiona might feel that what she had from Éric was as much as she wanted at the moment, yet she was conscious of an inequality about it. She was still less to him than he to her, simply because there was no other relationship of importance in her life, apart from those brought with her from childhood. More than that, she might pride herself on the equality of her dealings with men, but it was to Éric's flat that they went at night, and it was he who cooked for her or took her to restaurants, and he always refused to allow her to pay. She might have an independent existence when in London, or at work, but in Éric's company she was, in effect, as much a kept woman as the traditional mistress had ever been. She knew that was how he saw their relationship, and she feared that something of that estimation of her was beginning to creep into their working relationship too, though there was nothing precisely that she could put her finger on to bear out that impression. Now, she looked out at the wooded French countryside, the wide undulating fields and farms, glimpsed briefly as the train sped through, and thought, Time to put an end to it; time to move on.

It would hurt, a little, though rather less than if he were to be the first to make that decision. She would miss his company, and the sex – especially the sex. But in the long run she was sure she would not regret it. It was not something she felt should be done by phone or e-mail or fax. Next time she came to Paris, then, she would end it, at once, before he took her for a meal, or to the opera, before they went to his flat. She would book into a hotel before she left London and present him with a fait accompli. That decided, she felt better, at ease in her mind. She had allowed herself to be sucked into this relationship by simply following a very basic instinct. In future, she was going to take her life in hand; she would give herself time to think, to consider what she wanted from life, to ponder even what kind of person she was and where she was going and why – all those profound questions she had always meant to confront but had never quite found time for. Not that this was the moment to begin; one significant bit of thinking, one important decision was enough for one morning. She opened her copy of *Paris Match*, bought at the Gare du Nord, and began to read.

★ ★ ★

'There are a few things we need to discuss before Friday,' Keith's immediate superior had said to him, mid-morning. 'Can we go over them at lunch?'

Keith had refused. 'I've other plans. This afternoon, perhaps – or tomorrow morning, first thing.' He saw the look of surprise on the other man's face, and disapproval too, but did not care. After Friday they would no longer be colleagues anyway.

Shortly afterwards, he was driving back to Coldwell. It was foggy and cold, though all days seemed like that to him at present; he seemed to carry his own grey fog with him, permanently. In any case, he took in very little of what was around him and instinct alone kept him on the right road. Coldwell looked as cheerless as ever, when he reached it half an hour later, the streets a grey damp monotone. He turned off Front Street, along two other roads, left at the dilapidated corner shop, its window covered with a grille against vandals, into Hepburn Street. The fog was denser here, grey, thick, choking, almost like the smoke from a great bonfire; it concealed, until the last moment, the vehicles gathered at the further end.

Morning surgery had ended late, as usual, and there were still phone calls to be dealt with and patients coming in to collect prescriptions, though fortunately Elaine, one of the junior receptionists, was on duty with her today, so Jan was able to clear patients' notes away and deal with the usual post-surgery correspondence without too many interruptions. It gave her time to think and plan. Ever since she had phoned Don to arrange next weekend's trip she had been considering what clothes to pack. Something for tramping over archaeological sites, of course – inevitably that would be part of the weekend's programme. But Bath was a sophisticated city, with good shops and restaurants, so it was possible, even likely, that she would need smarter clothes too – something that would double up both for daytime tourism and evening meals out. And should that be something warm and wintry, or lighter, assuming good central heating? Then there was the question of what to wear in bed. Her comfortable winter pyjamas would hardly do. She had one deliciously slinky silk nightdress, but she had bought that some years ago for the first holiday she and Keith had taken away without the children – the only one, as it turned out – and it would feel like a sort of betrayal to take that with her to an assignation with another man. Perhaps she should see if she could buy herself something else before the weekend – but when? It wasn't easy without a car. Which was the other thing she had to consider. She could just about manage without a car while she was working here in Meadhope, though shopping anywhere but at the village shops was difficult. But once she began her new job, with several different surgeries within the group to manage, she would need her own transport. Maybe she should call at the local garage after work and see what they had to offer in the way of second-hand cars. That, of course, brought her thoughts back to the subject of money, and the need to get her finances sorted, disentangled from Keith's.

The phone was ringing again, but Elaine was at the other end of the office, putting cards away. Jan reached for the receiver. 'Meadhope Surgery, Jan speaking—' She had not even finished what she was saying when a strange strangled voice broke in.

Some nutter, she thought, as the voice gasped out something about 'my fault – you've got to come!' Then, she heard her name, clearly, and in that moment recognized the voice through the uncharacteristic notes of panic and despair. Keith – but not Keith as she knew him, for this man was sobbing incoherently into the phone about a fire, and Auntie Hilda and, again and again, how it was all his fault.

She tried to break in, 'Keith, listen, just hold on a minute, slow down! I can't make out what you're saying. What's happened?' But she might as well have saved her breath, for the terrible sobbing only grew fiercer and then the phone went dead. She dialled 1471 quickly, and recognized the number of Keith's mobile. She saw that Elaine was looking anxiously at her. 'I've got to go,' she said. 'Something's happened, I'm not sure what. Can you manage without me?'

'Of course,' said Elaine.

Jan reached for her coat, then remembered: no car – she had no car. It would take hours to get to Coldwell without one, if that was where Keith had called from. She picked up the phone and dialled a local taxi firm; good thing she'd been to the cashpoint on the way to work this morning. While she waited for the taxi, she gathered her things together, to be ready the moment it arrived.

It felt as though the journey went on for ever. The traffic seemed unusually heavy and obstructive – she could not remember ever having seen so many JCBs on the road, or tractors and trailers, even caravans, in winter, in this most untouristy of areas. She'd asked the driver to take her to Hepburn Street, and prayed she was right in assuming that was where Keith had phoned from. It was an assumption born of instinct, since he should really have been at work at this time of day.

When she reached it, she knew she was right: the fire engine parked outside the smoking gutted shell of Auntie Hilda's house told her that. The Mondeo was there too, parked at the further end, but it was empty and there was no sign of Keith in the little knot of neighbours standing at a safe distance watching the firemen dampening the last of the blaze. She asked the taxi driver to wait while she walked over to Ida Kelly.

'What's happened?' Stupid question, when that was only too obvious. 'Is Hilda all right? Have you seen Keith? Is he all right?'

'He's all right; he was at work – they got her out before he came. They took her to hospital. He went in the ambulance with her. She was conscious when they got her out. That's all I know.'

Cursing herself for not having brought her Mondeo keys with her, Jan ran back to the taxi and got the driver to drop her at the A & E department of the General Hospital where Ida said they had gone. There was no sign of Keith or his aunt in the waiting area, so she went to the desk to ask. After a moment or two they directed her beyond the swing doors at the further side of the waiting area. She found herself in a long passage edged by curtained cubicles. A nurse emerged from one, so she asked for Hilda Grey. 'She's my husband's aunt,' she added. Then she heard Keith's voice from close by, with that sobbing hysterical note still discernible beneath the familiar tones. She pushed the curtain aside and went in.

Hilda lay on the trolley, still and pale but breathing noisily, her hands bandaged. Keith sat beside her, one hand touching hers, as if afraid to cause her pain by clasping it. For a moment Jan almost failed to recognize him. She thought at first that he must have been caught in the fire himself, so dishevelled did he look; then she recalled what Ida Kelly had said, and took in that there were no signs of scorching about his clothes and face, no sooty marks. This was how he must have looked when he arrived at the fire, even perhaps (disturbing thought) when he went to work. Never the sharpest dresser, he had still never looked like this, utterly uncared for, neglected, with his clothes rumpled and stained, his face unshaven; and great dark hollows round his eyes. He looked utterly distraught, lost. From somewhere came an urge to run to him and hold him in her arms, to comfort him and reassure him. Yet he was too strange, he had clearly experienced too much since they were last together for her to understand fully what he was going through or know what kind of comfort to offer. More to the point, she had no idea if he would even begin to accept any sort of comfort from her. She thought he would almost certainly not. She stood there with the curtain falling back into place behind her and looked at him; he gazed at her, with an expression she could not read, except to see

262

that it was deeply troubled.

'How is she?' Jan asked at last. Her voice sounded very odd, forced, hoarse, as if it had not been used for a very long time, as if she had somehow forgotten how it worked.

For a time she thought he was not going to answer, even that he had been unable, for some reason, to take in what she asked, for he simply continued to stare back at her in silence with those eyes full of some sort of unexpressed pain and his mouth tightly closed. Then he cleared his throat – the sound was so sudden, so loud, that she jumped – and said, 'OK. She'll be OK.'

She had not thought what to say next when the curtain was pushed back and two porters came to wheel the old lady up to the ward, where a bed was ready for her. Saying nothing, either to one another or anyone else, Jan and Keith walked beside the trolley, along what seemed endless confusing corridors, up in a lift, along more corridors, until they reached the ward. There they were shown to a tiny waiting room while the old lady was put to bed. 'You can come and see her as soon as she's comfortable,' the nurse told them, closing the door on them.

They stood side by side in that cramped space, looking at one another. What shall I say? Jan wondered. What can I say? 'Keith...'

At that moment he spoke too, the words bursting from him. 'Jan, it was my fault...'

She did reach out to him then, though warily, running her hand up and down his arm. 'You couldn't be with her all the time; you had to go out to work. You did your best.' She had assumed at once that the fire had been caused, in some way, by the old lady herself.

Keith was shaking his head. She saw that he was very close to tears. 'You don't understand: I thought it ... I wanted ... It was a way out...'

Horror began to creep over her. What was he saying? She studied his face, searching for the truth. 'Keith, you didn't cause the fire!' The statement was a denial – confident, reassuring – but it was a question too, and she watched him with her heart in her mouth, praying that he would not take it as the cue for a confession. To her great relief, she saw the recoil in his eyes.

'No – no, of course not! But...' His voice was rough, rasping. 'This morning, I thought ... Jan, I wanted...'

She could hear the sobs then, dragged from deep inside him, harsh painful sobs, like nothing she had ever heard before, from him or anyone else. And she reached up and pulled him closer and felt his head drop against her shoulder and his hands cling to her and then he began to weep in earnest; this reserved, private man she had married was weeping like a child.

It went on for a long time. Eventually, the nurse opened the door, began to speak, said, 'Oh, I'm sorry. Come along when you're ready,' and left them again, closing the door.

Jan stroked Keith's hair – his lank unwashed hair – murmured meaningless comforting words – 'It's all right. It'll be all right. Hush now' – just as she might once have done to the children, while the sobbing went on and she wondered how on earth she was going to stop it and what she would do if he could not stop. 'Keith,' she tried again after a moment, 'hush now! Auntie Hilda is ready for us. Let's go and see how she is. You don't want her to see you like this. You need to be cheerful for her, positive.'

Somehow he managed to pull himself free, choke back the sobs; he even allowed her to pull out a tissue and wipe his face, as if he had been a toddler and she his mother. Then he stood gazing at her. 'Jan...'

She thought he was about to say more, but evidently he was unable to think of anything else to say, or perhaps simply could not find the words.

She took him by the elbow. 'Let's go and see Hilda. Ready now?'

He nodded and they walked along the passage and into the ward, where the old woman lay clean and calm in bed. She did not seem to know them at all, though at least there was none of the usual anxious bewilderment about her; she simply seemed sleepy. The ward sister came and told them that there was nothing seriously wrong with her physically; that the burns were fairly superficial and would heal as quickly as any wound on an old person's skin; but that mentally she seemed very confused. Jan confirmed that she had been in that condition for some time, though it seemed that Keith had already said something to that effect when the old woman was admitted. 'We've given her something to calm her and make her sleep,' the sister said. 'She needs rest at the moment. I can see you do, too. I suggest you go home and come back tomorrow.'

Jan made sure the hospital had her phone number – *their* phone number – and steered Keith out of the ward. 'We'll get a taxi back to the car and then I'll drive us home.' She tensed herself for his refusal, but he made no comment at all, simply waited while she used the public phone in the entrance and came meekly out with her when the taxi arrived. All the violence of his outburst upstairs had given way to a kind of numb silence, which, Jan thought, was probably just as well, at least until they were home again. Once, on the journey back to Meadhope, she thought that he was weeping, there beside her in the passenger seat, though quietly, heartbreakingly. She laid a hand on his knee for a moment, just to show that she knew and cared.

It seemed very odd to be driving back into the familiar gravelled area beside the house with this strangely transformed Keith at her side, almost as if she had plucked him safe from some disaster – as perhaps she had, as far as the disaster was concerned. It remained to be seen if he was safe again. She knew that some of today's breakdown was the result of shock, which time and reassurance would heal. But underneath she suspected there lay something much more serious, a depression deeper than anything she had guessed at until now. For that, he badly needed help, very probably more help than she could begin to give. But time enough for that when they were in the house again, drawing breath, learning to talk to each other as they had not done for years, had perhaps not done in all their lives; if Keith was willing to learn, as she was.

Not that talking was what he needed now. Keith seemed to have reverted to the helplessness of a child, so she had to take off his jacket for him, unbutton his shirt, show him the way to the bathroom to wash. 'I'll heat some soup. Come down as soon as you're ready.'

He ate some of the soup – though not much – and then had a bath and allowed himself to be put to bed. She wished there were some sleeping tablets in the house, but there weren't, so she hoped that the sleep he fell into almost at once would last.

When she was sure he was asleep she went back downstairs and telephoned Fiona, to let her know what had happened, or some of what had happened. She left out Keith's mental state (except to say he was exhausted and distressed), but did say that he was back at home with her. 'Can you let the others know, to save me making any more calls tonight?' she asked. But she did make one more call, to Don, to tell him, briefly, that she was very sorry, but she wouldn't be able to meet him that weekend. Because it was the simplest and most acceptable explanation, as well as having the merit of being entirely true, she told him about the fire, and how Auntie Hilda would need help, how they had to decide what was to become of her, once she was out of hospital. 'Let's just leave things as they were,' she suggested. 'The weekend away with you was a nice idea, but I can see it was a mistake. I'll speak to you sometime.' She guessed that there would be no further chance for her with Don, that this disappointment would be the last one he would take from her, but that was the way it had to be. Today had changed everything. Even if, in the end, she and Keith were not to patch things up somehow, she needed much more time than she had originally given herself, time for them both.

Keith's sleep didn't last; he woke almost as soon as she got into bed beside him and after that slept only briefly and fitfully. Often he lay weeping in her arms, in that terrible uncontrollable way he had at the hospital, apologizing as he did so, 'I'm sorry, Jan – I'm sorry!' Any hope she might have had that they could begin tonight to talk things through soon vanished. He was in no state to talk coherently about anything, even to think what he might want to say or take in what she might have to say to him.

Jan was relieved that there was no morning visiting allowed in the ward where Hilda was a patient, for it was obvious to her the next day, that Keith needed medical help himself. She telephoned the surgery to say she would not be in herself and to make an appointment for Keith with Dr Mead, the doctor he trusted most. For once, she used her position to ensure that there was one available, this morning, as soon as possible.

'I don't need a doctor,' Keith said, when she told him what she had done. He was sitting at the breakfast table, but had only drunk a cup of coffee and eaten nothing.

Jan sat down opposite him and took his hands in hers. 'You've had a terrible shock. You need some help just to tide you over. That's all. Trust me!'

'But I've got a meeting this morning. I've only two days to go. I can't miss work.'

'Yes you can. I've phoned them already to say you won't be in today. I don't think it'll make any difference. If they need to talk anything over with you, then you can pop in next week or sometime. That's if you're not fit tomorrow. I said I didn't know about that. And I phoned the hospital...' For a moment he looked as though he had no idea what she was talking about. Surely he could not already have blanked out all that had happened? 'They said Auntie Hilda had a peaceful night and is comfortable.' She leaned over and kissed him. 'Now, go and get ready. A shave might be a good idea.' She rubbed her hand over his cheek. 'A bit less scratchy to kiss.'

She wished he would smile, just once, show some sign of his old self. But it was a long time, a very long time, since she had seen that; she was not sure now if she could even remember the man he had been once. She had to force herself to be patient, to help him through this time. We'll get through! she told herself, and wished she was as sure about it as the words implied.

He looked more himself when, shaved and dressed, they set out to drive to the surgery – she was not sure he could cope with walking even that short distance without breaking down; the tears seemed to come without warning. She went in with him to see the doctor, sensing that he would need explanations from her too, if he was to make sense of Keith's condition. In the end, it was a fairly brief consultation; he prescribed a mild tranquillizer for Keith and told him to come back in three days. 'I think a psychiatric referral might be the answer, but we'll see, once the first shock's worn off. For now, you need rest, lots of it.' Dr Mead glanced pointedly at Jan as he gave that advice.

By the time, after a scanty lunch (though to Jan's relief Keith had eaten something), they set out for afternoon visiting at the hospital, Keith seemed calmer, subdued rather than on the brink of breaking down. He even seemed able to talk in a coherent manner of some of the implications of what had happened yesterday. 'Why did it have to happen now? Another two days and I'd have been there all the time!'

'Not all the time. You'd have had to go out some time.' She was about to add, 'She needs constant care, all the time,' and then thought better of it. It was not the moment to stir up past arguments. In any case, she suspected that he must already see the truth of her reasoning, without any need for her to repeat it. Or if, in the confusion and anguish of what had happened, he didn't quite see it yet, he would very soon. It would be much better if the final arguments, the final decisions as to what was best for Auntie Hilda, were to come from him.

It seemed that he was, for the present, too weary to continue the discussion any further, or consider the problem of the old woman's future. At the hospital, they found her looking better, though she seemed bewildered by their arrival and clearly had no idea at all who they were. There was, as far as Jan was concerned, nothing new in that, but it was the more marked now she was in strange surroundings, where she could not reach for some routine task to conceal her confusion, to give the appearance of normality. At the end of visiting, the ward sister asked to speak to them and said that though the old lady was making a quick physical recovery, they did not intend to release her until satisfactory arrangements had been made for her future. Medical staff and social services would make recommendations. For a moment Jan feared that Keith was about to object to such interference in their lives, but in the end he simply drew in a breath, opened his mouth; and then closed it again. Perhaps he too was seeing the merit of simply waiting to see how things worked out. One day at a time, Jan thought; one moment at a time. Let's deal with each of them as they come and not be in too much of a hurry to look to the future, to plan, to risk facing contentious issues. She was glad, though, that she had taken the trouble, in what now seemed almost like a past life, to visit the Old Rectory Retirement Home; she suspected it was going to be the answer.

At home again, she made them a simple supper of pasta and salad, and was glad to see that Keith was able to eat a little of it. As he ate, he said suddenly, 'I'm sorry about all this, Jan. I don't know what we're going to do.'

She knew better than to take that as a cue for discussing the future, but did take the opportunity to tell him one piece of news of which he had been ignorant until now. 'I got the practice manager's job, starting after Christmas. It should be enough to pay the mortgage, if we're sensible.' Even that, she thought, might be treading on dangerous ground, implying as it did that they had a future together, and also, perhaps, reminding him of his failure as a breadwinner. To her relief he gave no sign that he saw anything out of the way in her remark. In fact, he said, 'I thought you didn't want it?'

'Oh, I've come round to the idea.' It wasn't quite the truth, but that seemed irrelevant in the circumstances. 'The other piece of news is that they're all coming for Christmas – Fiona and Mel and Simon, and probably Simon's new significant other, Tamsin.' That was looking forward, it was true, but it was the hopeful, happy kind – on the surface at least – and she thought it could do no harm.

'That's nice,' said Keith, and his mouth

seemed on the verge of breaking into a smile. Then, with a genuine show of interest in something that had nothing to do with himself or Auntie Hilda: 'Who is this Tamsin?'

Thirteen

Jan found herself plunged suddenly from a life that had seemed to offer an abundance of opportunity and choice to one in which she had no choice at all, except to care for Keith and, because of him, his aunt. Of course, she did have a choice of some sort about it, or so she told herself. She could have turned her back on him, refused to have him home again. But she knew that had never been an option, or not so long as she was who she was.

So Keith was here, back at Mill House, shaken and ill, and she was caring for him. That was her task, her project, for the foreseeable future. Anything else, any other decision, had to be put to the back of her mind, put off until Keith was well again.

During the next few days, Keith ate little, slept much of the time, in the day as well as at night, and even when awake seemed to have no energy for anything but sitting slumped in a chair or wandering in slow aimlessness about the house, mostly following where Jan went, as if afraid that she might disappear while his back was turned. But by the time he saw the doctor again, the frequent outbursts of sobbing had all but gone and he was, as far as Jan could see, almost back to normal.

Except, Jan wondered, what *was* normal – the morose, uncommunicative man he had been for so long and still was, a brooding presence sucking all joy and lightheartedness from everything around him; or someone else whom she could now scarcely remember, the man she had described, in a letter written in the first flush of love, as delighting her with constant laughter? Was there anything left of that man at all? If so, would he ever come back?

She was relieved that Keith's return, and his appearances at the surgery, made it possible for her to talk to Anne, her closest friend at work, about his condition – though it was an expurgated version, leaving out, principally, the rift in their marriage, and concern for Keith's privacy made her cautious about how much she said. But to have someone to talk to, now and then, made her feel a little less alone than she might otherwise have done. Her mother too was given a sketchy account of what had happened, the essentials only; as for the children, they were simply glad their parents were together again and consequently felt less need than before to keep in touch, to Jan's frustration. Could they not see that she needed them now more than ever?

For in other respects, she felt more isolated than she had ever been in her whole life, especially at home, when the door of Mill House was closed against the world and she and Keith were alone together. There, her whole effort was concentrated on looking after Keith, on doing what she could to help him to recovery: she cooked him nourishing and (hopefully) tempting meals to encourage him to eat; she tried, gently, tactfully (and mostly without success) to get him to talk about his anxieties and fears and emotions; she urged him to go for walks, during which she exerted herself to be a stimulating companion, drawing his attention to amusing or beautiful sights – a bird or animal, a late blooming flower, a striking cloud formation, the way the light struck on water, the shape of a tree. Whether or not any of this had any effect at all, she was not really able to tell. After the first few days, she saw little perceptible change – if he was calmer than before, that was almost certainly due to the drugs he had been prescribed; he was certainly no more responsive or communicative. But Dr Mead seemed to think that for now there was no need for a psychiatric referral, that as Keith adjusted to the changes in his life, as the problem of his aunt was resolved, so he would gradually recover his spirits. But then Dr Mead had always been rather old-fashioned and dismissive of anything that did not have an obvious physical explanation.

One day at work, he took Jan on one side and tried to reassure her: 'It's just life, that's his problem. Nothing fundamental. He just needs a bit of help until the worst is over. That's what the tranquillizers and sleeping tablets are for. Don't worry. He'll be all right.'

As for Auntie Hilda, they went to visit her almost daily, in the evenings after work, on Wednesday afternoons when the surgery was closed, at the weekends – since Keith's medication prevented him from driving, he could only make the journey when Jan was able to go with him. Hilda had made a full physical recovery, but had been moved to a remote psychiatric ward at the hospital while the medical staff and social services carried out a full assessment of her condition. Keith hated the ward – 'full of loonies,' he said, with one of the occasional lapses into political incorrectness which came when he felt at his most bitter and angry. Jan didn't like the ward much either, feeling uneasy at the strange behaviour of many of the other elderly patients, behaviour that made Hilda seem positively sane. But it was after all only a temporary measure and Hilda seemed blithely unaware of what was going on around her. Jan knew – and she imagined Keith knew too – that at the end the recommendation would be that she should be transferred to a nursing home with full psychiatric facilities.

Meanwhile, Jan arranged for the house in Hepburn Street to be cleared of the charred remains of all the old woman's possessions, contacted the suppliers of state and work pensions and the building society and everyone else she could think of to report lost records, and dealt with the insurance company (thank goodness the house had been insured!), who were, slowly, carrying out the formalities that should lead to a payment that would help towards paying for the old woman's care – it seemed that, though far from wealthy, Hilda had rather more savings than would allow her to qualify for free residential care; but at least that would mean her relatives would have more of a say than they might otherwise have done as to where she should receive that care.

Life settled into a drab routine. Oddly, Jan found that its very dreariness assuaged her guilt about Keith, about having failed to see what was happening to him, about feeling angry with him for something he could not help. Now, in fact, she could see quite clearly that she was by no means responsible for what had happened, that she was only a very little to blame for his state of mind, if at all. It was not her fault that he had not confided in her in time for her to share his worries about the loss of his job and to help him come to terms with it – except that for so long she had been too wrapped up in the children to notice that anything was wrong. But it was Keith himself who had failed even to try to confide in her. Perhaps some sort of masculine pride, some feeling that it was not the man's part to admit to anxieties or to a sense of failure, lay behind his silence. But that was not her fault either.

As for Don, the affair that never was, even her revived interest in archaeology – they had all become things from the past, to be put aside, possibly for ever, certainly for the foreseeable future. She had a task to do that had nothing to do with them and to which she had to devote herself entirely, whole-heartedly. Her life, her needs, were on hold, while she did what had to be done for Keith. It was exhausting, draining; she found herself often longing for some temporary escape, for some time to herself. Yet there was another side to it all, a positive side, as she confided in Anne as they enjoyed a brief coffee break one particularly busy Monday morning.

'You should get away for a day or two

sometime,' Anne had advised, after observing how tired Jan was. 'You've got to look after yourself too.'

'I know that. But Keith's not well enough to be left, not yet. Don't worry about me. It's not all bad. In fact–' she smiled suddenly – 'I rather like feeling I'm the breadwinner. I'm the one keeping us going. It may be tiring making all the decisions, but it has its good side.'

'A bit of role reversal,' Anne commented. 'Not that you were exactly the passive partner before, as far as I could gather.'

She was right, but even so Jan knew that there was a difference, and it gave her a new insight which she took home with her that evening. 'I was thinking today,' she said to Keith as they sat over pizzas in the kitchen (she'd felt too tired to cook). 'I suddenly realized I'm quite enjoying being the breadwinner. I really feel rather proud about it. And I think its made me understand better what it must be like for you. You were always the provider, the one who supplied our needs. And now suddenly you're not. It must be so very hard. I wish I'd understood before now.'

Before she reached the end of what she was saying she could see she had (once again) misjudged the situation, seen an opportunity where none was. There was no lessening of the grim impassibility of Keith's expression,

280

no indication that he wanted to talk about how he felt. He simply shrugged. 'Don't suppose it would have made any difference.' He resumed his eating and the silence settled heavily over them again.

That'll teach me to try and engineer an intimate discussion, Jan thought. She searched her mind for some other topic, something that might divert him; something of innocuous banality. 'I've been wondering, shall we have a change from turkey this Christmas? How about goose?'

'Whatever you like. Turkey's OK.'

'There's always the problem of Simon, of course. I wonder if Tamsin's vegetarian too? But a nut-roast-cum-stuffing should take care of them.'

'Maybe she's vegan. What then?' There was just the hint of a teasing note in Keith's voice, and his gaze even met hers across the table. Jan felt a sudden astonishing lift of the spirits. Delight lit her face, gave her voice warmth and emphasis.

'Now, you've really got me worried! Christmas dinner without cream, eggs, butter, cheese...!' She chuckled. Then she looked across at Keith again and saw that the shutter was back in place, the tightness had returned to his mouth, the line between his brows. There had been a tiny glimpse of the old Keith, nothing more. Or had she simply imagined it? The momentary happiness drained from her. 'There's some fruit salad left from last night, if you'd like some.' Valiantly trying to recapture the lost moment, she went on, 'Good vegan fare!'

'No thanks.' He stood up. 'Can you manage if I go and watch the football?'

Can you manage? she thought sourly. When did I ever do anything else? She stacked the dishwasher, wiped down the table, checked the fridge and added a few items to her shopping list for tomorrow. No visit to Auntie Hilda tonight, which left a long evening ahead. Another long evening. Oh, if only she could have an evening to herself, just one evening when she could relax and do exactly as she pleased!

She took her briefcase from the hall and carried it up to the bedroom, taking from it a sheaf of photocopies of the applications for her present job, for which they were conducting interviews tomorrow. She sat down on the window seat, the papers on her lap, and found herself doing nothing, simply gazing out over the lights of the village. How long was all this going to go on? she wondered. How long before Keith was well? And what kind of man would emerge from it all? Would they find at the end that they still had nothing to say to one another, nothing to offer one another? If so, Jan would be back to where she had been before the fire slashed through their lives. The thought of returning to a single life did not frighten her, for she knew she could cope. What was more problematic was what Keith would do, once he was through the depression. Would he be able to recognize that their marriage was over, if that should be the case? Or would he want to hold on to the shadow of what he thought perhaps they had once had? And would she then feel she had to stay with him, simply to keep him from regressing into depression? There was no way of knowing, of course. It was pointless to wonder about the future.

She dragged her attention back to the papers she held and began to go through them, making notes as she did so.

She came home the next day to find to her astonishment that Keith had prepared a meal for them both, the one dish he could make well, a beef casserole, its savoury smells reaching her as she stepped into the hall. Keith himself was in the sitting room, asleep with the *Independent* draped over his lap, though he jolted into wakefulness as she came in and dropped a kiss on his forehead – she always made a point of offering him the small gestures of affection that might, in the end, make a difference. 'That smells good.'

He looked up at her, then put the paper aside and stood up. 'Thought it was time I earned my keep,' he said. There was, to Jan's surprise, none of the usual bitterness in his tone. Rather than trying to draw her attention again to his sense of failure, he sounded relatively normal, simply expressing a wish to be helpful. Jan felt inordinately grateful for that small advance, though conscious that the next moment it might have gone without trace.

'Let's go and eat then, if it's ready.' They had to eat early tonight, so as to be ready for the hospital visit. The kitchen table was already laid and Jan sat down, allowing Keith to bring the meal to the table and ladle it on to their plates. 'I could get to like this,' she said, 'dinner on the table when I come in from work, waited on hand and foot.'

'You've done it for me long enough. Only fair, I think.'

'Maybe you'd better extend your repertoire then,' she suggested with a smile. 'We can't have beef casserole every day.' She watched his face as she spoke, hoping she'd not gone too far.

'That had occurred to me.' He sat down and they began to eat. 'The hospital rang. They want to arrange a meeting with us and social services, to discuss their recommendations.'

Jan laid down her knife and fork. 'Oh. They've decided on something then.' It had been difficult to find anyone in the ward to discuss Hilda's case with, when most of their visits were at weekends or in the evening. 'Did you tell them we'd be in tomorrow afternoon?' Tomorrow was Wednesday, her half day.

'Oh, I forgot.'

She felt irritated, but said nothing. What was the point? To Keith every day probably seemed the same these days. 'I'll ring from the surgery in the morning and see if anything can be arranged at short notice. Otherwise, I suppose it'll have to be next week.' More delays, before they could finally address the question of Auntie Hilda, before they could move on from all the difficulties of her situation into some kind of resolution.

'Can't you take time off?'

With so much to do at work before she left the job, she knew it was hardly a good time, but in the circumstances no one would be likely to object. 'If need be. Let's see what happens tomorrow.'

It was perhaps a measure of how anxious the hospital was to free Hilda's bed for another patient that a meeting was, after all, arranged for the following afternoon. It took place in the ward sister's office, and was rather less daunting than Jan had feared. The sister herself was there, and the doctor who had been working most closely with Hilda, along with Susan McClure, a gentle little woman from social services – though Jan

285

supposed she must have been less self-effacing than she seemed, considering the nature of her job and its demands. The medical staff described Hilda's needs at length, and the social worker assured them residential care was essential and gave them a list of homes that had facilities for the elderly and mentally ill. At her use of the term, Keith broke in: 'But won't that prevent her from making any sort of recovery? A home's bad enough – people become institutionalized so quickly – but if she's shut up all day every day with people like that, she'll have no hope of getting better.'

'Mr Grey, your aunt is in an advanced state of senile dementia,' the doctor reminded him. 'She's not going to get better.'

'Please believe us,' put in the social worker, 'we wouldn't think of recommending such a place if we didn't believe it to be the very best option – in fact, the only option, in the circumstances. Hilda needs to be properly cared for, for her own safety, if nothing else. In a well run home she'll have all the stimulation she can possibly need. I don't think you'll find that anything will make very much difference, but she's been through a very traumatic time and I believe she'll be much happier for feeling secure. And that's what you want, isn't it?' She told them she wasn't allowed to recommend one home over another, but gave them advice on what to look for when making their choice. Scanning the list she had given them, Jan was relieved to see that the Old Rectory at Meadhope featured on it.

Once they were out of the hospital, she suggested to Keith, who had said nothing at all since they left the meeting, that she drop him off at Mill House, while she went to the Old Rectory to make arrangements for his aunt's admission. 'No way!' he objected. 'Do you think I'm going to have my aunt shut up in some place I've never even seen? I want a good look at it first.'

Jan struggled to think what to say. She was afraid that the whole experience of visiting the home and making arrangements for his aunt to move there would be too much for Keith in his present fragile mental state, that it would only intensify his depression and make him more incapable of making any rational decision. This afternoon's meeting had already brought on a resurgence of the bitterness and anger that had seemed to recede during the past days. But she sympathized with him too. Indeed, his mood chimed with her own unease at the prospect of enclosing the old lady in a place full of other patients in various stages of mental decay. In hospital that had been only a temporary arrangement, and there had been plenty of nurses and visitors coming and going; in the Old Rectory it would be permanent, until her life ended. But was it really the best option for her mental and physical welfare? Was it not indeed a poor return for all her love and care of Keith? If she, Jan, felt like this, how would Keith feel, in his present uncertain mental state, at seeing where they proposed to place his aunt? But she found she could not bring herself to say, 'You should let me go alone, in case you find it too upsetting.' Instead, she found herself admitting that he had a point, while she wondered how she would cope if she still found the place acceptable, but Keith continued to react as negatively as she feared he would to any possible residential home. 'We'll go straight there then.'

To Jan's relief, the home looked as welcoming as it had before, as clean and sweet smelling, as bright and flower filled. Eileen Quigley, the matron, remembered Jan, welcomed them warmly and listened to their story with sympathy and apparent understanding, and then led them to the locked door which led through to the EMI unit – for the elderly mentally ill, as she explained. This was the part of the home that Jan had not seen before – she had not then even realized it existed – and she stepped through the door with a feeling of apprehension, for herself but especially for Keith. She glanced at him, noting the familiar set greyness of his expression and feeling the knot of anxiety tighten again inside her.

It was a relief to find the corridor beyond the door as bright and fresh smelling as the rest of the home. From it, at one end, French windows opened on to a small sunlit garden, with a gravelled area and shrubs and a bed with a few late chrysanthemums still in bloom. There was a table set on the gravel, with chairs tipped on to it, so Jan supposed there were times when the residents sat out there. There was a lounge much like the ones on the other side of the door, bright, full of flowers, the television on. A number of residents sat dozing or mumbling to themselves around the room, though none seemed to be watching the television. In one corner, a teenage careworker knelt on the floor beside an old lady's wheelchair, holding her hand and talking to her softly, soothingly. Jan heard the words, 'Darling' and 'we all love you, Annie, you know that...' until the old woman's initial whimpering faded to silence. Further on, in a large room (it had a piano in it), a uniformed careworker was standing in the middle of the room leading the residents who surrounded her – nearly all women – in simple wheelchair exercises, and most of the patients seemed to be enjoying it, even those who were muttering to themselves or shouting ribald abuse. There were two other careworkers in the room, helping the residents exercise – it was clear to Jan that the staff–resident ratio was much higher in the EMI unit than elsewhere in the home. But as in the area outside the locked door, here each resident had a single room, some en suite, small but bright and clean and furnished with many of the occupants's own belongings. Not that Auntie Hilda had any personal things left to bring with her, Jan thought, with a sudden pang of sadness. How was she ever to be made to feel at home?

And it *was* a disturbing place, there was no denying that. To see so many old people in various stages of mental decline, all under one roof, was upsetting, and to think of Auntie Hilda, much less severely afflicted than many of the residents they saw, coming to live among them, was painful even to Jan. She glanced at Keith and saw the frown and the hard line of his mouth, and could only guess at the strength of his feelings, the revulsion even.

The tour continued, with Jan asking an occasional question, every one of which was answered courteously and in full, though Keith said nothing at all and she was only too aware of his unhappiness. At the end, they were led out of the unit, feeling a sense of relief as the door was secured behind them, and then taken back to Eileen Quigley's office, where Jan thanked her and said that they would think things over and almost certainly take up the offer of a place at the home.

Once outside in the car, Keith said, 'Why did you say that? You don't really suppose I'm going to let them shut my poor aunt up with all those other nutcases, do you? She'd lose every last shred of sanity before she'd been there a week.'

What could she say? She knew exactly what he must feel, for she was feeling it too, to some degree. 'I imagine she wouldn't see it as we do. She wouldn't realize there was anything wrong with them. She might not even know they were there.'

'You don't believe that, do you? Surely to God there must be a better solution than this?'

'I don't imagine any other home would be any better. In fact, I'm sure many of them would be much worse.'

'But you don't know. We have to look. Unless we're going to have her to live with us. And I'm beginning to think...'

Jan felt a rising sense of panic. Once she had thought that was enough of a possibility to speak of it to the children and to Keith himself. But that was before she had realized how seriously ill not only Hilda was, but Keith himself. 'No, Keith,' she said firmly, forcing herself to sound calm, rational, 'it wouldn't work. For one thing, you're not well enough at present to cope. Maybe when you're better we can reconsider.' It was said simply to mollify him, for she knew that she at least was not likely to reconsider. 'But for now – well, a home is the only serious solution. It just has to be the best we can find.'

'Then we'd better start looking.'

Jan tried to argue; the Old Rectory was the only such place in Meadhope; it was convenient, enabling them to visit often, with ease; she was sure it was pretty good, as such places went. When Keith was unmoved, she drove home and suggested they talk about it again the next day, hoping that by then he would have had time to see the sense of what she said. But he would have none of it; the search for a suitable home must continue immediately. He took the list Susan McClure had given them and found the two next nearest homes, and suggested they call on them at once.

There followed days in which every spare moment was taken up with visiting every home even in the further reaches of the county which had the appropriate facilities. They saw places that smelled; places where both buildings and residents were dirty and uncared for; places where the residents were clearly drugged into compliance; places where there were no single rooms and so no privacy; places with harrassed, over-stretched staff; places with only one tiny cramped day room, with no space for any activities to be provided; places where even as visitors they felt unsafe, with residents suffering from dementia wandering unchecked and unsupervised by staff, so that those who were less afflicted seemed frightened and there seemed more than an acceptable number of patients with injuries of one sort or another; places that they were admitted to only after making an appointment some time ahead, so that they were suspicious even of the good things they found. They also saw homes that were as good as the one at Meadhope, but none that were better. They visited local libraries and read the inspection reports lodged there, sometimes finding that a home that seemed clean and well run was in fact lacking in some area that had not been obvious to them. Time and again, Jan, feeling increasingly depressed at the whole business, at seeing so many deranged old people, so many plastic flowers and chintzy curtains and over-loud televisions such as she would have hated, asked herself how, if she could not have borne to live there, could they expect Auntie Hilda to do so? She felt increasingly depressed by it all, and it was quite clear that the whole business was doing Keith no good at all. She tried, time and again, to persuade him that she could be trusted to do the visiting for him, to ask the right questions and look for the right things. But he would not listen.

Hilda was his aunt, he owed her everything, so he had to do this for her. So Jan resigned herself to a worsening of his condition, to weeks longer of treatment than he might otherwise have needed. The fits of weeping, which she'd thought were over, returned several times during those wearisome days.

Meanwhile, the hospital was growing impatient with the delay in moving the old woman. 'We do have a shortage of beds,' the sister said at last. 'If arrangements are not made by the end of this week, then we shall have to make them for her. The Pines in Coldwell can take her.' They had seen the Pines; the staff were kind and hard-working, but it was cramped and old-fashioned, with most rooms shared, only a single television-dominated day room and few activities laid on for the residents besides an occasional visiting concert party. Auntie Hilda, a devotee of Classic FM, had always hated concert parties of the kind that belted out 'the old songs' to a captive audience. 'No thank you. I never liked those songs when I was young; I don't see why I should have to listen to them in my old age,' she had said, very firmly, when invited some Christmases ago to an old people's party laid on by the local Rotary Club.

'We'll make the arrangements today,' Jan promised the sister. As they walked away, she saw that Keith looked bent and weary, as if he knew he could not fight any longer, as if stooped to accept the burden on his back; the burden of allowing his aunt to suffer what was, at his most optimistic assessment, second-best care.

Jan slid her arm through his. 'I'm sorry, love, but I do think the Old Rectory is the best we can do. It may not be ideal, but there just isn't an ideal.'

'It shouldn't have to come to this!' he returned bitterly, but that was – to her relief – the only objection he made.

By the end of the week, Auntie Hilda was installed in her own bright sunny room at the home. To their surprise, she seemed to feel almost instantly at home, even though she had no belongings of her own to relieve its shiny impersonality, beyond the basic necessities that Jan had bought for her. In particular, the fact that the room looked over the enclosed garden of the home seemed to delight her. She went at once to the window and stood gazing out, clearly enraptured by the birds fluttering among the shrubs. She had never lived in a house with a garden, and now, Jan thought, she looked almost as if she had woken and found herself in Paradise. Jan glanced at Keith, and saw that he too was struck by his aunt's obvious pleasure; he looked, not troubled, but pensive. She linked her arm through his.

'We'll bring her a radio from home – that

one in the small bedroom that we never use. Then she can listen to music again. And there must be some old photos and ornaments and things up in the loft, something that might remind her of the past.'

Keith soon freed himself from her clasp, but Jan still felt relieved as they left the home. It looked as if the worst was over for Hilda. They could begin to move on, to find a way of living with this new situation. Now perhaps Keith too could put the past behind him and step into the future, finding healing as he did so.

Meanwhile, it would soon be Christmas – she *could* allow herself to plan for that one part of their future. She did not particularly look forward to Christmas itself, which was likely to be very fraught, especially as she wasn't sure how Keith would cope with it. But at least she would enjoy having the children about her. She knew she mustn't let their presence establish a barrier between her and Keith, as it had done so effectively for years; but it would be good to have cheerful adult company about her again. She looked forward to their coming so much that she hardly dared to allow herself to think of it.

Fourteen

There was a bitter wind with flurries of snow on the day Fiona came home for Christmas. She was earlier than she had originally intended; suddenly growing sick of London and work and her life in general, she had taken a week's holiday that was due to her so as to spend more time at Meadhope. It had seemed a good idea, until the three hours of inactivity on the train had given her time to think, to wonder what she was coming home to. In the impulsive moments of putting in for her holiday, booking her train tickets, she had been filled with thoughts of Mill House as she remembered it – warm, loving, welcoming, a haven of normality, security, love. It was not until she was established in her forward-facing window seat, with a squalling baby on one side of her and a teenage girl opposite talking non-stop in a very loud voice into her mobile phone, that it came to her that her parents' home would not, now, be as she remembered it. Her parents might be together again under one roof, but after all that had happened, how could things ever be as they once were, especially as her father was now suffering from some kind of break-down? But it was too late to change her mind. She had made her choice and here she was, on a train moving inexorably north-wards. She tried to quell the apprehension rising in her, tell herself that it would be all right, it would be as if she had never been away, things would be just as she remem-bered them.

She stepped out of the warm crowded train at Durham station, pulling her coat closer round her as her eyes swept the waiting throng for her parents. Then she saw her mother, coming her way, all smiles. She looked exactly the same, unchanged in spite of all that had happened. In fact, it was possible, looking at her, to believe that noth-ing had happened, nothing had changed, everything at home was exactly as it always had been. Fiona felt comforted, reassured.

She kissed her mother, who took her bag from her, ignoring her token protest; they walked to the car, parked in the roadway, because there were, as usual, no parking spaces. 'New car!' Fiona exclaimed, looking at the silver Micra parked there. 'What hap-pened to the Mondeo?'

'Company car, so they wanted it back.' Jan patted the roof of the vehicle. 'Someone in Raby Street was selling this – one owner from new. I got the AA to check it over for me first. It seems a good little car.'

Fiona scrutinized her mother's face, the face of this capable woman who was clearly now in charge of things at home – as perhaps she always had been, if not so overtly. She wondered what Jan's feelings now were towards her father, how much she had after all changed, under that reassuringly normal surface; but Jan's expression was simply that of one concerned to get the bag and themselves into the car before the snow came any faster and the driver of the car hemmed in by Jan's parking returned to find he couldn't get out.

'Christmas weather,' Fiona said, as they set out, the windscreen wipers swinging against the thick, sticky flakes. Her mother went into a light-hearted account of the past few days' weather, until Fiona broke in on a pause for breath and asked, 'How's Dad?'

'Oh, he has bad days and good days. But he's much better on the whole. It'll all take time, we know that.'

'I suppose so. It *was* some kind of break-down, was it?'

'Yes, I suppose it was. Too much stress, coming all at once.'

'And what about you – are you looking forward to the new job?'

'I haven't thought about it much.' Nor had she. She had not thought much beyond Christmas; there had been planning enough in that to keep her from looking any further into the future. In any case, anything beyond Christmas was too problematic, too difficult. As for the new job, she knew that in reality she gave it little thought simply because she could not take it very seriously. It was a temporary necessity, a stopgap, until such time as she knew what she was going to do with the rest of her life. But she had no intention of confiding this view to anyone. 'What's your news then? Have you heard anything from Sam?'

'We don't keep in touch,' said Fiona, with a curtness that intrigued Jan, because it hinted at some hidden hurt. Could her daughter be regretting the ending of that relationship after all? But had there not been some other relationship since?

'Do you still get to Paris often?'

'Not lately. That job's finished. Anyway, Paris can get boring after a time.'

'Paris! Boring!'

'Even Paris, Mum.' She yawned, as if to emphasize the point.

So the Paris relationship has ended too, Jan thought. Was Fiona right, in what she had said once: was it possible to have a relationship without strings, without commitment, on one side or the other, without hurt to someone when it ended? As she would perhaps hurt Keith, when in time he was well again, if she were to decide there was no future for her in their relationship ... Could she do that? Or would she feel she must go on doing as she was doing now, caring for him as one might care for a sick friend or relative, even though there was no longer any remaining trace of the man she had once loved enough to want to commit herself to for life?

Some days ago, searching the loft for anything that might cheer Auntie Hilda's room, she had come across a bundle of old letters and had untied the ribbon that bound them and begun to read them. They were all letters she had written to Keith during the months before their marriage, and their tone had astonished her. She sounded so meek, so adoring, so deferential to his judgement, so unfailingly eager to please. It was like reading something written by a different person. She could not remember that she had ever been like that, could not even imagine it now. Yet there it was in black and white. When, then, had the change come about, from that meek wifely creature (not yet a wife) to what she was now? It could have been no sudden overnight change, for if it had been she would surely have remembered how it happened. Had she simply, slowly, begun to realize that Keith was not, after all, right in everything he said and did, that he did not know everything? Had she simply absorbed more of the changed understanding of the role of women than she had realized at the time; she who had reached maturity before the great wave of early feminism, and had been too busy raising children and building a home to read its seminal texts? And what, she wondered, had it been like for Keith, to find that the deferential woman who looked up to him in all he did, had become critical, independent, quite able to manage without his views and judgements? She had grown used to thinking how much he had changed, to wondering where and when the man she had married had gone. Now she was faced with the thought that he might feel the same way, about her.

She'd tried to talk to him about it; asked him, 'What sort of woman did you think you were marrying?' to which he had replied impatiently, 'I don't know! I just wanted to marry you, that's all,' and then walked out of the room.

She realized suddenly that Fiona had asked her a question, which she had completely failed to hear; her daughter was now repeating it, her tone exasperated, her expression concerned. 'I'm sorry, what did you say?'

'I hope you've got more of your attention on your driving than you have on me.'

'Of course.' She grinned at her daughter. 'I drive on automatic pilot. Don't you know that by now?'

'Anyway, I was asking about Auntie Hilda. Does she still like the home?'

'She does seem to, thank goodness.' It was the one truly good thing that had come out of the past awful weeks, for even Keith had not been able to find any fault with the arrangements that had been made for her. Though her mind was as clouded and confused as ever, she was clearly happy with almost everything about her new life. 'In fact, you're back in time to take part in the EMI unit's carol concert, lucky you! It's on Tuesday night. Mince pies to follow.'

'I can't wait!' said Fiona. She peered through the windscreen, seeing through the swirling snow that they had reached the end of the built-up area on the city's fringes and were now out in open country, making slower progress because of poor visibility and an increasing thickness of snow building up on the road. Her mother looked calm enough, though concentrating hard on her driving. 'It's getting worse,' Fiona observed.

'Oh, it's just a shower. You'll see, the sun'll be out again in a moment.' She slowed behind a gritter, which scattered them with grit and salt, and let the car fall back a little. 'Not the best thing for the paintwork.'

'It used to be Dad who was the one who worried about the car.'

'Ah, but he didn't own it, in the end. This

is the first one we've had in years that's ours, properly ours.'

At least she still spoke of 'ours', Fiona noticed, not 'mine'. That was something. She wished she could ask probing questions, the sort of questions she would have asked a friend in her mother's position, but for all their apparently equal and comfortable relationship, Jan was still her mother and Fiona her daughter and it did not seem quite proper to ask such things. The snow was easing now, thinning to a few light snow-flakes; the road surface was already becoming visible again through the swiftly melting snow. Jan chose her moment and moved out to overtake the gritter.

'You were right,' said Fiona. 'Sun will be out in a moment. Pity the snow's not lying properly – I'd like a white Christmas.'

'Let's get you all safely here first,' said Jan. 'Then it can do what it likes.'

They discussed the plans for the next few days, who was arriving when – Mel two days before Christmas, Simon and Tamsin on Christmas Eve. 'Have you spoken to Mel lately?' Fiona asked. 'Simon phoned me up in a great state the other day – he thinks she's been taken over by some sort of cult.'

'Really? Whatever gives him that idea? I spoke to her on Thursday night and she sounded perfectly normal.'

'She's started going to church, he says.

Some sort of funny church – you know, all born again and alleluias, that kind of thing.'

Jan laughed. 'Sounds terrible! I admit, that kind of thing wouldn't be to my taste, but it sounds harmless enough.'

'You knew about it then?'

'She said she'd been to some sort of church social with a friend from work, that's all. I was just glad she sounded a bit happier, that she's made some friends. I've been worried about her.'

'Me too, and Simon. But getting caught up in some dodgy religious cult is no solution, even if it makes her think she's happier.'

'Why don't we wait until we know a bit more about it?' Jan suggested. 'If she starts giving away all her money to this church, or refusing to have anything to do with us, that's the time to worry. If she simply enjoys the social life of some rather simple-minded religious organization, I can't see any harm in it.'

'Maybe not.' Then Fiona said, 'But I do wonder if we should have done something, so she wasn't so lonely.'

'I know – me too. On the other hand, there's only so much her family can do, if she's away from home. That's the thing when you go to a new place – you have to make friends and make yourself part of the community before you can feel at home. It takes effort, and it's hard at first, but there it is.'

'I didn't have any problem when I went to London.'

'No – you had ready-made friends, people like you, doing the same work, who worked in the same office. And you went with Sam. That was work and social life taken care of.'

Fiona's reply was a murmur, though whether of agreement or evasion, Jan could not be sure.

They drove in silence for some time; the sun was fully out again now, brilliant on wet roads and roofs, and the white caps of the distant hills. Jan pondered what they had been saying, and Fiona's reaction. There were many questions she would have asked, about Fiona herself, about her social life without Sam, about her feelings for Sam, if she still had any, which Jan suspected she did. But Fiona was an adult now, not a child to be questioned, guided, advised. She would deeply resent any unasked for intrusion into her privacy. If she were to confide in her mother, that would be different – though even then Jan would know better than to offer advice, unless it were asked for. As it was, she had to keep her thoughts, and her questions, to herself.

It was Fiona who spoke next, and then it was to ask a question herself. 'Mum, when you first came to Meadhope, did you find it hard to make friends, or did you feel at home right away? It always seems such a friendly place.'

'So it is. And of course I came here with your father, straight after we were married.' She tried to remember that time, so long ago, but it eluded her. They had lived, then, in a stone terraced house – much like Auntie Hilda's in size and amenities – with a yard and a view of the houses opposite. She could bring that to mind, because it still existed, in the least attractive part of Meadhope. But of the life she had led within its walls she recalled very little, only small snapshots taken out of time and context, mostly concerned with decorating and furnishing that first home of theirs; the two of them painting a room – the front room, she thought, with one wall in a fashionable brown that made the whole room close in on them. She remembered the dark colour in front of her face, the brush that left its bristles behind, laughter, the cause of it long forgotten. That Jan, and that Keith, seemed like strangers now, more strange even than Jan St John, the student, less recoverable, since there seemed less trace left behind. They used to go together to salerooms, in the hope of picking up cheap furniture for the house – she recalled that too, pleasurably, but without detail. 'I don't think we had much time for a social life,' she said after a moment. 'There was too much to do in the house, to get it right. And then you came along.' The smell of paint had been unbearable while she was pregnant, so that had put a stop to the decorating. 'Pushing a baby round in a pram,' Jan added, 'is the quickest way I know to make friends. After that, we were in.'

'You must have been very young.'

'Younger than you are now.' She didn't want that to sound like a criticism, so added hastily, 'But things were different then. I was quite old for a first baby, by the terms of those days. And you were still expected to give up your job when a baby came. Women didn't think in terms of a career in the same way men did. That all changed soon afterwards, but I was too early for it.'

'I can't see me ever wanting kids. Even if you don't have to give up your job to have them, they still get in the way of a career. I've seen that at work – most of the people I know who have babies start falling behind, even with nannies and nurseries and all that. Maybe they just haven't the same drive, or there are too many distractions, I don't know.'

'Children certainly alter your priorities. I don't suppose there are that many super-women out there who can cope with everything, work and children, with the same singlemindedness.'

'We're supposed to.'

'Women have always been expected to do the impossible, whether it's juggling work and children, or being the angel within the home. The trouble is we expect it of ourselves too, and then get depressed and guilty when we fail – the children aren't perfect, the work doesn't get done well. As I see it, most of what we do – what any of us do – is a case of trial and error. Especially parenting. Why else are there so many baby books all saying completely different things? And other kinds of advice too. *How to be a Superwoman* – wasn't that one of them?'

'So you're a failure if you don't wash your light bulbs.' Fiona laughed. 'My generation just want to be perpetual students – or that's what we thought. Then one day we start to get an urge to settle down, and we don't know how to go about it.'

'Are you feeling like that then – that you want to settle down?'

'I wasn't, not at all, especially after the break with Sam. But, lately – oh, I don't know. Settle down isn't the right word – begin to take life seriously perhaps. I expect it's Christmas. It does funny things to you.' Alarmed to find how close she had come to revealing more about herself than she intended, she asked suddenly, 'You haven't met Tamsin yet have you? I wonder what she's like.'

They speculated on the little they knew until they reached the fringe of Meadhope; by now it was snowing again, though languidly, only hinting at the beginning of a shower.

Keith must have been listening for the car's arrival, for he opened the front door as they approached it. He was smiling, to all appearances his old normal self; the self that, long ago, Jan must have ceased to know except at a very superficial level. She wondered if, seeing him like this, Fiona would wonder what all the fuss was about, would begin to doubt that her father had ever been ill. In fact, it struck her for the first time how very much better he was, how much progress he'd made in the weeks since the fire. It was likely that the return of their children would help him further towards full recovery. 'Lunch is on the table,' he said, and came to kiss Fiona.

They went inside, and, while Fiona took her bag up to her room and tidied herself, Jan followed Keith into the kitchen, where the table had been set with a salad, bread and cheese. 'I'm impressed,' she said. 'You've been busy.'

'More than you think. I've been making some calls this morning and checking on a few things. My redundancy payment should be through any day – by the end of the week, they said.'

'Thank goodness for that. I was afraid they were going to say you weren't entitled to it anyway.'

'Why, because I missed those last few days? No, they couldn't do that.'

'But you thought that was possible once, didn't you?'

'Not really,' he said. She wondered if the intensity of his initial depression was already fading from his memory, as he recovered his spirits. Perhaps this was a sign that he was now over the worst; she hoped so, while a small voice whispered to her that they might be coming closer to the moment of truth, when they had to face the reality of their relationship, when they could no longer go on simply living in the present.

They could hear Fiona running water in the bathroom. 'Any post this morning?' Jan asked. The postman hadn't come before she left for the station.

'A couple of things.' Keith reached on to the dresser and handed Jan a telephone bill ('very timely,' she murmured ruefully) and a letter with a Scottish postmark addressed to her in a tidy, unformed hand she recognized after a moment's consideration. 'Sam!' she exclaimed. 'I wonder what he's writing about.' She looked round to make sure Fiona was not about to come into the room, and then slit it open. Inside was a Christmas card, with a note added at some length. His address had changed, Sam told her, because he'd moved in with Kirsty, a librarian working in the small town where he'd been living.

There was insufficient space for him to write much, but enough to convey his happiness and even his hope that this relationship might become, perhaps was already, the most significant thing in his life. Jan passed the card to Keith for him to read.

'I wonder how Fiona will take it,' Keith wondered, as she was doing too.

'I think we'll keep it out of sight for the moment.' Jan slipped it back into the envelope and pushed it under the phone bill, which covered it completely.

Fiona joined them and they ate their meal, while she entertained them with anecdotes about her work – she could be an amusing conversationalist when in the right mood – and questioned them further about the less painful aspects of their lives during the autumn. Afterwards, while Keith went to see if he could finish the *Independent* crossword, Fiona helped her mother clear the table and load the dirty dishes into the dishwasher. Putting the unused cutlery away in the dresser drawer, she knocked the two letters; Sam's fell on to the floor. She stooped to pick it up then stood still, gazing at it. 'Oh – Sam!'

'Yes,' said Jan, watching her face with concern. 'A Christmas card.'

'Did he write anything – about himself, I mean?'

She knows, Jan thought. 'You can read it.'

Fiona did so. Her expression was, at the very least, unhappy. 'Didn't take him long,' she said. There was a note of bitterness in her voice.

Jan stopped herself from making any comment; she simply sat down at the table near her daughter, who read the card again, laid it down and then stood where she was, her face not fully visible, though Jan wondered with sudden alarm if she was close to tears.

'Damn!' she said. 'Why should I care? Why do I care?' She slumped down abruptly on a chair beside her mother. 'I don't mind, really. It's his life – good luck to him. It's just that – well, somehow he's got it all sorted.'

'And you haven't?' prompted Jan gently.

Fiona shrugged. 'Oh, I don't know. I love my job; that's not the problem. It's just there doesn't seem to be anything else. Clubs, the gym, lots of friends. But it's all a bit pointless. I thought I didn't want commitment – I don't, I think. I don't know. In any case, there isn't anyone I'd even want to *think* about that way.' She gave a sudden rueful laugh. 'You know, Mum, I even found myself reading one of those dating agency leaflets – you know, the sort that match up busy professionals. Isn't that pathetic?'

Jan put an arm round her and gave her a quick hug. 'Not really. It's very hard meeting people when you're busy. My generation met our partners at university' – though not me, she thought – 'but for you, that's far too young to settle down – wisely, I think. But work does limit your horizons and your choices. Instead of hundreds or maybe thousands of possibilities around you, there are only perhaps dozens, and most of those will be ineligible for some reason.'

'And how! It's not that I want marriage – it's not that I see it as important. I just want someone I care about who cares about me.'

'You've only been parted from Sam for a few months. Plenty of time yet.'

'He's already found someone. And he was the one who was dumped.'

How to answer that one? 'I suppose he needed someone then. Shouldn't you be glad?' Even as she spoke she thought it was probably the wrong thing to say. The next moment she found herself wondering fleetingly – without coming to any sort of answer – how she would feel if she and Keith parted and Keith were then to find another woman. It was somehow impossible to imagine, or so she told herself. 'I suppose sometimes it's easier to cope with something if you feel guilty about it. Only there's no need to feel guilty any more about Sam.'

Fiona brushed the remark aside. 'I didn't anyway. Why should I? There was nothing left for us, for either of us. It's just that he hadn't seen it then. Obviously he has now.

Anyway, of course I'm glad for him.' She stood up, stretching. 'I'm whacked. I'll be going to bed soon. Shall we go and watch the news?'

Jan, hanging back to set the dishwasher going, watched her walk towards the sitting room, and found herself wondering what was going to become of this beloved daughter of hers, so unwilling to admit to any sort of need. Perhaps, after all, her apparent independence was not so enviable as she had thought. Life could never be without complications, unless you were entirely without feelings.

Fifteen

By the end of Christmas Eve, a decorated tree dominated the hallway at Mill House, there was holly above every picture, garlands crossing the sitting room, a holly wreath hooked on the front door, and the noise of young people in high spirits filled the house. The whole place was transformed, alive as it had not been for months. Keith looked happier than he had done for ... oh, longer than she could recall, Jan thought, with the

315

now-familiar pang of guilt. Even last Christmas, looking back, she thought he had been subdued, withdrawn, though she had been too busy, too wrapped up in the young ones, to realize.

Tamsin had blonde hair, long-lashed brown eyes, a slight but curvaceous figure and enough self-confidence to cope without too much awkwardness – beyond a certain charming hesitancy – with the family scrutiny of her. It took little more than a day for them to forget they had not always known her, and from the start she was included as one of them in all their customary Christmas activities. On Christmas morning, after the usual stockings, full of silly small gifts, they followed breakfast with church – or Jan did, and Keith too, to her surprise and pleasure. Mel also came down with her coat on, to accompany them; she was not then, Jan thought – with reassurance rather than relief, since she had never been unduly worried – so lost to a cult that she could not take part in normal churchgoing. The others stayed at home, with instructions to keep an eye on the turkey and peel the potatoes. By the time their elders came back from church – calling at the home to collect Auntie Hilda, who was to join them for lunch – the house was full of the smells of good food and the table was set, embellished with elegant crackers supplied by Fiona, and a floral arrangement of holly, candles and red ribbon which Tamsin had concocted from materials rooted out by Simon, including a few Christmas roses picked from the garden. Jan stood gazing at the table, with the sights and smells and sounds of a family Christmas around her, and suddenly felt awash with happiness and gratitude. For now at least, for today, for this moment, all was well. What lay ahead did not matter for now, could be left until later. What was important was to enjoy this day, to savour every moment of it.

Dinner lasted for hours, then there was a minimum of washing up (with much laughter), presents (for everyone, in equal measure), a long chat on the phone with Jan's mother, a family expedition to the Old Rectory to return Auntie Hilda (who seemed glad to be back in familiar surroundings, having appeared rather overawed by all the people she did not recognize at Mill House), and then a walk over the frosty fields. After that, came a tea which no one claimed to want but all managed to eat to some degree, an evening of television, chat, nuts and fruit and yet more alcohol, and the day was over.

Then Jan and Keith were alone in their room, getting ready for bed, at the same time (which was unusual in itself, these days).

'It's been a good day,' Jan said, as she sat at the dressing table removing her make-up.

She could see Keith in the mirror, though he was stooping to pull off his socks and had his back to her.

'Yes,' he said. 'They're good kids.'

'I like Tamsin.'

'Simon's done all right for himself there,' Keith agreed. That was all, but it was more of a conversation than they had held for a long time, and they even went so far as to exchange a kiss before putting the light out; it was the first time Keith had responded in any way to one of Jan's token kisses. Once the light was out, he drew her into his arms. 'Thank you, Jan. It's been hard for you. But thank you for sticking by me.' Jan felt too full of emotion to do more than kiss him again.

From downstairs, where the younger members of the family were still up, came the faint sounds of music and laughter. It had indeed been a good day, and enough for the moment, enough to be going on with.

The following morning, Jan got up first, to a silent house and a kitchen full of empty glasses and plates no one had felt awake enough to put in the dishwasher before going to bed, especially as the dishwasher had not been emptied from its previous use. Jan busied herself with the leftover tasks, and wondered if anyone would feel like bacon and eggs for breakfast, when eventually they came down. By the time she'd had her own bowl of cereal, Keith was up but no one else, so she set about dismembering the remains of the turkey. 'I'm going over to see Hilda,' Keith said, and left her to the silent house. The happy glow of yesterday had gone as if it had never been, the moment of tenderness last night might never have happened; he was once more the Keith of the past long months, the taciturn, unresponsive man who lived with Jan but in a separate gloomy world of his own.

Well, it was over, or the main bit was. Now there were only the last few days to enjoy before the youngsters left – two days, since they were all spending the New Year elsewhere. She dreaded the prospect of their going, of being left once more alone in the house with Keith, even a recovering Keith. It had been such a joy to be able to laugh and relax, to enjoy real companionship, to have congenial people to talk to, about anything and everything – or not quite everything, for she could not talk about the loneliness of living with their father. Even now, with the house full of their sleeping offspring, it was a relief that Keith had gone out; she felt the familiar sense of a burden lifted, of being able again to breathe. She told herself she must not think beyond these few days, or she would spoil what she had now. In any case, perhaps Keith was dreading the future too. She had to continue to try and understand his feelings, his needs.

By the time Mel – the first to come down, probably because she had been the least drunk last night – reached the kitchen, the turkey meat was packed into boxes and bowls and distributed between fridge and freezer, and the carcase was packed into Jan's largest pan, with carrots, onions, celery, peppercorns and a bayleaf, being turned slowly into stock.

'Boxing Day smell,' observed Mel, sniffing the air appreciatively. She took a bowl from the cupboard, filled it with muesli, poured milk over it and sat down to eat. 'Another good Boxing Day thing – simple ordinary food. Not that yesterday's wasn't wonderful,' she added hastily, with a grin. She took a few mouthfuls, then paused and glanced round at her mother; it was the first time they had been alone together since her arrival at Mill House. 'How are things, Mum? I don't mean Dad – I can see how he is. But the other – oh!' She floundered into silence, then tried again. 'I suppose I'm trying to ask if everything's OK again now.'

'You mean, are we going to stay together?' Jan was glad that she was bent over the dishwasher, so that her daughter could not see her face. 'To be honest, Mel, I don't know. So much has happened, and most of it's still in the melting pot. And your father's not fully well yet. I really don't know.'

'Oh.'

Jan glanced at Mel, and saw the disappointment in her face. 'Whatever happens, nothing's going to be done lightly. And whatever happens, it'll be for the best.'

'I hope so.' Another pause, then she asked, with a note of hesitancy, 'Mum, was there anyone else?'

Jan could feel herself colouring, so continued to keep her face averted. What was the truthful answer, and did she want to give it anyway? She considered for a while, then said, 'No, there wasn't. There could have been, but there wasn't.' After all, Don had been irrelevant to the fracturing of her relationship with Keith, an incidental complication that had never really come to anything. The fracture would have happened anyway, had in fact already happened. It might all have come about rather differently without Don somewhere in the picture, but ultimately, she thought, the result would have been the same; would be the same, when eventually they reached that point.

'Who was he?' Mel asked, with a lively note of curiosity.

But at that moment, to Jan's relief, Simon came in, with Tamsin at his elbow, asking brightly, 'What are we doing today, then?'

'What do you want to do? I always think a walk on Boxing Day is a good idea.'

'Let's go to the Roman Wall,' Fiona suggested, coming in too.

Simon's groan was cut off abruptly when he realized Tamsin was saying, 'Oh yes, I would love that! I've only ever seen pictures of it.'

Jan was doubtful. 'Do you think we can get there in time to see anything before it gets dark? The days are so short now.'

'We can start straightaway,' said Fiona. 'A slice of toast each then we can be off. We can have lunch in that nice pub – you know, the one we found that very wet day.'

Jan had a dim recollection of a family outing long ago when they had taken refuge from pouring rain beside a roaring fire. There had been good hot soup and much laughter, she remembered. 'Your father's out, at the home. But you can go – Mel can drive you all.' She had driven home in her new car.

'Oh no, we all have to go!' Fiona gulped down the coffee she had poured herself. 'I'll go and find Dad.'

But there was no need, for he was coming in the front door as she reached it. 'Dad, we're going to the Wall. Five minutes to get ready.'

Jan did not catch his response, though she heard him go upstairs; but by the time they were assembling in the yard with warm jumpers and rainproof coats, he was there too, silent still, and unsmiling, but a willing member of the party. They travelled in

322

separate cars, for he went with Mel and Fiona, while Simon and Tamsin climbed into Jan's Micra. They drove away from the house into the still grey day and the empty roads.

They parked in the small cark park at Steel Rigg, and there climbed out and walked up to the highest and most dramatic point on the Wall, to gaze out over the landscape as once, when it was wilder, more open, less tamed, Roman soldiers had gazed, wondering perhaps what forsaken territory they had come to. It was grey and cold, with a few thin flakes of snow in the air, and the wind cut their faces, but it was clear and they could see for miles.

'Wow!' breathed Tamsin. 'What a place!'

The others pointed out familiar landmarks, picked out distant hills, showed where the fortifications that lined the Wall could be seen, and one or other of the forts and turrets and mile castles that marked its length. 'There's a fort there, just to the left of that knot of trees,' Simon told Tamsin. 'See, you can just make out the humps in the ground. Close to, you wouldn't see much.'

'It's a turret,' Jan corrected him, 'not a fort.' And she was there, on a cold summer day, working at her first job on leaving university, scraping at the soil to see what, in the six weeks that was all they had, might be revealed to their eyes. She glanced round at Keith and saw that he was looking at her, with an intent, unreadable expression; so he was remembering too. 'I've taken part in a dig there, so I should know,' she said, as she knew Keith was expecting her to say.

'So that was it!' Fiona looked excited. 'Was that the dig where you met Dad?'

Again, a glance exchanged between husband and wife, longer this time, grave, neither of them knowing quite what the other was thinking, what, precisely, they remembered of that time. 'Yes, that's right.'

'Let's go and look. Can we get to it?' Simon was eager, and the others too.

'I think so,' said Jan.

So they got back in the cars and drove a little way along the military road and parked in a lay-by which gave access to the footpath that led to the turret. Simon had been right; here on the site there was little to see, just a few scarcely discernible bumps, grass-grown, like the undulations in so many of the fields round here which gave nothing away to the unpractised eye. 'It doesn't look as if it had ever been excavated,' Tamsin said.

'Ah, but you can see, here, where some of the work was done.' It was Keith who had spoken, to Jan's astonishment. She watched as he showed where trenches had been, where this and that artefact had been found, what lay under this insignificant patch of earth, or that. He was right too, about all of it; she who had worked over this ground remembered it all very well, now that she heard Keith talk, but she was not sure if she could have recalled it in such detail if he'd not prompted her memory.

Keith led the way across the site, slowly, describing every step of the way to a fascinated Tamsin; and his own three children too. Jan followed behind, remembering other things besides the course of the excavation. In those days there had been a rough shelter – a sheet of canvas stretched over a wooden frame – set up close to the wall that bounded the site, so as to provide cover for the pot washers. Otherwise they'd worked in the open, which mostly meant in cold wind and rain, even though it was late summer. Jan remembered sore fingers that were never warm; but she also recalled excitement, enthusiasm – and Keith...

'How come Dad was here?' Mel asked softly, clearly not wanting to interrupt Keith's flow of explanation.

It was all so long ago; Jan struggled to bring the past to mind. 'Do you know, I can't remember exactly. It was something to do with his job, something the council wanted him to check on. They'd given us a grant, I think. No, come to think of it, he didn't work for Northumberland County Council, so it couldn't have been that. Maybe he was on some sort of course, working with the council here for a week or so – I think that was it. Oh, I don't know – you'll have to ask him.' In the end it hadn't mattered why he had come that first time. After that, he'd come again and again, before and after work and at weekends, staying for hours at a time, watching what they were doing, asking questions – and hadn't he even done some digging himself before the excavation was over? Surely he had, or he wouldn't have remembered it all so well.

She looked across to where he stood now, by the wall that bounded the far edge of the site, his hands gesturing towards the nearest indentations in the ground. What was he seeing? The bared earth, hands gently, tenderly scraping the surface away with trowels, that meticulous, immensely careful work that she used once to love so much? Watching Keith, Jan realized with a sudden shock of recognition who she was reminded of as he described what he saw – Don, speaking to his students, carrying them with him by his enthusiasm, bringing the past alive. How strange, how odd, that she should see a likeness between the Oxford archaeologist with all his knowledge and experience and her husband, redundant council surveyor. But it was there, it was most certainly there. She made her way slowly towards Keith; she could see now how intent his expression was, how absorbed in his memories, probably scarcely aware of his audience. He had come back time and again because she was there, she'd always known that. Today, she was reminded that there had been another reason, another pull on him; he had been fascinated by the whole process, drawn to the actual work they were doing. She was beginning to recall more fully now, how he had questioned and watched, how at the end of each day they had talked eagerly together of the progress of the dig, as they made their way to the pub where the whole team were staying, or sat over drinks long into the night, or went for drives in his battered old Morris Minor, or walked on fine evenings over the hills in the growing dusk. Keith had become part of the team, accepted, welcomed into their company and their work.

By the time she reached Keith he had stopped talking and the others had wandered off to look at the site for themselves. He remained, leaning against the wall, deep in thought. 'I've just remembered,' she said. 'That last night here, the night we got caught in the rain near the Temple of Mithras. You decided you were going to give up your job and go and study archaeology. It's funny, I'd forgotten all about it. I didn't dream it, did I?'

'No.' He looked sombre. 'I was the one did the dreaming.'

'What happened then to stop it?'

He almost smiled, but there was bitterness

in his expression too. 'You did; you and the children. Remember?'

She felt the hurt of it, the sense of loss. Of course; they had married soon afterwards, taken out their first mortgage, set about raising a family. For that, Keith had needed a job, since in those days it was still difficult for a mother of small children to continue doing paid work, and besides her earning power was much less. Had the bitterness and depression started so long ago, the disappointment with life? 'That must have been hard.'

'Not really. No, it seemed well worth it, at the time.' He was looking at her now, directly, studying her face as if discerning – or trying to discern – the young woman he had met in this place and so quickly come to love; to love more, then, than any hope of changing the direction of his life. 'In any case,' he added suddenly, 'I wasn't the only one who gave up dreams and ambitions. You did too.'

Which was true, though she had never thought of it like that, or not until the reunion had reminded her of what might have been; even of what still might be. She gazed back at her husband, and for a moment, with a flash of recollection, saw the young Keith standing there, much as he was now; thick chestnut hair, brown unlined face, dark gentle eyes that could brighten into enthusiasm – and laughter, for now she did remember the laughter of which she had written long ago to Rosemary; a great deal of laughter. 'If you could go back,' she said now, 'would you do things differently?'

He thought a little, giving the matter serious attention; then he said, 'No. No, I don't suppose I would. Though maybe I wish some of the other things, later on, hadn't turned out as they did.'

Warily, afraid to break the present mood, not wanting to risk sending him back inside himself, away from her, she said, 'For that I have to take some of the blame. If only for not realizing what was happening, right from the start.'

'Maybe – who's to say? What I do know is that I let my job take over my life. It became too important, took too much time. It was never worth all that sacrifice.'

She reached out then and slid her hand into his and felt his answering clasp. 'If you'd had work you loved, that wouldn't have mattered. I know we can't bring back the past. But there's still the future. I can see,' she went on, 'that you had to give up your dreams then; that you felt you couldn't give up your job. But you haven't got a job now.' She paused, looking at him, waiting for him to understand what she was saying.

He shook his head. 'It's much too late. Much too late.'

'Why? Because you're no longer interested? I was watching you just now.'

'Oh, I don't know.' He shrugged. 'I'm too
old, too tired.'

'Not just now, not while you were explaining it all. You looked years younger. You're
tired because you've worked too long and
too hard at a job you never really liked that
much – and, perhaps, because I haven't
taken the trouble to include you in all our
lives, to make you feel wanted. That's what
makes you feel old.'

'You may have a point. But am I wanted,
that's what I want to know?'

And she too needed to know the answer to
that question, because it was the one she had
not yet faced, not yet felt able to face. She
looked at him, seeing not just Keith the
husband who had for so long excluded her,
however unwittingly, from his life and its
stresses, the man whose presence had lately
become hard for her to bear; but Keith the
eager young man, who had loved both her
and the work she did, but had only been able
to choose one of those enthusiasms.

She had her answer. What lay between
them, in spite of all the pain of the past
months, went too deep to be lightly thrown
off; and what had drawn them together all
those years ago was still there, dormant,
perhaps almost defunct for lack of nurture,
but capable of revival, if they were both to

work at it. She had been drawn to Don because he seemed to offer her a way back to an enthusiasm long past, but he could only ever have offered her a partial return, for Keith too was a part of that past. To recover what had been lost, they must make the journey together, or try to do so.

She linked her arm through Keith's, glad that he made no move to draw away from her but simply looked down at her expectantly. 'I'm going to be earning a good salary when I start the new job next week,' she said. 'Enough to pay the mortgage and keep us both, so long as we're sensible. And we've got your redundancy money. That should fund an archeology course, easily.'

'But it's the middle of the academic year. I can't start anything now.'

'You don't have to. Get your application in for next autumn and fill in the time by reading and going round sites, anything to give you a good start.'

'But – but what about you? You'll be missing out.'

'No I shan't, because you'll be able to tell me about it, get me up to date on all the latest thinking. And eventually, when I retire, we can do all sorts of things together. It'll be a new life for both of us. We've done the bringing up children bit, as best we can. Now it's time for new things, a new life.'

She could see the light rekindled in his

eyes; and then he smiled suddenly, the old dear familiar smile she had not seen for so long. 'Maybe you're right. Maybe I should give it a try.' She turned to put her arms about him and he folded her into his embrace and bent his head to kiss her.

'Mum! Dad! Can we go and find that pub? We're starving!'

They went across to where Simon stood by the gate. 'You never did have much of an attention span for Roman ruins,' said Jan. 'Come on then.'

EK